Dark Gambit
RELIANCE

THE CHILDREN OF THE GODS
BOOK SIXTY-SEVEN

I. T. LUCAS

Dark Gambit Reliance is a work of fiction! Names, characters, places and incidents are products of the author's imagination or are used fictitiously and are not to be construed as real. Any similarity to actual persons, organizations and/or events is purely coincidental.

Copyright © 2022 by I. T. Lucas

All rights reserved.

No part of this book may be reproduced in any form or by any electronic or mechanical means, including information storage and retrieval systems, without written permission from the author, except for the use of brief quotations in a book review.

Published by Evening Star Press

EveningStarPress.com

ISBN-13: 978-1-957139-41-8

Marcel

As Marcel lay awake, holding Sofia tightly against his body, wave after wave of anxiety swept through him.

When he'd told her his greatest sin, his crime, she'd been so supportive, so understanding, but would she feel the same when she woke up?

Would she want to tie herself to a murderer?

Cordelia's husband wasn't the first human Marcel had killed, but the others had been invading marauders, and he'd been defending his people. Those killings had been in the line of duty, sanctioned and justified.

Cordelia's husband had been a different story.

He'd murdered the man in cold blood. Well, in hot blood, but that was irrelevant.

Marcel had taken a life that hadn't been his to take.

He'd appointed himself the judge, jury, and executioner, and he'd convicted the man based on the words of a beautiful liar who'd had him wrapped around her little finger. He'd never stood trial for his crime, and his only punishment had been his self-inflicted flagellation and dreary existence.

What if Sofia decided to reveal his secret?

Perhaps he should just reach into her mind and suppress the memory of the murder story. He hadn't thralled her last night, but he'd done it the day before, and it was a little too soon for another thralling session. Still, given that he no longer needed to continue thralling her after every bite, it was probably fine to do it again.

Now that she knew he was immortal and that his venom bites came with several great benefits, like the possible gift of immortality, Sofia might be more inclined to forgive him his past sins.

Except, he didn't want her to be with him only because of what he could do for her. He wanted Sofia to love him for who he was, but maybe the first step toward that goal was learning to love himself.

Marcel had carried the guilt for long enough, and maybe it was time to confess his crime and submit to whatever punishment Edna deemed suitable.

Hopefully, it would be just a token whipping and some prison time.

Edna wouldn't sentence him to entombment three hundred years after the fact, right?

Enough time had passed that perhaps she wouldn't judge him as harshly.

Then again, he had nothing to say in his defense. Stupidity wasn't a mitigating circumstance, and neither was an emotional disturbance. Or was it?

He hadn't been thinking straight. He'd been in love, and Cordelia had played him like a skilled violinist, tugging on his heartstrings.

If only witchcraft were real, he could have claimed that he'd been bewitched. Three hundred years ago, that line of defense might have worked in a human court, but it wouldn't have worked in Edna's. Unless Cordelia was a powerful immortal who could manipulate his mind, she had no other power over him.

Except, she had.

She'd bewitched him with her smiles and her tears and her delicate touch, but he couldn't use that in his defense. It was entirely his fault that he had not only fallen for her deceit but had also committed a terrible crime to please her.

At the time, Marcel wouldn't have minded entombment. Hell, he would have welcomed it to escape the guilt. But now that he had Sofia, he didn't want to miss even one moment with her, and that meant keeping his crime a secret and living with the guilt because he couldn't guarantee that Edna would be lenient.

"Stop," Sofia murmured. "Your thoughts are so loud that they are waking me up." She opened her eyes and gave him a sleepy smile. "Last night was amazing. I thought I would be afraid of your fangs, but you look kind of cute with them."

"Cute?" Marcel arched a brow. "Those are deadly instruments."

Sofia stretched her long body, pressing her small breasts to his chest. "Instruments of pleasure. What a trip." She kissed the underside of his jaw. "If women knew what your venom can do, they would be beating down your door and offering you sex or lots of money just for a chance to experience that. It's like the best psychedelic on the market."

He cupped her round bottom. "How many psychedelics have you tried?"

"None, but I've heard people describe their experiences. I wanted to try it, but I was afraid. I don't like having no control over what's happening to me."

He gave her lush bottom a squeeze. "Last night, you didn't seem to mind giving up control to me."

Her expression turned serious. "That's because I trust you. I know that you will never do anything to hurt me, and you'll protect me with everything you have."

"I don't know how you can still think that after what I told you."

"Nothing has changed for me." Sofia put her hand on his chest. "What happened with that evil woman and her husband is ancient history, and you were a different man back then. If you were a human, you would have died and been reborn again at least four times by now, and the knowledge of what you had done would have been lost. The slate would have been wiped clean. It's only because you are immortal that you keep on suffering endlessly. If you ask me, you've been in hell for the past three hundred years, and you've paid for your crime. It's time for a new beginning." She smiled and rubbed herself against him. "With me. And since I'm going to transition and become a new person as well, we will have a new beginning together. Isn't that great?"

Marcel suspected that Sofia was still loopy from the residual effect of the venom. Otherwise, she wouldn't be so optimistic and cheerful.

Kian wouldn't be happy about them starting the process so soon. They were supposed to wait until after Sofia's death had been faked, but Marcel just couldn't tell her that last night. Her eagerness to start the process had infected him, and he'd thrown caution to the wind.

When her tummy rumbled, he asked, "Are you hungry? We can get breakfast at the lodge."

"I don't want to share you with anyone yet, and I don't want to dip my feet back into reality and face the day. Let's stay here and make love like there is no world outside of this bunker, and we are not planning to take down Igor."

Yep, Sofia was definitely loopy, but her happiness was contagious, and Marcel didn't mind following her advice and forgetting that anything existed outside of the two of them. They could stay in bed and make love until they passed out from exhaustion, and when they woke up, they could do it again.

Kian

"Your phone is ringing," Syssi said sleepily.

"I heard it." Kian tightened his arms around her. "I'm choosing to ignore it." He kissed the tip of her nose.

"What if it's an emergency?"

"It's always an emergency. I'm tired of all the emergencies I have to deal with."

"Just answer it, please."

He let out a breath and turned around to snatch the phone off the charger. It had stopped ringing, but seeing that the call had been from Eleanor, he decided to return it. She wouldn't have called if it wasn't important.

"What's up?"

"Did I wake you up?"

"No. I was already awake."

"I just wanted to give you an update on my talk with Sofia."

Alarm bells ringing in his head, Kian pushed up on the pillows. "Did she lie?"

"No, she believes that everything she told us is true, and she didn't hide any additional information except for the fact that her grandfather is Igor's second-in-command, but she's already told Marcel about that without any compulsion on my part."

This was indeed big news, and he was glad that Eleanor hadn't waited to call him.

"What does it mean for us?"

"Not much. I had a long talk with her while she was under my compulsion, so I know she was telling me the truth. Her relationship with Igor's second-in-command doesn't afford her any special status in the compound. She believes that it gives her only a slight advantage over other human Kra-ell offspring, allowing her to attend university for the past seven years and perhaps more leeway in choosing her bed partners. But that could be her take on it. The pureblooded Kra-ell don't believe in the concept of love, and having or showing emotions is considered a weakness. Her grandfather might care for her, but he doesn't show it. In any case, it makes me reassess our hypothesis about the tracker that was embedded in her. I don't think that he wanted his grand-daughter to get caught just so he could follow the tracker to wherever she was taken. I suspect that they embed trackers in all the humans who are allowed to leave the compound. They want to keep tabs on them."

"That makes sense, but I still like the idea of driving the cat with the tracker around to see if we can catch something in the net."

"Poor cat," Syssi murmured. "She didn't sign up for getting Sofia's tracker."

"Neither did Sofia." Kian patted her arm. "The tracker is tiny, and Julian gave the cat an anesthetic."

"She didn't suffer," Eleanor said. "And she's getting more petting than ever. But back to the tracker. If it has a tail, catching it will be easier than traveling all the way to Karelia and capturing the Kra-ell guarding the entrance to their secret tunnel. And what's even more important, Toven won't have to go there either and drag Mia with him, which he will have to do because she enhances his powers, and he can't free the Kra-ell from Igor's compulsion without her help. Did you talk to him about it? He might refuse, and without him and Mia, we have no plan."

"Not yet." Kian turned the speaker on and put the phone on his lap. "I'll talk to him today, but the truth is that I don't want him to go there either. It's too dangerous. I'm waiting for Turner to come up with a plan before we make our next move, and I hope he can come up with something that doesn't involve Toven and Mia going to Karelia."

Eleanor snorted. "Good luck with that. Turner is smart, but he's not a miracle worker."

"Some say that he is, but we'll see. Did Marcel tell Sofia about her genetic potential?"

"He did, but he made a mess of it. The guy is not a smooth operator, and after Sofia told him about Valstar being so high up in Igor's organization, he started treating her like a suspect again, and she blew up. Given all the information she'd volunteered, it was uncalled for. I had to step in and calm things down. I took her on a long walk on the beach, explained that the clan is all about doing good things for humanity, about our efforts to free trafficking victims and rehabilitate them, and ended with explaining in more detail about immortals and Dormants. When I was done, she was all smiles and ready to get induced. I hope that Marcel didn't ruin all my good work with some other brain fart."

"Being suspicious is not a brain fart, but I know what you mean. Marcel is an engineer. Enough said."

She chuckled. "They are a special breed, aren't they? But as someone who is mated to the ultimate drama king, I sometimes long for the calm logic of the engineer types."

"Do I sense discontent?"

"Not at all. I love Emmett, and I'm very happy to have a man with flair. It's funny how atypical he is for a Kra-ell. Between the two of us, I'm more Kra-ell than he is."

"Hey, maybe you are Kra-ell," Syssi said. "You certainly have the look. You're tall, skinny, and your hair and eyes are dark. You are also a compeller."

Kian's brows took a deep dive. It hadn't occurred to him, but Syssi was onto something.

"Frankly, I don't care either way," Eleanor said. "But if I am descended from the Kra-ell, then the Kra-ell and the immortals must be really closely related for me to transition so quickly. I wasn't bonded to my inducer. I didn't even have any feelings for him. He was just a hookup." She chuckled. "Given my compulsion ability, I actually suspect that I came from Toven's line. Maybe my grandmother was a naughty girl."

"I hope that your theory is the correct one," Syssi said quietly. "The Kra-ell are only long-lived, not immortal."

Eleanor let out a breath. "Even if I'm their descendant, a thousand years is a very long time, and my mate will enjoy a similar lifespan. Besides, in a thousand years, we will most likely figure out how to turn everyone immortal."

Darlene

When Darlene woke up and opened her eyes, the sight that greeted her was not pleasant. The bedroom was in shambles. Eric was passed out on the bed and smelled as if he had showered in booze, yet she felt amazing.

As she remembered him tearing the bed apart, she sat up and gave the room a second look around. The bed frame was gone, but no evidence of splintered wood remained, and the mattress was somehow still supported and not on the floor. The pictures on the walls were hanging crookedly to some degree, the two bedside lamps were gone, and the dresser had been pushed aside, probably to vacuum the debris from under it.

It seemed that Eric had gotten much stronger during the days following his transition. When he was human, he couldn't have gotten free of the chains by demolishing the bed frame.

Was Max still around?

She lifted her hand to the spot on her neck where he'd bitten her and patted the skin. It wasn't tender, and there was no crusted blood or bumps where Max's fangs had penetrated her skin.

He'd bitten her through the nightgown, but Eric must have loosened the tie that had secured the high collar because the strings were hanging loose on both sides of the opening. Other than that, her nightgown was none the worse for wear, which was a miracle given what the bedroom looked like.

How had she survived it intact?

Darlene remembered the bed frame groaning as Eric had pulled on the chains, but then she'd found herself under him while the posts had toppled down.

"Oh, my God, Eric!" She tried to move him to his side so she could examine his back.

Those posts were massive. How was he sleeping on his back with fractured ribs?

"What?" he murmured sleepily.

"Wake up. You need Bridget to examine you."

"Why?" Eric cracked one eye open and then shielded it with his hand to protect it from the light streaming through the window.

"To check your back. The bedposts fell on you."

"I'm fine." He reached for her, pulling her against his body.

"Ugh, let go. You stink of booze."

"I do?" He cupped his hand over his mouth and exhaled. "Oh, I do. My bad. Max and I finished two bottles of whiskey last night." He lifted both hands with two fingers each. "Another perk of being immortal is incredible tolerance for alcohol. I can outdrink any human now."

Great. They had been celebrating while she'd been out of it.

"What happened?" She pulled away from him and fanned in front of her face to stave off the stench.

"Max was right. When he bit you, I lost my shit and wanted to attack him. Fortunately for him, my priority was to shield you from the toppling posts, so I pulled you under me, and he managed to escape." Eric lifted his arm and flexed. "I'm as strong as a gorilla now. I didn't expect that to happen so soon after my transition."

"Did Max see me naked?"

"He didn't see anything. I made sure of that. He returned to the bedroom to release me from the chains, but I was covering you."

She wasn't sure how that had worked while there had been wooden poles on top of him and he was naked, but it was healthier for both of them to pretend that Max hadn't seen anything.

"What about your back?"

"I'm immortal now, baby. Sticks and stones can't hurt me." He scratched at his side. "I'd better get up and wash the stink off. I want to kiss you and do other things to you."

Her lips curved in a smile, but the smile wilted as she imagined Eric and Max sitting in the living room and getting drunk while talking about her.

"What did you and Max talk about while you were imbibing all that whiskey?"

"This and that. Do you know that Dalhu made nude portraits of Amanda and that she had them hanging in their house? She only took them down after Evie was born."

"I didn't know that, but I wonder how you got to discuss Amanda's nudes. Were you talking about my nightgown?"

Eric's sheepish smile confirmed her suspicion. "Max said that immortals are not as prudish as humans and that nudity is not a big deal for them."

"I don't care." She tucked the hem under her knees. "Anyway, this thing's going into the trash because I'm never repeating this exercise. If I don't transition from Max's bite, we are waiting for you to grow fangs and venom."

The smile slid off his face. "I don't think I could go through that again either, but I need to know. Did you enjoy his bite?"

How to answer that? She enjoyed the effects of the venom. It had been an incredible trip, and the sense of physical well-being she felt now could most likely be attributed to the venom as well, but she hadn't enjoyed the bite itself.

"It hurt, but that wasn't the biggest issue. I wouldn't have minded if it were you. It felt wrong getting bitten by Max." She searched for better words, but every analogy she could think of didn't fit.

Max was a friend, and he was an attractive male, but she didn't want him.

"It just felt wrong. But then the venom hit me, and the effect was mind-blowing." She brushed a strand of hair off his forehead. "I have no doubt that it's going to be even better when it's you."

His smile was brilliant. "I'm positive that it will be the best you've ever had."

"Since Max's bite was the only other one, and it wasn't great, it's not such a big challenge to do better."

"Oh, yeah?"

"Yeah." Darlene slapped Eric's arm playfully. "Just go brush your teeth already, so you can come back to bed." She pulled the nightgown over her head and handed it to him. "Put this in the trash bin, will you?"

His eyes blazed with an inner light. "Yes, ma'am."

Sofia

Sofia yawned and stretched her arms over her head. "I think we have no choice. We need to get out of bed and get something to eat. I'm starving."

Smiling, Marcel caressed her bare back. "I can make a dash to the kitchen, raid the refrigerator, and bring the loot back here."

"Go for it." She cupped his cheek and pressed a kiss to his lips. "I'll take a shower while you're hunting for food to bring back to the cave."

Grunting like a gorilla, he punched his chest. "Me, Tarzan. You, Jane. I bring food. But first, shower." He kissed the tip of her nose and then jumped out of bed and sprinted for the bathroom.

She loved seeing Marcel smiling and joking around. He'd been so scared of her reaction to his confession, and the truth was that it had been a shocking revelation, but from a human's perspective of time, the crime had happened so long ago that the statute of limitations should have kicked in. Not that he could stand trial in a human court, but his clan laws were probably similar. Did premeditated murder even have a statute of limitations?

Had it been premeditated, though?

Yeah, it had been.

Marcel had followed Cordelia's husband home, not to have a chat with him or even to give him a warning. He'd planned to kill the man.

So why couldn't she bring herself to be repulsed by it or even judge Marcel harshly for it?

Perhaps her savage one-quarter Kra-ell was overriding the three-quarters human? Or maybe it was the influence of growing up with purebloods and hybrids and absorbing their attitudes? Or perhaps she was just blinded by love the way Marcel had been with that bitch.

Cordelia deserved to forever walk in the valley of the shamed.

Or did she?

Would the Mother of All Life fault her for plotting to get rid of her husband if he'd wronged her?

Probably not.

"Ugh, religion is so frustrating."

"Did you say something?" Marcel called from the bathroom.

"I was talking to myself."

With a sigh, Sofia tossed the blanket aside and slid out of bed. She needed to use the bathroom, but despite making love to Marcel in every possible position, she wasn't comfortable peeing in front of him yet.

Instead, she grabbed a fresh outfit and went to the bathroom in the next room over.

When she returned to the bedroom, she found Marcel sitting on the bed with his phone pressed against his ear.

"Perhaps I should start the coffee." She turned to go back out.

Marcel looked up. "It's Turner. He wants to speak with you."

"Now? Can't he wait for me to have some coffee?"

It surprised her that the strategist worked during the weekend. Not many humans were willing to give up their free days. Should she be glad or worried that he did?

Marcel had reassured her that his people were just collecting information and that they were not planning to attack the compound, but maybe they were going to help Jade and the others free themselves. Did that require working on a Sunday?

They must deem the matter urgent for some reason.

Perhaps Jade had contacted them with new information?

"Here." Marcel handed her the phone. "I'll make you coffee." He activated the speaker. "Sofia is here, Turner."

"Thank you," Turner said. "How are you this afternoon?"

Was it afternoon already? She hadn't checked the time.

"I'm very well, thank you. What can I help you with?"

"I need to know the wording Igor used to phrase his monthly compulsion sessions with you."

Sitting on the bed, she let out a breath. "It was more or less the same thing every month with only a few slight variations. I was to keep the existence of the Kra-ell a secret. I was to keep the location of the compound a secret. I was to do everything in my power to protect the compound and its inhabitants, and I was never to do anything that could endanger the compound and its inhabitants. I was to report to the security office any suspicious activity that might endanger the compound, and I was to follow the commands of my superiors in order of their hierarchy. Igor's command overruled commands given by Valstar, Valstar's commands overruled that of everyone under him, and so on. When I was away, I had to call once a week to report, and I had to come back in person once a month."

"Do you know if others received the same commands?"

"Igor held weekly assemblies which everyone in the compound had to attend, and he repeated the same instructions, except for the two last ones that were specific to me and the other students who got to leave the compound. Other humans got private one-on-one sessions with Igor only once in a while, if at all, and I don't know how often the hybrids and the purebloods got private sessions with him, but I think it was quite often."

Turner sighed. "That's what I thought. Igor is very thorough."

He sounded as if he admired the guy, which annoyed her, but she could understand how the strategist might be appreciative of another's talent.

"Does it make a difference?" She was afraid to hear Turner's answer.

"Regrettably, yes. Even if it was possible to deliver a message to your father, neither he nor your aunts could deliver it to Jade without reporting it to someone. The term Igor used was 'anything suspicious,' and delivering a secret message to Jade would definitely fall under that description."

Sofia's heart fell.

Turner was right. How come it hadn't occurred to her? She should have realized that her father and aunts would be bound by the compulsion. Now that she was free, it was so easy to forget the effect Igor's compulsion had on her life. She still had to contend with Tom's, but it didn't feel as oppressive and heavy-handed as Igor's.

"Here is your coffee." Marcel handed her a cup and sat down next to her on the bed.

"Thank you." She took a small sip. "So I guess the idea of helping a rebellion led by Jade is out."

"Don't worry. I will come up with a way to free your people. I have a couple more questions. Are Jade and Igor exclusive with one another?"

"Igor is not for sure, but I don't know about Jade. Maybe she's just more discreet than him. None of the purebloods are exclusive. It goes against the Mother's teachings and their tradition."

"That's what I thought, but I wanted to make sure. My last question is, how do the pureblood and hybrid females wear their hair?"

"Either loose, braided, or in a ponytail. Why?"

"If we find a way to supply a few main players with compulsion-blocking earpieces, they will need to hide them under their hair."

Hope surged in Sofia's chest once more. "The hybrid and pureblooded males wear their hair long too. Well, most do. I've seen two hybrids with modern haircuts. Maybe they were sent on an undercover mission."

"Excellent. That will make it easy for them to hide the earpieces."

"How are you going to get the devices to them? And wouldn't Igor's compulsion force them to report that?"

Turner chuckled. "Patience, Sofia. I'm still working on it."

Marcel

Sofia returned the phone to Marcel. "The fantasy was nice while it lasted. I got carried away imagining tiny robot spiders and drones, and I forgot the human element that's under Igor's compulsion."

"We all make mistakes. Well, maybe not Turner." He returned the phone to his pocket. "Do you still want to stay here while I get food? Or do we go together?"

"Let's go to the dining hall. But if Roxie or anyone else from the retreat sees us, we tell them that we just came back. I don't want her to think that I returned without coming over to say hello."

"Of course." He offered her his arm. "If you want, we can go around and dine in the paranormal enclave's private dining room. It's where the clinic is."

"Am I allowed in there?"

"You are with me now, and you know about immortals, so you're governed by a different set of rules."

With all the back and forth between him and Kian, Marcel wasn't sure what he had gotten permission for and what he had not, but since he'd already told Sofia the biggest secret, he assumed that everything else fell under that umbrella.

"Can I rejoin the retreat?" she asked.

"You can if you want to, but I'd rather you spent your time with me."

"Don't you have a job to do?"

He put the code into the keypad. "I'm on an unofficial vacation. The team I was supervising was sent home."

She arched a brow. "Am I your new job?"

He paused just outside the door at the top of the stairs and pulled her into his arms. "You are my everything."

She didn't smile. "Do you love me?"

"Are you still doubting my feelings for you?"

"You've never said the actual words."

"Neither have you."

Sofia frowned. "Haven't I? I was sure that I had."

He shook his head. "We both admitted to having fallen for each other, which is basically saying the same thing, just without the word love in it."

"The Kra-ell don't believe in love."

He took her hand and led her out of the cottage. "We are not Kra-ell. Someone once told me that the definition of love is not being able to stay away from your beloved or being unable to imagine life without her. Since both are true for me, I must be in love with you."

Sofia rolled her eyes. "That's the most unromantic way to tell a woman that you love her, and it's also so you. I can't believe that in your youth, you were ruled by your emotions. You're so logical and analytical now."

Marcel's good mood took a nosedive. "I was a different man back then. I don't think that guy is still in here." He touched a hand to his chest. "I think that he died three centuries ago."

For some reason, his comment had Sofia smile brilliantly. "Here is a solution to your feelings of guilt. You killed yourself along with Cordelia's husband, so you've already been punished, and you can let go of the guilt."

This time Marcel couldn't blame the venom for Sofia's dismissive attitude toward the crime he'd committed. He hadn't bitten her this morning, and the venom from last night was long gone from her system.

"I wish I could, but I can't. Once this crisis is over, your people are free, and things go back to normal, I'll walk into our judge's office, confess my crime, and accept any punishment she deems appropriate."

"Don't." She stopped and lifted their clasped hands to her chest. "What if the judge sentences you to life in prison? I just found you. I can't lose you."

"I don't think she will, but she might sentence me to whipping or a short entombment." When tears started spilling from the corners of Sofia's eyes, he lifted their hands to his lips and kissed her knuckles. "If she gives me a choice, I'll choose the whipping. I don't want to be away from you even for a few days."

"Then don't do it. You don't need some judge to absolve you of your crimes. Let me be your judge and determine your punishment."

He smiled. "And what would that punishment be?"

Sofia resumed walking. "Community service of some sort. Eleanor said that your people rescue trafficking victims and help rehabilitate them. You can be one of the rescuers. You used to be a Guardian, so you have the skills." She tilted her head. "I doubt you'd be any good in helping with the rehabilitation, though. Your bedside manner leaves a lot to be desired."

"Oh, yeah? What about my in-bed manner? Does that leave a lot to be desired as well?"

Sofia shook her head. "Men. No matter what species, you are always insecure about your performance. Yours was fine."

He stopped in his tracks. "Just fine?"

Laughing, she tugged on his hand. "It was exceptional."

"That's better." He let Sofia drag him behind her for a couple of moments. "The dining hall is on your left."

"Oh." She changed direction. "So, what do you think about my idea?"

"It has merit, but I enjoy what I'm doing now much more than I ever enjoyed being a Guardian."

"Perfect. Then it will be a real punishment for you."

Toven

As Toven climbed the steps to Bridget and Turner's house, the door opened and Turner stepped out. "Good afternoon. Thanks for accepting my invitation. I didn't want to drag everyone to Kian's office on a Sunday."

"No problem. I'm glad to help in any way I can."

"Hello." Bridget walked over and offered him her hand. "Where is Mia?"

"She opted to stay with her grandparents. They were a little upset about having to cut their weekend in Arcadia short."

Turner led him to the couch where Vrog and Aliya were sitting. "I wouldn't have asked for you to come if it wasn't important. I need to test the Kra-ell's susceptibility to thralling and shrouding."

"You mentioned that when you called." Toven offered his hand to Aliya, who looked anxious. "Don't worry. Thralling and shrouding don't hurt."

"I know. I can do a little of that myself on humans. But that's the thing. What works on Vrog and me might not work on the purebloods. And if the male holding Jade is as powerful as everyone says, he might be immune."

"Not every compeller is immune," Turner said. "Eleanor is immune, but Emmett is not. Annani successfully compelled him to reveal the numbers of his Swiss bank accounts, and we all know that he wouldn't have volunteered them."

As a knock sounded at the door, Bridget walked over to open it. "Hello, Kian."

"Hello, everyone. Apologies for my late arrival."

"No apology needed." Bridget motioned for them to move to the dining table. "I prepared some snacks."

Looking at the place settings, Toven lifted a brow. "Are we expecting more people?"

"Yes." Turner pulled out a chair for Bridget. "Onegus and Yamanu are going to join us in a few minutes. I want to conduct an experiment. We will start with Bridget. Her thralling and shrouding abilities are good, but Onegus's are better, Yamanu's are superior, and yours are divine." He chuckled at his own lame joke. "Bridget, you go first."

She smiled at Aliya. "Ready?"

"Yes."

"I'll start with an illusion. Here it goes."

No response registered on Aliya's or Vrog's faces, so Toven concluded that they didn't see Bridget's illusion.

"Nothing?" Bridget asked. "Not even a flicker?"

"Nothing," Aliya said. "What was your illusion?"

"A rainbow unicorn. The little kids love it when I project it into their minds. They forget all about my checkups and vaccinations."

Turner glanced at his watch. "I'd better open the door for our two other guests."

Toven cast Kian a sidelong glance. "Why don't you give it a try?"

Kian shrugged. "Turner wants me to observe, not to participate."

That was odd. What could Turner's motives be? Was Kian still uncomfortable about showing the extent of his powers in front of Toven? Was he embarrassed about not being as powerful as a god? Or was he powerful but didn't want to show his hand?

If so, it was uncalled for and somewhat offensive.

So far, Toven had provided his assistance whenever he'd been asked. He was part of the family, and it was time they treated him as such.

As the two Guardians walked into the living room, and a round of hellos and how-are-yous ensued, Toven crossed his arms over his chest and waited for the show to begin.

"Vrog and Aliya didn't see Bridget's illusion," Turner told Onegus. "You go next."

The chief nodded. "Do you also want me to thrall them?"

Turner looked at Vrog. "Only if you agree to be thralled." He shifted his gaze to Aliya. "I only mentioned illusions when I invited you."

"I don't mind," Vrog said. "I have no secrets to hide."

"I don't have any either," Aliya said.

"I'm not going to sift through your memories," Onegus said. "I will plant new ones."

That was less intrusive and Toven approved.

"I'll start with the illusion." Onegus looked at the two of them.

Aliya frowned, and Vrog leaned forward.

"Do you see anything?" Turner asked.

"I see an outline of a shape," Vrog said. "Is it a butterfly?"

Onegus chuckled. "Close. It's a baby dragon."

"I only got an impression of wings," Aliya said.

"Let's try the thrall." He looked into Aliya's eyes.

She gasped. "It worked. I remember seeing a baby dragon, but I know that's a fake memory."

It worked on Vrog just as well.

"My turn." Yamanu rubbed his enormous hands together.

"I see it!" Aliya exclaimed. "It's a cute little alien with big black eyes."

Yamanu smirked. "Correct."

"But it's not solid," Vrog said. "Is it supposed to be a ghost?"

The smile slid off Yamanu's face. "Damn. I was sure you would see my illusion." He shifted his eyes to Turner. "Should I thrall them now?"

"We can try that later." Turner looked at Toven. "It's your turn, Your Majesty."

Toven cut him a glare. "You're lucky that you are immune. I would have set your house on illusionary fire for calling me that."

"Hey," Bridget protested. "It's my house, too."

Toven smiled at her. "For you, doctor, I would have created a much nicer illusion."

"Can you cast different illusions for different people at the same time?" Kian asked.

"I can. But today, I'm going to treat all of you to the same one."

Closing his eyes, he imagined them sitting in the opera house, watching and listening to the *Phantom of the Opera*.

Since Rosalyn loved that opera and even sang along to the recording, he knew it well enough to recreate it in his imagination.

"Amazing," Bridget whispered.

"What do you see?" Turner asked.

"The *Phantom of the Opera* is on the stage of a large concert hall, and we are all sitting in a private booth, dressed to the nines like royalty. I love it."

Kian chuckled. "Who needs a Perfect Match machine when we have Toven to entertain us."

"Why did you stop?" Aliya asked. "It was so beautiful."

Toven gave her an apologetic smile. "That's all I remember. But if you enjoyed it, stop by our house at any time, and Mia's grandmother will gladly put it on for you and join you to watch it. It's her favorite musical, and when I'm in the mood, I sing the duet with her."

Like all gods, he had a great singing voice, and whenever he capitulated to Rosalyn's pleading for him to sing with her, she was so delighted that he had no heart to refuse.

"I would love that." Aliya cast Vrog a sidelong glance. "But I would love even more to see it in an opera house like the one Toven showed us."

"That was the Metropolitan Opera house in New York." Kian pushed to his feet. "If you want to go, you will have to wait for this crisis to blow over first."

Kian

Kian had hoped that Yamanu would be enough and that he wouldn't need to get Toven involved on the ground in Karelia.

Were they actually going to do it?

He felt as if he was getting dragged into action before it was actually needed. If not for Jade's message to Emmett, they wouldn't have known about Igor, and Igor wouldn't have known about them. But now the clan had one of Igor's subjects, and she was possibly Marcel's fated one.

Once again, the situation had the Fates' signature all over it, and Kian resented being used by them to further their plans.

"The purebloods," Turner said. "How many of them were strong compellers? And could they compel each other?"

Vrog put down the glass of water he'd been sipping on. "All purebloods could compel to some extent. But it only worked on hybrids, humans, and animals. They couldn't compel each other."

"Then how come you still feel compelled to help Jade?" Kian asked.

"I'm a hybrid, and she could've compelled me, but she didn't. I took a vow to serve her loyally to the day I die, and I take my vows seriously, but I also vowed loyalty to the clan, and I will not betray it even if it means betraying the one I made to Jade."

"The Mother punishes vow breakers." Aliya's olive-toned skin turned a shade paler. "They are doomed to forever walk in the valley of the shamed."

Vrog took her hand. "I've been a good steward of the tribe's money, and I will give it all back. That should satisfy the Mother."

Aliya didn't look sure at all, but she nodded. "I'll pray for the Mother to accept your gift."

"It's not only mine. Half of those funds are yours."

The sale of his school brought Vrog a nice chunk of money, and he'd planned to use it to open a new school near the village, but since Kian had offered to finance the project, Vrog got to keep his money.

Aliya shook her head. "I never thought of the money as mine."

Turner lifted his hand. "Let's get back to the reason we are here. Are you sure that Jade couldn't compel the other purebloods?"

"I'm not," Vrog admitted. "Perhaps Emmett can answer that question better than I since he has the ability. He says that he can even compel purebloods, but Emmett likes to boast, and I'm not sure I believe him." Vrog grimaced. "Don't base any of your military decisions on what he tells you. He's not a bad guy, but he's not very Kra-ell in nature."

Vrog had said it as if being a Kra-ell was a badge of honor.

"Maybe that's a good thing." Kian reached for the cookies Bridget had put on the table. "The Kra-ell are too bloodthirsty for my taste, pun intended."

"Indeed." Turner leaned back in his chair. "I'll sum up what we've learned so far, and then I'll tell you my plan."

That was unexpected. "Is it ready?"

"I still need to iron out a few details, and naturally, it's up to you to act on it or not, but you asked me to prepare an actionable plan, which I did."

"Let's hear it," Onegus said.

"Given the intel we have, spiders are not an option," Turner started. "The ones that would go unnoticed by the Kra-ell guards are too small to carry a charge that will allow them to traverse the distance from the first tunnel all the way to the compound and then roam around the compound itself. We can't drop them from the air either because they are too fragile for that. So as far as using them for spying, it's not going to work. Personally, I don't like them, and I never use them on missions. They are good for urban settings when you can drop one in a hallway and have it crawl under a door to eavesdrop on a meeting. They are useless in rough terrain."

"What about drones?" Kian asked.

"Drones are better. We can use the same tactic we used on the Doomers' island. A small drone will piggyback on a larger one and get dropped directly over the compound, but that will do us no good, either. I asked Sofia to tell me the precise wording of Igor's routine compulsion, and it turns out that everyone in there is compelled to report anything suspicious to security. What it means is that delivering a message or a pair of earpieces is out of the question as well. The only way we can collect information is by capturing a pureblood, breaking Igor's compulsion, getting the pureblood to reveal the compound's military setup and anything else that we need intel on, and then thralling and compelling him to forget that he'd been captured."

Kian groaned. "That means sending Toven to Karelia along with Mia, and that's not going to happen."

"Why not?" Toven asked. "I'm willing to go, and so is Mia."

Kian gaped at him. "Are you willing to take your fragile mate into enemy territory?"

"I can protect her." Toven affected a haughty expression. "You keep forgetting that I am a god. I can freeze the minds of any would-be attackers in a five-mile radius. No one would be able to get close enough to do Mia any harm."

"Can you really do that?" Onegus asked. "Five-mile radius is a damn big area."

Toven shrugged. "I might have exaggerated a little. In any case, though, no one will get within shooting range of my mate."

"Provided that you are aware of them," Kian pointed out. "What if they sneak up on you?"

"We can mitigate that," Onegus said. "A team of Guardians can form a shield around Toven and Mia."

"Hold on." Turner lifted his hand. "I'm not done explaining my plan."

Toven

Toven nodded. "Go ahead, Turner."

"Thank you. My plan is basically going back to what we talked about before the ideas about spiders and drones muddied the water, but with the inclusion of Jade. The first step will be to drive the cat around with Sofia in the car. Eleanor could pose as Sofia, but that would only work from a distance, and I wouldn't risk it. Sofia should be in the car, and a team of Guardians should follow her in another vehicle. Hopefully, she will have a tail, and we will catch it. And hopefully, it will be a pureblood. If not, we will start from stage two of my plan, but let me finish with stage one first. Since only Toven can break Igor's compulsion, and since he needs Mia to fortify his power, he needs to be on standby in the area." He turned to Toven. "If you liked the house I secured for you before, I can arrange the same one again."

"Mia loved the house overlooking the ocean, and she loved being needed." Toven drummed his fingers on the dining table. "But the truth is that I might not need Mia to break the compulsion on a pureblood. I was careful with Sofia because she is human and fragile. When I pushed too hard, it had an adverse effect on her. I won't be as gentle with a Kra-ell pureblood."

"That would be a great way to test it," Turner said. "If you can break through the compulsion without Mia's help, you might not need her for the second stage of the plan, and that would make Kian happy." Turner looked at Kian. "Right?"

Kian groaned. "Nothing about this is making me happy. Please, go on."

"I believe that we need to act as swiftly as possible." Turner looked at Toven. "You will need to fly out tonight. I want to deploy the cat tomorrow morning."

"That's not a problem."

Mia's grandparents might be upset about her leaving again, especially after she had told them what the previous trip had been all about, but they wouldn't put up too much of a fuss. They were proud of their granddaughter's unique ability to enhance other paranormal talents.

"Thank you." Turner dipped his head. "It's a real pleasure working with you, Toven. Kian will send additional Guardians along, and they will have tranq guns with them." He looked at Bridget. "You need to calibrate those darts to knock out pureblood Kra-ell."

"No problem. I'll use the recommended dose for gorillas." When he gave her a perplexed look, she laughed. "I'm just joking. I'll use the recommended dose for male tigers. They weigh about the same as the average adult human. The Kra-ell are taller, but they are slimmer, so they should weigh about the same."

"The Guardians need titanium chains to secure a pureblood," Onegus said. "For the interrogation."

Toven chuckled. "As long as the Guardians keep the Kra-ell asleep until they bring them to me, no chains will be needed. I can paralyze them without uttering a single word."

"Right." Turner nodded respectfully. "But let me remind you that a pureblood is the equivalent of a god, not an immortal, and you might not be able to seize his mind. I'd rather err on the side of caution, and so would Kian."

Turner was right. Toven had been thinking about the Kra-ell as he would about immortals, but that only applied to the hybrid Kra-ell. The purebloods might not be as powerful as the gods, but they might be more resistant to thralling than immortals. Most gods couldn't control each other's minds, and he was no exception. Mortdh and Ahn had possessed the ability to some extent, but since it was illegal to use thralling on another god, Toven hadn't witnessed either of them breaking that law. He'd only suspected they could do that based on rumors.

"I agree. Chains are needed."

"Also," Turner continued. "Even if you can break the compulsion on the pureblood without Mia's help, I'd rather you did it with her. A lot rests on that pureblood not reporting to Igor about getting captured and interrogated."

Toven nodded. "I understand."

Onegus cleared his throat. "Should we wait until we take the cat for a ride to send the team to Karelia?"

"No." Turner flipped the page on his yellow pad. "It's a long flight, and they need to do reconnaissance work in preparation. They should go as planned and wait in St. Petersburg for further instructions. I had a local contact arrange lodging for them and supply them with everything they need."

"He can't supply them with exoskeletons," Onegus said. "We can't fight the Kra-ell without them."

"We are not fighting the Kra-ell just yet." Turner tapped his pen on the yellow pad. "Their job will be to catch one of the guards at the entrance to the tunnel, but they will have to wait for Toven to arrive. Naturally, Sylvia will be instrumental in disabling the cameras on the way to the tunnel, but she doesn't need to go with the first team. She can join Toven and Mia when they go."

Kian lifted his hand. "Hold on. You said that if we catch a tail in Safe Haven, Toven might not need to go to Karelia."

"I said that he might not need Mia, but I prefer for her to join him."

Kian

The more Turner's plan unfolded, the less Kian liked it. Sofia's idea to help Jade start a rebellion had appealed to him much more, but what Turner had said obliterated that idea.

"If we catch a pureblood using the cat with the tracker as bait, why do we need to bother with the guards at the entrance to the tunnel unless your plan is to invade the compound?"

"I was getting to that." Turner made a checkmark on his yellow pad. "We need the guard to deliver a message to Jade that will not trigger Igor's compulsion to report it to security. The guard will invite Jade to go with him hunting for a Veskar, at a specific time and at a specific spot, and it will be veiled as an invitation to have sex. Jade will suspect something because of the mention of Veskar, but since she won't be sure, it won't trigger her compulsion to report it. Even if Igor finds out about it, the mention of Veskar would be meaningless to him."

Turner shifted his eyes to Vrog. "I hope that a Veskar is not a ferocious giant rat."

Vrog chuckled. "It's the size of a squirrel. To invite Jade to hunt for it would be taken as an insult, but it could also be taken as a joke or a pun, so it might work."

"How do you plan for us to get to their hunting grounds without them noticing us?" Onegus asked.

"With an amphibian vehicle. There are many rivers and small lakes in the area, and the rivers are not boat-friendly. The Kra-ell can't monitor all the waterways, and they have no reason to do that given that they are not easily navigable."

"They probably have guards posted at strategic points," Onegus said. "It would be remiss of them not to do that, and Igor doesn't seem like the sort of guy who would overlook anything."

"Obviously." Turner nodded. "After interrogating the guards, we will find out how he addresses that problem, and we will adapt accordingly. He doesn't have limitless resources, and he needs to prioritize. Areas that are difficult for humans to traverse will be less guarded."

"What do we do once we catch Jade?" Kian asked.

"Toven frees her from the compulsion, and we give her earpieces. Hopefully, she will be able to solve the problem for us by killing Igor, but we can't count on that."

"She can't kill him," Onegus said. "Leon and Marcel briefed me in detail about what Sofia told them. Sofia was searched every time she came for her monthly compulsion reinforcement sessions with him, once at the gate, again at the entrance to the office building, and a third time right before going into Igor's office. The guy is super careful, and he's not relying solely on his compulsion ability for safety." Onegus cast Toven a meaningful glance. "If he has a weak human searched before allowing her in his presence, I'm sure he has Jade searched much more thoroughly for weapons, and I doubt that she's strong enough to overpower him physically with her bare hands."

"Didn't Sofia say that Jade is Igor's top breeder?" Kian asked.

"She did," Onegus said. "Sofia also told Marcel and Leon that Jade doesn't hide her hatred for Igor. A paranoid guy like him would be even more careful with someone he takes to his bed. Sofia also mentioned that he's guarded at all times. In addition, we should assume that he carries weapons and sleeps with a gun under his pillow. If we want to do away with him, we should aim a missile at the office building and take out the compound's entire upper echelon."

"That's part of the last resort contingency," Turner said. "If possible, I prefer for the Kra-ell to take care of the problem for us. The less we reveal ourselves to them, the better. Jade is a clever female, and she might come up with a solution." He smiled. "If Igor sleeps with a gun under his pillow, she might be able to get ahold of it."

They should be so lucky.

"What if she can't do anything?" Yamanu asked. "Where does the shrouding and the thralling come into play?"

"The shrouding and thralling are also part of the last resort contingency plan in case all the previous steps are exhausted without producing the results we want. The next step in my plan is for Jade to start recruiting other purebloods who might join her rebellion. If she can get a couple of strong males who are willing to help her, we can free them from Igor's compulsion, supply them with earpieces, and have them kill Igor. Once he's gone, the rest will be easy. Toven can free everyone from Igor's compulsion without revealing who he is. As far as they are concerned, we are a group of paranormally talented humans."

"I'm starting to like your plan," Kian said. "If it works, we just leave Jade in charge and keep our eye on her. We can't let her treat the humans in the compound the way she'd treated those who served her tribe. Whoever wants to leave will be allowed to do so after we confuse their memories, and those who decide to stay will get paid for their services. We will have to monitor her to make sure she follows the new protocol."

"What's your contingency plan in case the assassination plan fails?" Onegus asked.

"If it fails, we have to go in. Igor will kill the males, find the earpieces, and know that someone is helping them. He will immediately connect the dots and come after Safe Haven."

Kian shook his head. "We don't have enough Guardians."

"We don't," Turner smirked. "But we can make them think that we do. That's where the shrouding comes in. Toven and Yamanu will project an image of our warriors in their exoskeletons multiplied tenfold. Igor and his cronies will think that they are being attacked by a large alien force."

"He won't surrender," Vrog said. "The Kra-ell fight to the death."

Turner leveled his pale blue eyes at the guy. "Igor spits in the face of Kra-ell tradition, but you are right; he won't surrender. Like any other despot, he only cares about his own skin, and he will try to escape. We need to make sure that he doesn't."

Eric

"Here you go, sweetie." Darlene handed Evan a big piece of watermelon.

Eric turned to Idina. "Do you want some?"

"No." She didn't even look up at him.

"Why not? Don't you like watermelon?" He knew that she did.

"I don't want the juice to make my new dress dirty."

"I can tie a napkin around your neck and put another one over your lap. How's that?"

She eyed him with her dark gaze. "Promise that I will have no juice stains on my dress."

"I promise." He took his napkin and hers and covered her up. "All good?"

Nodding, she extended her small hand. "Watermelon, please."

"You didn't say thank you," Karen admonished.

"Thank you." Idina still held her hand out. "Watermelon, please."

"Here you go." Darlene handed her a chunk and turned to Karen. "How are you holding up without Gilbert?"

"The better question is, how am I holding up without Berta and Cheryl. Gilbert was never a big help around the house or with the little ones, but I had Berta. I feel so guilty for letting her go without even saying a proper goodbye. She's been with us for so many years."

"Berta is great." Kaia handed Ryan a juicy piece. "She'll find a new job in a heartbeat. Also, Gilbert promised to pay her six months' worth of work as severance pay. She might take a long, well-deserved vacation."

"What about Cheryl?" Darlene asked. "Is schoolwork keeping her busy?"

Karen nodded. "Between homework and waitressing for Callie, she can barely catch her breath, but I'm so happy that she no longer has her nose in that Instatock app all day long."

"Does she enjoy waitressing?" Eric asked. "It's hard work."

"She does," Kaia said. "She gets to spend time with her two new besties, and Callie pays her well. I'm so happy that Cheryl loves it in the village. I was worried that she wouldn't."

Darlene sighed. "Our reservation at Callie's is in two weeks. I can't wait for our turn in Callie's place."

"It's beautiful," Kaia said. "But right now, it is too big for what she can manage. She has about twenty, square tables sized for couples, while the dining area can easily hold ten times as many. Callie tried to fill the space up with couches and big planters, which adds to the exclusive vibe and provides the diners with a sense of privacy, but if she manages to hire more people, she can add more tables and serve more clients."

"What's the decor like?" Darlene asked.

Kaia pursed her lips. "It's modern with island vibes. I liked it a lot. In fact, I told William that I want to decorate our house in the same style."

Eric waved a dismissive hand. "I don't care about the decor. How was the food?"

"Delicious." William's eyes started glowing. "It's good that the waiting list is so long, or we'd be dining there every day."

Kaia glared at him. "What's wrong with my cooking?"

"Nothing, my love. You are an excellent cook, but I'd rather you rested after a long day of work instead of spending an hour or more on food preparation."

"Good save," Eric murmured.

"It's the truth." William lifted his hand to his nose as if he was still wearing glasses and needed to push them up.

"What did she serve?" Darlene asked. "I heard that it's a fixed menu, and you get what you get."

"There were five courses," Kaia said.

"The appetizer was mushroom crostini, and she served it on beautiful crystal plates." Kaia gestured with her fingers to indicate the size. "About this big. The second course was a salad made of mixed greens, beets, goat cheese, and almond slivers."

"The third course was soup." William licked his lips. "It was the best butternut squash soup I've had the pleasure to sample, and I've sampled many in the fanciest restaurants. She made tiny croutons from red bell peppers, all of different heights, and they were centered in each soup bowl, looking like high-rise buildings surrounded by an orange lake. It was such a pretty presentation." He shifted his eyes to Eric. "It makes a difference, you know. The presentation, the decor, the sounds in the background, all come together to create a one-of-a-kind culinary experience. Callie nailed it."

"There were three different main courses." Kaia wiped the juice from Ryan's chin. "One was almond-crusted tilapia with roasted vegetables. The second was seafood paella, and the third was a vegetable paella for Kian and the other vegetarians. The fifth course was a choice of marzipan cake, chocolate cake, coffee, and tea."

"You forgot to mention the champagne and the wines," William said. "Callie told us that she will be serving champagne every day for an entire month to celebrate the opening. She wants everyone to feel like they were at the opening night."

"That's so nice of her," Darlene said. "I wonder what she'll serve when it's our turn. I hope the seafood paella will be on the menu for that night."

After Idina and the boys were moved to the den, Karen got that conspiratorial look on her face that warned Eric about what was coming next.

"So, did you do it?"

Darlene frowned. "How did you know that we were planning it? Did Eric tell you?"

"Don't be mad. He told Gilbert. You know why."

Darlene sighed. "Yeah. You are in the same boat as me."

"I wish." Karen winced. "My grandfather is not a god."

"Right." Darlene looked at Eric. "Just tell them. But try to be mindful of how I feel about it."

He nodded. "It was awkward as hell," he admitted. "Especially for Darlene. Max chained me to the bed, which I thought was absurd, but he was right. When he bit Darlene, I wanted to tear him apart, and I discovered that I was as strong as a damn gorilla. I pulled on the chains and toppled the posts. Those were not twigs. They were massive. I would have never been able to do that as a human."

Karen looked at Darlene with alarm in her eyes. "Are you okay? Did you get hurt?"

Darlene shook her head. "Eric protected me. The posts fell on him, but since he's immortal now, nothing broke, and he was as good as new the next morning."

William smirked. "Welcome to the club, Eric. Our civilized veneers hide dangerous animals. Most of the time they lie dormant, but when our mates are threatened, the beasts come out."

"Max didn't threaten me." Darlene looked down at her plate. "He was doing us a favor."

"The beasts are mindless," William said. "They are all instinct and very little thought. Max was smart to chain Eric to the bed."

Eleanor

"Got it. Thanks, Julian." Eleanor ended the call, put the pen down, and turned to Sofia. "Julian sent the referral to the cardiologist, and he gave me the precise wording for the fake diagnosis."

They needed to start building the case for Sofia's fake heart problem, and a visit to the cardiologist's office was the perfect excuse for a road trip that would include the cat with the tracker, killing two birds with one stone so to speak.

Sofia shook her head. "Marcel told me that it's not permitted to thrall humans unless it is done to protect the secret of immortals' existence or their lives. How are you going to justify thralling the doctor?"

"Easy. You are a potential immortal, and if we don't fake your death convincingly enough, your life will be in danger. Besides, I'm not going to thrall anyone. Marcel is going to do that. I can only compel." Eleanor leaned her elbows on her thighs and rested her chin on her fist. "A diagnosis by a human cardiologist who is in no way connected to us will be more convincing than just your word."

"Igor knows that you have compellers. He might suspect that you compelled the Safe Haven doctor to send the referral to the cardiologist, and since you are coming with me, they might suspect that you compelled that doctor as well."

"Good point. We should also plant some fake test results to make it look more legit." She dialed Julian's number again.

"What did you forget?" the doctor asked.

"Sofia pointed out that Igor knows we have compellers, so having a couple of doctors write fake diagnoses is not a problem for us. Can you have Roni plant fake test results in the cardiologist's files?"

Julian groaned. "I can probably get some, but it's not something that I can do in the next hour or two. When are you seeing the cardiologist?"

"In about three hours. I can also compel him to swap results with another patient or copy them and put them in Sofia's file."

"That would be much easier. Don't have him swap, though. Just copy them. We don't want to endanger someone's life."

"Got it. Thanks, Julian." She ended the call, pushed to her feet, and put the phone in the pocket of her jacket. "You didn't say anything about my new look." She turned in a circle.

Sofia frowned. "I don't think that my hairstyle looks good on you."

That wasn't nice. Eleanor thought that she looked great with her hair pinned up. "It's not about looking good. I just need to look like you from a distance."

"No, you don't." Sofia put her hand on her hip. "Since we've decided that I'm going too and you don't need to pretend to be me, what's the point?"

Eleanor shrugged. "I put a lot of effort into making myself look like you, and I didn't want to let it go to waste."

"Are we ready to go?" Marcel asked.

"We are." Eleanor picked the cat off the windowsill and turned to Leon. "Are your guys ready?"

"They are waiting for you in the parking garage."

"Good. I hope Cecilia behaves and doesn't pee or puke in the car. Cats are not fond of moving vehicles, and Emmett will be furious if she has an accident in his Lamborghini." Eleanor handed the bundle of fur to Sofia. "You hold her."

"I'm prepared in case she has an accident." Sofia scratched under Cecelia's chin. "I put a couple of towels in my bag to put over my legs during the drive."

"Good thinking." Leon opened the door for them. "Have fun, kids."

"Thank you, Daddy." Eleanor blew him an air kiss.

"It's going to look strange," Marcel said. "Why would people take a cat to a cardiologist's office?"

"People do all kinds of crazy things." Eleanor started pulling out the pins that were holding her hair up. "Maybe we will have the cat's heart checked. I can pretend to be an eccentric cat owner who wants her cat treated by a human doctor."

Sofia chuckled. "You can just thrall them to ignore Cecilia. We don't want anything to seem unusual about my doctor's visit."

Marcel shook his head. "If we pick up a tail, and they are Kra-ell, I can't thrall them not to see the cat, and we are doing all this to flush them out. Maybe we should leave Cecilia in the car with Asher."

"That will look even weirder," Eleanor said. "It doesn't make sense for Sofia's guard to stay in the car while she goes to see the doctor."

Everyone in Safe Haven knew that Eleanor was with Emmett. That was why they were taking Emmett's new Lamborghini, and the Guardian was posing as himself, a guard to watch over Sofia. The doctor's visit needed to look legit, but all the rest needed to look suspicious enough for the tail to get intrigued and follow them all the way to the beach house.

It would have been even better if Emmett had accompanied them, but that was too dangerous.

Keeping his real identity a secret was crucial.

It was a mess, and despite the cheerful attitude Eleanor fronted, she was worried about her and Emmett's future in Safe Haven.

Unless they eliminated Igor, Kian would order all the immortals to leave the resort. She would have to find a solution for her paranormals, and the clan would have to move the expensive equipment they'd put in the lab out of there.

Emmett would be devastated, and she didn't have an alternative solution for him. They couldn't uproot the community and have it move to a different location, and even if they could, it wouldn't make a difference. The community members depended on the income generated from the retreats, and if they kept running them in a different location, they would be easy to find.

She and Emmett had only two options. They could go back to the village, where they would be safe, or stay in Safe Haven and live in constant fear. Except, Kian might not give them the option to stay and force them to move back into the village. If that happened, she would have to convince him to get a new location for the paranormals.

Eleanor had invested too much effort into the program to give it up.

Sofia

"That went well." Sofia entered the back seat of Emmett's fancy sports car and took Cecilia from Eleanor. "You were so good in the doctor's office." She tickled the cat's ear.

"She was." Eleanor sat behind the wheel of the fancy car. "How did I do playing the crazy diva who wants a cardiologist to check her cat's heart?" She eased into the traffic.

Sofia laughed. "You were hilarious. It was so hard not to laugh. I thought that you would thrall them to ignore Cecilia. That's such a nifty talent. I wish I had it."

"I can't thrall, remember? I can only compel."

"Why not? Marcel said that all immortals could thrall to some extent."

"Yeah, but those who transition as adults have a hard time doing it. Thralling needs to be practiced from a young age."

That was a shame. Sofia had hoped she would gain the ability once she transitioned, but apparently, that wasn't going to happen. Still, it wasn't a big deal considering everything else she would gain.

She was one-quarter Kra-ell, so maybe she would gain a slight compulsion ability.

The truth was that Sofia wasn't sure how thralling and compelling were different from each other. Eleanor had been the one who had dictated to the cardiologist what to write in his diagnosis, but Marcel had to thrall him to forget that he'd been told what to do. Then Eleanor compelled the doctor to take the test results of another patient and copy them to Sofia's file, and Marcel had once again thralled him to forget that the results weren't hers. If frequent thralling could potentially cause brain damage, the poor doctor might have suffered some. He'd even printed out everything for her to show her physician in Finland.

"Igor is going to flip when he sees the bill Riley sends him for your medical examination." Eleanor chuckled. "What do you think he will do?"

"I have no clue. Probably ignore it. Did you pay for it?"

"Yeah, but don't worry, it didn't come out of my own pocket. Kian will pay the credit card bill."

"Where to now?" the Guardian asked.

"I'm hungry," Eleanor said. "Can you look online for a place to eat?"

Asher pulled out his phone. "Anything specific that you have in mind?"

"Somewhere pets are allowed."

Cecelia lifted her ears as if she understood what Eleanor had said.

"I think she's hungry." Sofia smoothed her hand over the cat's back. "Should we give her another snack?"

Cecilia's ears twitched, and she tried to leap from Sofia's arms.

Sofia chuckled. "Now I'm sure that she understood what I said."

"Here you go." Marcel handed her a snack.

As the cat settled in her lap and started chewing, Sofia smiled. "I'm growing attached to this girl. I wonder if Anastasia would be willing to part with her."

Eleanor looked at her through the rearview mirror. "Where do you think you'll be taking her?"

"To your village. After I transition, that is."

"Are you sure that you will?" Eleanor asked. "I don't want you to get your hopes up and then get disappointed."

Sofia clasped Marcel's hand. "I strongly believe that I will." For Marcel's sake as much as for her own. "The Fates brought us together for a reason. Perhaps we are supposed to form a bridge between our people."

"Right." Eleanor glanced at the rearview mirror. "So far, it doesn't look as if anyone is following us, which is a serious setback to Turner's plan."

"He has a contingency," Marcel said. "If we can't catch a pureblood here, we will catch one in Karelia and get information out of him. We need to do that regardless, so we can get the guard to give Jade a message. The team is already on its way."

It was such a relief that they hadn't picked up a tail, but it was also tinged with disappointment. After her initial reaction to the news about the tracker, Sofia had entertained the absurd hope that maybe its purpose hadn't been to find out more about the people running Safe Haven, but for her protection, and that perhaps Valstar himself had followed her to the Oregon Coast to keep an eye on her and rescue her if she needed rescuing.

Right. Talk about delusional.

When they got to the restaurant, the hostess looked at Cecilia and smiled. "Pets are welcome, but only on the patio. Is that okay?"

"It's great." Eleanor kissed the top of the cat's head. "Cecilia was such a good girl at the doctor's office, and she deserves a reward. Do you have fish on the menu?"

"We do. She will love the tuna."

If anyone was watching them, which Sofia doubted, Eleanor had just given a great performance to reinforce their story.

"What about your friends?" Sofia asked Asher. "Shouldn't we invite them to join us?"

"It will blow their cover," the Guardian said. "They have to wait in the van."

"I hope they brought snacks," Eleanor said.

"I'm sure they did." Marcel opened the menu. "And if they didn't, they can get something at a drive-through while we are here. No one is going to attack us in a crowded restaurant."

Marcel

Marcel's phone rang twenty or so minutes into the drive back to Safe Haven.

"We have a tail," Morgan said. "Two men in a gray Honda Accord. The back windows are tinted, so there might be more, but I doubt it. Two is more than enough to follow the tracker around."

Asher, who had taken over driving, looked at Marcel through the rearview mirror. "I didn't see it, and I've been watching out for it the entire drive. I still don't see it."

"They are very subtle about it," Morgan said. "They never get close. The only reason we spotted them on the way back was that the traffic was so light they couldn't disappear among the other cars."

"I wonder what they thought about the doctor's visit," Marcel said.

Morgan chuckled. "I'm sure that they were disappointed. They probably expected us to haul Sofia to some secret location for interrogation, and all they got was a cardiology clinic."

They had hauled her to a secret location when they had taken her to Toven, but that had been without the tracker, and the tail hadn't known that she'd left Safe Haven.

"Maybe they thought that the clinic was a cover for our headquarters," Asher said. "We are heading toward the house. You know the plan."

"We do." Morgan ended the call.

Next to Marcel, Sofia sat ramrod straight, and given her pinched expression, she was fighting tears. "I hoped..." She hesitated. "I don't know what I hoped for. It was stupid."

Marcel wrapped his arm around her shoulders. "Did you hope for a rescue?"

She nodded. "It's not that I wanted to be rescued. I wanted to know that my grandfather cared enough to send someone to retrieve me."

"Maybe that's why they have been following us. When they saw that we took you to see the doctor and then to a restaurant, they probably reported to Valstar that everything you told him and Igor was true. You were on an outing with your new boyfriend, the one who you seduced to pump for information, and Eleanor and her brother were with you. You didn't need rescuing."

She let out a breath. "You are right. So it's all good. Igor got the confirmation he needed. I just hope that we don't blow the story up when we capture them."

"That depends on whether they show their hand when we execute our plan."

"What are we going to do with Cecilia?" Sofia asked.

"We will take her with us, of course." Eleanor pulled out a mesh backpack from her satchel. "I'll strap her to my chest and carry her like a baby."

For the next hour or so, the tense silence in the car was only interrupted by the cat's purring and from time to time, by Morgan's calls with updates about the Honda. The Guardians had deployed a small drone to follow it from a safe distance.

The tail had no reason to get close. The tracker informed them where Sofia was, or rather where the tracker was. The question was whether they would follow on foot once they could no longer follow with the car.

When Asher stopped at the designated spot, the four of them got out of the car, Marcel and Asher put their earpieces in, and Eleanor put the cat in the backpack.

"Sorry about this, kitty." She strapped the backpack to her chest and patted Cecilia through the mesh. "That's the best I could do on short notice."

It was getting dark, and as they started the climb up the rugged mountainside, Marcel took Sofia's clammy hand. "I won't let you fall."

"I'm not afraid of falling."

"It's dark, and you can't see as well as we do."

"I know you will keep me safe. What I am worried about is whether they will follow on foot. There is nothing on this mountain. They might think that we are just getting some exercise."

Eleanor snorted. "Right. A human with a heart condition and a crazy lady with a cat climbing a mountain in the dark for fun. No one would think that."

"They are out of the car," Morgan said in Marcel's earpiece. "Two guys. They look human."

That was a disappointment. Hopefully, they were at least hybrids and not some humans Igor had hired to follow Sofia.

"We will wait until they are a good distance away before we check the car," Morgan said.

When Marcel repeated that for Sofia, she let out a breath. "Thank the Mother. It worked. They took the bait."

"Don't thank her yet." Eleanor stopped to readjust her backpack. "Let's see if we can catch them. They might hear the drone and bolt."

"With all the noise from the ocean, I can't hear myself breathing," Asher said. "When they hear the drone, it will already be too late. Morgan and Bradley are right behind them."

That was why they had chosen that exact spot for their deception. The mountain practically rose up from the water, and the surf crashing to shore was loud.

"We need to keep going." Marcel tugged on Sofia's hand. "They need to focus on catching up to us."

The hope was that the guys following them would suspect that they were taking Sofia to a secret location hidden in the mountain and that they would follow to find out where the entrance was.

Straining his one free ear, Marcel tried to identify the drone's buzz, but he couldn't hear a thing over the surf. The higher they climbed, the noisier it became instead of getting quieter.

They were nearly all the way to the top when Morgan spoke in his earpiece. "We got them. You can come back down."

Sofia

"What if they have trackers on them? Or in them, as may be the case." Sofia had her hand on Marcel's shoulder, using him as her guide on the way down. "Don't we need to take them to the clinic first to remove them?"

The moon was out, so it wasn't entirely dark, but the lava rocks the mountainside was made of were nearly black, and there was very sparse vegetation. She could barely see where to put her foot down.

"We can't remove the trackers," Eleanor said. "We need those guys to appear intact and to go back to reporting to your grandpa."

Sofia gritted her teeth. Eleanor hadn't realized that referring to Valstar as her grandpa was painful to her. They were blood, as the Kra-ell called their purebloooded relatives and sometimes to the hybrids, but never their human descendants.

She was nothing to Valstar.

"Tom's place is not far from here," Asher said. "Morgan and Bradley will carry them over so it will appear as if they walked there."

"Isn't that dangerous?" Sofia asked. "Igor will know where to find Tom."

"Tom will leave as soon as we are done, and we are not going to use that house again."

"I thought it was his home."

Marcel stopped his descent. "It was rented for the meeting. I thought I told you that."

She rubbed her temple. "The headache I got when Tom tried to break through Igor's compulsion must have messed with my memories. I can barely remember anything about that night." She tightened her hand around his bicep. "Did you do anything to me to make me forget?"

"I didn't."

"I hope you're not transitioning," Eleanor said.

Sofia's heart leaped, in part from fright and in part from excitement. "Why? Is forgetfulness one of the signs?"

"Not that I know of." Eleanor kept going. "But every transitioning Dormant experiences different symptoms, and with you being the scion of a different species, I expect your transition to be even more different."

"What are the usual symptoms?"

Eleanor shrugged, jolting Cecilia in the backpack that was strapped to her chest. "I can only tell you about my experience. I was feverish, lightheaded, and then I lost consciousness."

That didn't sound like fun, but given that immortality was the prize, it was worth going through a lot more than that.

"Are we walking all the way to the house?" Sofia asked.

She was in good shape, but she was getting fatigued.

"Yes." Marcel slowed down. "I can carry you on my back."

As if she would let him do that. "No, thank you. I can walk. But I don't understand why we need to. The idea was for the guards to wake up and remember that they watched us go into the house, hobnob with some rich people, and go out. They wouldn't have done it on foot, and neither would we."

"We needed them to get out of the car," Marcel said.

By the time the house came into view, she was dragging her feet, and her legs ached so badly that she was considering letting Marcel carry her the rest of the way.

"Are the Guardians already there?"

"They had a big head start," Asher said.

"But they were carrying dead weight." Sofia winced. "That was a bad choice of words. I hope the Kra-ell are not dead."

"They are not." Marcel squeezed her hand. "Morgan informed me that they are chained and ready for interrogation and that we should leave the cat with the tracker in Tom's rented car. It's open, and the key is inside. We don't want the tracker to be too close to the two. They are supposed to be spying on you from afar, not to be right next to you."

"Eleanor and I can stay with the cat," Asher offered. "Just get us food and something to drink. For the cat too."

"We will do that." Marcel tugged on Sofia's hand. "Come on. It's just a hundred feet more."

She groaned. "There are stairs to climb. I don't think I can do that. How did Tom get Mia and her wheelchair up there? Is there a hidden elevator in the house?" She prayed that there was.

"He carried her and the chair." Marcel smiled. "You know that I would be more than happy to carry you up there." He wrapped his arm around her waist and propped her against his body. "But since you are so damn proud and stubborn, I'll just help a little."

Sofia didn't want to tell him that it wasn't just the physical exertion that made the stairs seem so ominous. Once she climbed them and the door opened, she would see who had been following her, and she was afraid to find out who it was.

Toven

Toven leaned against the dining table and observed the two Kra-ell males chained to the iron chairs the Guardians had brought from the outdoor garden. Both could pass for humans, which meant that neither was a pureblood.

That was disappointing.

How much would they know?

Was it even worth the risk of detaining them?

Beside him, Mia gaped at the males, wide-eyed. "I expected them to look more alien, but they look a lot like Vrog. A little different, but they could easily be mistaken for humans."

"They are hybrids." Toven sighed. "We've gone to a lot of effort to lure them into a trap, and they probably don't know much more than Sofia."

"The hybrids serve in Igor's army," Morgan said. "They should know about the compound's military capabilities."

"I hope so."

As a knock sounded at the door, Morgan walked over to open it for the others, and Mia wheeled her chair around to greet them.

"Sofia." As she opened her arms, the girl bent down to hug her.

"Hi, Mia." Sofia straightened and looked at the two chained males. "Neither of them is a pureblood."

"Do you know them?" Toven asked.

She nodded. "The one on the right is Dima, and the one on the left is Anton."

The girl looked exhausted, and as he motioned for her to take a seat on the couch, she gave him a grateful nod.

"Those are Russian names," Toven said when she sat down. "Is that common?"

She nodded. "Almost all of the hybrids get named by their mothers, who are mostly Russian, and they choose names they are familiar with."

"Are they good guys?" Mia asked.

Sofia shrugged. "Dima is a jerk. I don't know Anton well, but I didn't notice him doing anything mean. They are both young. About my age."

"I assume that they are not high on the totem pole." Marcel sat next to her.

"They are not. I'm not important enough to justify sending higher-ranking people to follow me around."

Things weren't adding up. "And yet he put his second-in-command in charge of your mission." Toven crossed his arms over his chest. "What are we missing here?"

He hadn't posed the question to the others but rather to himself.

Nevertheless, Sofia answered. "Maybe he figured that hybrids were good enough to deal with a bunch of humans. They can also blend in. If he needed them to get into Safe Haven without arousing suspicion, it would have been easier to do for males who could pass for humans."

Those were valid points, but Toven had a niggling suspicion that those hadn't been Igor's reasons. The problem was that he couldn't come up with an alternative.

He turned to Morgan. "How long until they wake up?"

"I don't know," the Guardian said. "Julian supplied us with darts that can knock out Jaguars, but that might be overkill for these dudes. Neither of them weighs more than one hundred and sixty or seventy pounds. They have the bodies of teenage anime characters."

Toven stifled a smile. The description was apt, and just like those anime males, the hybrids were much stronger than they looked. "Will splashing them with cold water help?"

"I don't think so," Marcel said. "The drug needs to get metabolized."

"Well then, we just have to wait." He looked at Sofia. "Now that you've identified them, I no longer need you here, and I prefer that they don't see you. I suggest that you stay in the bedroom during the interrogation. If I need to ask you something, I'll send Marcel over."

Sofia swallowed. "What are you going to do to them?"

He smiled. "Don't worry. I don't need to beat them up to get them to talk. But I won't be as gentle with them as I was with you."

She winced. "That was gentle? I felt as if you were trying to pull out my brain through my eye sockets. I'll gladly rest for a little bit, though." She looked down at her dusty clothes. "But I don't want to dirty your bed."

"We are not staying the night," Mia said. "Housekeeping will come tomorrow and change the bedding."

"Still, I don't like the idea of getting into a clean bed with dirty clothes. I'll just take off my pants and jacket. The T-shirt underneath is okay." She glanced at the Guardians. "I hope none of you needs to get into that bedroom."

Morgan lifted his hands in the air. "No worries. No one other than Marcel and Mia will go in there."

"Thank you. Before I forget, Eleanor and Asher asked for some food to be sent down to them. And if you have something for our cat, that would be great."

Mia's eyes widened. "I'm such a bad hostess. I didn't even offer you anything to drink. You must be parched after the long walk you had."

"I'm on it," Bradley said.

Mia glared at him. "I might be in a wheelchair, but I'm not helpless."

"Of course not." The Guardian rubbed a hand over the back of his neck. "May I help, though?"

"Yes, you may." Mia turned her chair around and drove toward the kitchen.

Kian

"Let the show begin." Marcel positioned the tablet so the camera faced the two bound and tranquilized hybrids. "Can you see them clearly?"

"We can," Kian said.

He, Turner, and Onegus were watching the interrogation from his office, and like they had done with Sofia, they wouldn't be visible to the other side, and only Marcel would hear them through his earpiece. If they had any questions, he would relay them.

As the tranquilizer effect started to wear off, and the males became cognizant of their situation, they began struggling against the chains holding them.

"Stop," Toven commanded. "Look at me."

Their struggle ceased immediately.

"That was impressive," Turner murmured.

It was, but it was nothing compared to the ease with which Toven broke through Igor's compulsion.

"You can talk about any and everything that Igor has ever commanded you not to reveal, and you will answer all my questions truthfully and without holding anything back."

He'd said that he wouldn't be as gentle with the hybrids as he had been with Sofia, and Kian had expected him to do a quicker job of releasing them from Igor's compulsion, but as he watched the god break through it in mere seconds, he was just as impressed as Turner was.

Perhaps the lingering effects of the tranquilizer had made the hybrids' brains easier to manipulate, or perhaps it had been the experience Toven had gained by going through the process with Sofia, or maybe the compulsion just didn't stick as strongly to hybrid minds.

"What is your name?" Toven asked the one on the left.

"Anton," the hybrid answered with a slight Russian accent.

Toven was fluent in the language, but he knew that Kian and Onegus weren't, and he continued the interrogation in English.

"What's your position in Igor's organization?" Toven asked.

"I'm a guard."

"What were you sent to do?"

"Follow Sofia."

"Why?"

"We were told that Sofia is investigating something, and if she leaves Safe Haven, we were to follow, find out where she was taken, and report back."

Kian glanced at Turner. "You were right."

The guy smirked. "Am I ever wrong?"

Toven crossed his arms over his chest. "Were you told to help her escape if she was in trouble?"

"We were not given instructions for such contingencies."

Toven turned to look at the other hybrid. "What is your name?"

"Dima."

"What's your position in Igor's organization?"

"I'm a guard like Anton."

"Why were the two of you chosen for this mission?"

"We speak good English," Dima said.

"Did you study it in the university?"

Dima snorted. "Hybrids don't get to study outside the compound. Me and Anton learned English from watching American movies and playing video games."

Toven turned to look at the tablet. "I wondered why two pawns were sent to investigate instead of someone more senior. Now we know why."

"Who are you?" Dima asked.

"I'm the one asking the questions. What kind of weapons does Igor have in his arsenal?"

"Assault rifles," Dima answered, and it didn't seem as if he was even trying to resist Toven's compulsion. "We also have sniper rifles and grenades. The swords and javelins and other kinds of old crap that he insists we train with are stupid. What can a sword do against an assault rifle?"

Obviously, Dima didn't like or even respect his boss.

Toven graced the hybrids with a smile. "Not much. Those weapons are obsolete, and training with them is just busy work. I feel for you, buddy."

Kian had never heard Toven talk like that. He cut a glance to Turner. "What was that? Is it part of the negotiation technique?"

Turner nodded. "It's a classic move. The interrogator befriends the interrogated to create a feeling of *we are the same*. We understand each other. It's especially effective if the interrogated has grievances against his superiors and his allegiance to them is shaky."

"Dima is under compulsion," Kian said. "Toven doesn't need to employ more tricks to get the guy to talk."

Turner shrugged.

"Watch what you say about Igor, Dima," Anton warned.

"Why? Is he here? He's not here, and this guy is just as powerful, if not more. I want to get out from under

Igor's boot, and I want to get out of this alive." Dima looked at Toven. "You freed us from his compulsion, but if you offer us asylum, I will not only tell you anything you want to know but come work for you willingly. No compulsion needed. If you know who we are, you also know what we can do." He pulled on his chains. "We are valuable."

Toven ignored the comment about their abilities and shifted his gaze to Anton. "How do you feel about your friend's offer?"

The guy looked uncomfortable. "I have a family."

Toven nodded. "What if you didn't have family in Igor's compound? Would you still be loyal to him?"

Anton shook his head. "If I didn't have a family, and I wasn't under Igor's power, I would have left a long time ago and made a life for myself where no one knew me."

That was what Emmett had done. Hybrids were not happy to be under the purebloods' rule, even when the rule was not as oppressive as Igor's. No one wanted to be regarded as a second-class member of their community.

"Why is that?" Toven asked. "Aren't you treated well?"

"I'm tired of being treated as an inferior," the guard admitted. "I'm young, so if there was a way for me to climb the ranks, I would have hope of improving my standing in the community. But I know that I will never rise above the station I hold now."

Dima nodded. "We are not even allowed near the hybrid females. Only the purebloods get to breed with them."

"Dima!" Anton hissed. "You're such an idiot."

It seemed that Anton was under the impression that their captors didn't know who they were, which was ridiculous, given the titanium chains. They wouldn't have been needed to bind humans.

"It's okay, Anton," Toven said. "We know all about the Kra-ell, the purebloods, and the hybrids, and the discrimination the hybrids are subjected to."

"Did Sofia talk?" the guy asked.

"I'm the one asking the questions, remember?"

Anton nodded. "So you know who we are."

"You are half Kra-ell and half human."

Anton's eyes changed shade, a purplish sheen appearing over his nearly black irises. "Are you going to experiment on us?"

Toven shook his head. "No harm will befall you at our hands. No one is going to experiment on you or even examine you. We just want more information to confirm what we already know and expand on it. Once we are done here, we will put you back in your car with no memory of what happened here."

"He's making them less apprehensive," Turner said. "Compulsion works better when people are not terrified."

The chief nodded. "I don't know about compulsion since I don't use it, but it's always easier to deal with people when they are not in a state of panic."

Toven continued, "I understand that you're unhappy about not having access to the females of your kind. Is that the main reason for your displeasure? Or is there more to it?"

Anton nodded. "Our children, if we have any, will be born human, and we will outlive them. The human part of me has a hard time with that."

Vrog and Emmett had voiced the same dissatisfaction with Jade, so it wasn't a big surprise to hear these males echo them. The question was whether there was dissent among the purebloods as well.

"Ask him if the pureblooded males are all loyal to Igor by choice," Kian told Marcel.

As Marcel repeated the question, Dima shrugged. "Maybe they are, and maybe they are not. They don't tell us."

"You seem like a smart guy," Toven said. "People don't express themselves just with words. They talk with their facial expressions and their bodies. Have you noticed any displeasure with Igor's rule?"

"No," Anton answered. "They worship him like a god. And why wouldn't they? He takes care of them. They are at the top of the hierarchy."

"What's your opinion, Dima?" Toven looked at the hybrid.

"Anton is right. They have no reason to resent Igor. All the purebloded females want to breed with him. Even Jade, who hates Igor's guts. That's the Kra-ell way. They embody the survival of the fittest philosophy."

The females didn't choose the purebloded males because they wanted to produce the best offspring. They had been compelled to comply with the purebloded males' demands.

Kian looked at Turner. "Since he's wrong about the females, he might be wrong about the males as well."

"He's not necessarily wrong." Turner leaned back in his chair. "The other females might hate Igor just as much as Jade does, but their tradition and maybe even their instinct is to breed with the most powerful male. That doesn't mean that they are loyal to him. The moment he loses his power, they might tear him apart with their bare fangs."

The glow in Turner's eyes as he spoke was disturbing.

Kian shook his head. "Sometimes I worry about you. You have strange fantasies."

Turner shrugged. "I'm just stating the facts as they are without running them through a sensitivity filter. We both know that the Kra-ell are vicious."

Marcel

The interrogation hadn't taken long, and Toven had exhausted everything the guards knew in less than an hour.

What had surprised Marcel was that Igor hadn't sounded like the evil monster dictator he'd imagined him to be. The compound was run efficiently and was guarded well, but their two captives had no horror stories to share. Evidently, they didn't know about the history of most of the pureblooded females and how they had ended up in the compound, and they didn't think that the human females' obligation to breed with hybrids was such a big deal either. To them, it was a cultural thing, and since they could point to many human cultures who still treated females as breeders with no rights, Marcel couldn't even fault them for thinking that.

Evil came in many shades of darkness and compared to some human dictators, even contemporary ones, Igor was only dark gray.

Most of the community members had no ability to communicate with the outside world, but Igor didn't limit access to information. They could place orders for any movie, book, or video game they wanted, and their allowance was small but sufficient for acquiring those and other small luxuries.

There were no official days off, but the guards had reported plenty of free time. They'd also confirmed what Sofia had said about the humans being pretty much left to their own devices. Those who didn't perform to the standards expected of them were punished by fines and lost privileges, but capital punishment of humans was so rare that the two guards hadn't heard of any in recent years. Igor was less lenient with the hybrids and the purebloods, though, ruling them with an iron fist. Then again, according to Jade's surviving tribe members, she had been tough on her people as well, so it might be the Kra-ell way.

"You will fall asleep and wake up in three hours in your car," Toven said to finish his thralling session.

When the hybrids' heads dropped over their chests, the god let out a breath. "That should be enough time for the grogginess of the tranquilizer to fade."

Toven had thralled the Kra-ell hybrids to forget that they had ever been captured, replacing those memories with them watching from afar as Sofia hobnobbed with a bunch of rich people in a secluded beach house.

They wouldn't even remember hiking up the mountain behind her.

"Let's take them back." Morgan unlocked Dima's chains.

"Don't forget to clean their boots," Marcel said.

"Right." Morgan lifted the hybrid and draped him over his shoulder.

After Bradley did the same for Anton, Marcel called Asher to tell him that he and Eleanor could come up.

Following Turner's instructions, Asher had gone back to pick up the hybrids' Honda and had driven it to a spot overlooking the beach house. Then he and Eleanor had gone back for the other two vehicles.

When the door opened, and Eleanor walked in with Asher and Cecilia, the cat leaped out of her arms and ran into the bedroom where Sofia was resting.

"Those two have bonded." Eleanor walked over to the dining table. "Hello, Kian." She waved at the blank screen and then turned to Toven. "Did we learn anything useful?"

The god nodded. "We learned quite a lot from Dima and Anton."

As Marcel deactivated the earpiece and switched on the tablet's speaker, Kian turned his camera on.

"We know the schedules of the guards at the tunnel entrances and at what intervals they are required to call in," Kian said. "We also know the frequency of patrols in the hunting grounds and the way they monitor the waterways running through the area."

"We also learned a lot about how the compound is run," Marcel added.

"Can I come out now?" Sofia walked in with Cecilia in her arms.

"Of course." Marcel pulled out a chair for her.

She yawned. "How did it go?"

"Better than I expected," Toven said. "Anton and Dima might not know what Igor's agenda is, but they are very familiar with the day-to-day operations of the compound. They served as guards at the entrances to the tunnels, they also served in the office building, the security office, and a number of other stations, and they trained with the purebloods. They told us what weapons Igor has, how many times a week the purebloods go hunting and many other details that will help us plan our next step."

"Did they give you any trouble?"

Toven chuckled. "They are not fans of Igor. Dima was willing to switch masters in a heartbeat. Anton would have done so gladly as well, but he has a family to think of. Dima, for some reason, was not concerned with that. Do you know why?"

Sofia shook her head. "His father is a jerk like most of the purebloods, and his mother died a long time ago. Once the hybrids reach puberty, they leave the human quarters, so I didn't have much contact with him after that." She grimaced. "He wasn't nice to me when we were still kids, and he wasn't nice after he left either. Anton's mother married a human after she was released from her breeding duties, and he has a human sister that he's surprisingly close to. It's not common."

Mia shivered. "Being forced to breed is awful. I really want to free all those poor women."

Toven put a hand on her shoulder. "You will."

Sofia frowned. "She will? How?"

"It's a long story, and we need to get moving. I thralled those two to sleep for three hours, and we need to be long gone by the time they wake up."

Sofia nodded. "I should contact Valstar tomorrow and tell him a story to corroborate what Anton and Dima will report about this evening."

"Tell him that your boyfriend and your new best friend, i.e., Eleanor, took you to a private fundraiser." Marcel wrapped his arm around her shoulders. "You mingled with the paranormal community's rich backers, and you learned more about their breeding program by eavesdropping on their conversations."

"What did I learn?"

He chuckled. "That they plan on producing superhumans who will take over the world."

She elbowed him. "Seriously. I need something less vague."

"How about influencing elections?" Turner suggested. "Rich people with no paranormal talents do that, so it will sound reasonable."

"Whom do they support?" Sofia asked. "I need specific details to sound truthful."

"I'll check and let you know. I don't know who is running for what in Oregon."

Nodding, Sofia looked at Toven. "How strong is your thralling? Do you think it will hold?"

"I know it will. They were as susceptible to my mind manipulations as humans are. If I can thrall the pure-bloods as easily, we will have much less trouble freeing the compound."

Kian

"I need to go," Onegus said as Kian ended the video call and closed his laptop. "If you need me when Toven calls, you can put me on the line."

"I will." Kian rose to his feet and looked at Turner. "Care to join me on the roof? It will take at least fifteen minutes for Toven to load his and Mia's belongings into the car and get on the road, which gives us enough time to get comfortable on the roof with a couple of cigars and some whiskey."

Turner smiled. "Lead the way."

By the time Toven's call came, the two of them were puffing on their cigars.

"Hello, Toven. I assume that you are on your way to the airport."

"We've just left," Toven said. "Did you have time to discuss what we've learned?"

"Turner and I only talked about it briefly. The bad news is that you still need to interrogate the pureblood guarding the entrance to the tunnel, but the good news is that we've learned most of what we needed to know from the hybrids, so you won't need to ask him a lot of questions, and it won't take long to interrogate him. That means less exposure for you and Mia and the Guardians."

"True," Toven said. "I also need to find out whether the purebloods are susceptible to my thrall. They might not be, and that will leave me with only compulsion to work with, and that's not as safe. The guy will walk around with the knowledge of me and of what I asked him to do, and his facial expressions might give away that something is not right with him."

Turner put his cigar on the lip of the ashtray. "Can't you compel him to act as usual?"

"I can, and it might be enough, but people's expressions often change involuntarily without them giving it any conscious thought."

"It's a risk I'm willing to take." Kian took a small swig from his whiskey. "The problem is what's next? What do we do if the purebloods aren't susceptible to shrouding? Our plan doesn't work without the ability to create convincing illusions."

"We abandon the mission," Turner said. "We can help break Igor's compulsion for Jade, which will give her a short window of opportunity to kill him, but we can't risk giving her earpieces. Since we can't attack the compound by creating an illusion of a larger force, we can't let Igor know that Jade had help. Without the earpieces, there will be no proof of our meddling."

Kian didn't like that.

He'd been opposed to invading the compound, but after listening to the two hybrids, his gut feeling had changed. It wasn't because of sympathy for those males, and it wasn't because of Jade and the other females' plight. There was nothing new about those factors. What was new was the realization that those two young hybrids were not all that different from immortals and that their hopes and aspirations were the same as everyone else's.

Having three Kra-ell hybrids as members of his community should have made him realize that sooner, but up until now, he'd thought about them as the exceptions, and he'd thought about the Kra-ell males in Igor's compound collectively as the enemy, as the other, the alien.

The clan's relationship with the hybrids shouldn't be adversarial, and once Igor was out of the way, they might be able to form an alliance. It also helped that Igor's arsenal was so basic and that getting rid of him might not be as difficult as Kian had assumed. On the other hand, the tracker Julian had removed from Sofia was a sophisticated piece of technology, so there was that.

"We can launch a rocket into the office building," he said. "There might be some unintended collateral damage, and innocents might be killed along with Igor and his inner circle, but it will be effective."

Turner shrugged. "That's up to you. My prime objective when designing this mission was to minimize casualties. A successful shroud would have done that."

"I'm not sure about that." Kian puffed on his cigar. "Who knows what Igor would do when under siege? You assume that he will try to run, and Jade will just take over without a struggle. What if he decides to launch an attack of his own?"

Turner arched a brow. "With what? He has no rocket launchers."

"He might. The hybrid guards might not be privy to everything he has. What if he salvaged some end-of-days alien weapon like Mortdh used on the gods' assembly? If we take down the office building with him in it, he won't have time to launch it."

"I agree with Kian," Toven said. "We will still need to shroud the area, though. Otherwise, after we blow up the office building the Russian army will show up, and they don't lack weapons."

"Indeed." Turner lifted his cigar. "In either case, the mission requires major prep work. To release Jade from Igor's compulsion, we need to get to the hunting grounds unnoticed, and to do that, we need an amphibious vehicle. The good thing about Russia is that you can get anything you want if you can pay for it. My contractor has secured the vessel for our use. The supplier only rents it per month, so we will have to pay for a month even if we use it for only a couple of days. Then there is the insane deposit he demands, but if we return the vehicle in the same condition we got it, the supplier will refund it."

Kian grimaced. "How much?"

"The deposit is three million dollars. But the monthly rental is only two hundred thousand dollars."

"Only?" Kian emptied what was left in the miniature bottle down his throat. "Those Kra-ell will owe us big time."

"They might be able to pay you back," Turner said. "Igor stole all of the money that Jade's tribe had in the bank. He probably did the same to the other tribes he attacked. We just need to find where he hid that money and recompense ourselves from their accounts."

Toven

"How many people can the amphibian carry?" Kian asked.

Toven had wondered the same thing.

"The one we are getting can carry forty. I figured it will be enough for what we need. We are not deploying the entire force via the river. When we get the boat, we will need to test if it can navigate the rivers that crisscross the hunting grounds. Since it's a Russian Navy vehicle, I also asked for Russian uniforms in case we are discovered. The Guardians will have to pretend to be Russian soldiers on patrol. Igor's guards wouldn't dare attack them."

Kian chuckled. "Excellent plan, save for one small detail. We don't have anyone fluent in Russian except for Morris, and he's our pilot. We need him and Charlie to fly the rest of the team in when the time comes."

Immortals had an easy time learning new languages, but they learned mostly by spending time in different countries and absorbing them during their visits. For some reason, Russia had never been a popular destination.

"I'm fluent," Toven reminded them. "But you have nothing to worry about when I'm there because I can shroud the amphibian."

"They won't have you with them when they test whether the river is navigable. The Guardians can manage the humans, but as the test Turner conducted with Vrog and Aliya demonstrated, they can't thrall the hybrids, let alone the purebloods."

"There is a simple solution for that," Turner said. "They can thrall a real Russian to be their spokesman. If Igor's patrol finds them, the human in the Russian Navy uniform will tell them that they are running a drill."

Kian nodded. "Sometimes, by overthinking a problem, we don't see the simplest solutions. Do you have another one for how Mia will travel over the rough terrain?"

"I'll carry her on my back," Toven said. "I will need a harness, though, so my hands are free."

"I don't want you to carry me," Mia protested.

Toven took her hand. "That's the only way, love. It's either my back or you stay behind." He smiled. "You know that carrying you is not an effort for me. I can run for miles with you strapped to my back, even with all the Kevlar you'll have on you."

He wasn't taking any chances with her. Mia would be covered in Kevlar from head to toe.

She sighed. "I'd rather ride on your back than stay behind. I'll just pretend that I'm your secret weapon."

"It's not a pretense. You *are* my secret weapon."

"I can get a harness," Turner said. "One of those that are used for parachuting practice should work with only minor modifications."

"So, what happens after we free Jade from Igor's compulsion?" Mia asked.

"We ask her if she can kill Igor," Kian said.

Toven frowned. "We already deduced that Jade wouldn't be able to do that without a weapon, and we assumed that she must be searched every time she sees Igor. Did you come up with a way for her to smuggle in a weapon?"

Mia squeezed his hand. "I have an idea. In movies and in books, assassins sometimes use a thin wire to cut their victim's throat. Perhaps Jade can hide it in her hair."

"I'm sure that the guards don't take any chances," Turner said. "They check the hair too."

"She's his breeder," Kian said. "The guards are not with them in the bedroom. Maybe she could strangle him while he sleeps, or maybe she can get her hands on some poison. We won't know until we talk to her."

Mia squeezed Toven's hand again. "If Jade tells us that she can't kill Igor, can we just take her with us?"

"If that's what she wants, sure," Turner said. "Or if she wants to take a few key players with her, she can arrange a hunting party with just those people, and we will take them all. But that's only if we decide not to invade the compound."

"We can't do that in any case," Kian said. "Humans cannot be included in a Kra-ell hunting party, and we can't leave Sofia's family behind. Even if we only take Jade, Igor will know that it was achieved with Sofia's help, and he will retaliate against her family. We promised her that we would not let that happen. I'm not willing to sacrifice innocent humans to save a few Kra-ell."

"I agree," Toven said. "When are Mia and I flying out to Russia?"

"As soon as possible," Turner said. "I want you in place and ready to deploy. Do you want to fly commercial, or do you want us to fly you with the clan's private jet?"

"We can borrow Kalugal's," Kian said. "He's not going anywhere anytime soon."

"Does he know about the situation we are dealing with?" Toven asked.

Kian chuckled. "I'm sure he does. We didn't keep the Kra-ell situation top secret, and your grandnephew has a way of finding out about things even when we try to keep them classified. I'm still trying to figure out how he does it."

Toven frowned. "You don't sound concerned."

"I'm not. We swore alliance to each other, and it was reinforced by Annani's compulsion. He's not going to sell us out, and he doesn't know enough to use it for his own benefit, either. It's just his way of getting under my skin."

Kian was obviously fond of Kalugal, and it seemed that he enjoyed the games they were playing. Perhaps he needed someone to challenge him, and Kalugal was the only one who could and was up to playing games with his cousin.

"I'm still waiting for an answer," Turner said. "Commercial or private?"

Before Kian had suggested Kalugal's jet, Toven would have said commercial. The clan needed their two jets and their pilots to fly the additional Guardians and equipment to Russia. He didn't want to tie either of them down only so he and Mia could travel in comfort. But flying on his grandnephew's posh jet sounded like a treat for Mia.

"If Kalugal agrees to loan us his plane, we will take it. If not, we will fly commercial."

"He'll loan it to us," Kian said. "Will you be ready to fly out tomorrow? You'll need warm clothing. Karelia is very cold this time of year."

"Aren't the rivers frozen over?" Mia asked.

"Not yet," Turner said. "But they will be in less than a month. That's why it's important to push forward at a fast rate. The Kra-ell will increase patrols during the wintertime. It's not likely that they get unexpected visitors during those months, but since the rivers can be crossed on foot while frozen, they need to guard against the unexpected."

"We can get warm clothing in St. Petersburg." Toven put his hand on Mia's thigh. "Would you like to go shopping in one of the most beautiful cities in Europe?"

She gave him a brilliant smile. "Is that even a question?"

Sofia

After Asher parked Emmett's car in the garage, the four of them got out.

Eleanor held Cecilia to her chest. "Do you want her?" she asked Sofia. "Or do I return her to Anastasia?"

"I want to visit Roxie, so you should take her back." When Eleanor lifted a brow, Sofia added, "You said it was okay."

The retreat would end in four days, and despite everything that was going on, Sofia wanted to spend some time with the friends she'd made and was not going to see again.

"It is, but you still need to report to Valstar about your hobnobbing with the rich campaign contributors."

"I'll do it tomorrow. It's too late today."

Eleanor shrugged. "It's only a little after eight in the evening but suit yourself. I'm going to retire for the evening." She winked. "I suggest you do the same." She turned and walked away.

"See you tomorrow," Asher gave them a smile before following Eleanor.

Marcel wrapped his arm around Sofia's waist. "Let's find Roxana."

She shouldn't be surprised that he offered to accompany her. It wasn't because he couldn't stand being apart from her, and it wasn't a gesture of love. He wanted to ensure that she didn't tell Roxie anything she shouldn't.

"You don't have to come with me."

"I know, but I want to. It's on the way to my bungalow. We can go there after we say hello to your friend."

She hadn't expected that. "Am I allowed in your section?"

"Now that you know about us, there is no reason for you not to be allowed. I want you to see my bungalow, and if you like it better than the bunker, we can stay there from now on."

"Of course, I like it better. It's not underground. I like having windows."

"It's very small."

"I don't care. Should we go to the bunker first and collect our things?"

"Yeah. It will be more believable that you were away if Roxana sees you with your luggage."

It was a short walk from the underground garage to the cottage, and since the side door opened to Emmett's private garden, they didn't encounter anyone from the lodge.

Less than fifteen minutes later, she was packed and they were on their way.

As they passed through the lodge, a few people waved hello at her, but Roxie wasn't there, and neither were the two other women she'd befriended.

"She might be in our room." Sofia tugged on Marcel's hand.

"It's too early for her to be asleep."

Sofia smiled. "She might be busy doing other things."

"I didn't know that the retreat instructors assigned homework."

Stifling a laugh, Sofia kept walking. "Not the kind of homework you have in mind."

Understanding dawning, Marcel halted. "Maybe we shouldn't stop by at this hour."

"It's okay." She leaned closer. "With your exceptional hearing, you will know whether it's okay to knock."

He winced. "I'd rather not spy on Roxana's bedroom activities."

"She wouldn't mind." Sofia pulled on his hand. "Roxie likes to boast about her conquests. I think the free-love philosophy of the community was what drew her to the retreat, not her paranormal talent." She leaned closer to his ear. "I don't think she really has talent. She claims to have precognition, but she failed all the tests we did. I scored better than her at the card guessing game."

"What about your talent? Is it real?"

"The truth is that I'm not sure," she admitted. "Here is my old room." She pointed.

Marcel got closer and listened for a moment. "It doesn't sound like Roxana is engaged in sexual activities. She is talking with another female." He took a step back and waved at the door. "Go ahead."

Sofia had been gone for days, so she couldn't just walk into her old room. Instead, she knocked.

"Who is it?" Roxie asked.

"It's me, Sofia, and I have Marcel with me, so don't open the door if you're indecent."

The door was flung open, and Roxie flew at Sofia, with her pink robe flapping behind her and exposing her thighs.

"Sofia." She pulled her into a crushing hug. "Where have you been?"

"I can't tell you." She hugged her friend back. "It's a secret."

Roxie let go of her, took a step back, and gave her a once-over. "You look tired and bedraggled." She tilted her head to glare at Marcel. "What did you do to her?"

"I took her rock climbing."

"Oh, well, that explains it." She looked at Sofia, waiting for her to either confirm or deny it.

"We visited Marcel's friend in a house overlooking the ocean, and we hiked part of the way." Sofia swiped her hands over her dirty pants. "Perhaps I shouldn't come in."

The room had only one chair, and she didn't want to dirty one of the beds.

"Nonsense." Roxie took her hand and dragged her in behind her. "You can sit on the chair, and Marcel can sit on the desk. Or even better, Marcel can sit on the chair, and you can sit on Marcel."

Kian

As the doorbell rang, Okidu rushed to open the door. "Hello, Master Kalugal."

"Hello to you, too." Kalugal swaggered into the living room. "Good evening, cousin. Where are your lovely wife and daughter?"

"Syssi is putting Allegra to sleep."

Allegra had outgrown the small crib in their bedroom, and Syssi had decided it was time to get her used to sleeping in her own room. She tucked her in every night and read her a story. Their daughter was too young to understand it, but her mother's voice soothed her and helped her fall asleep.

"That's a shame. I wanted to kiss those chubby cheeks of hers."

"How is Darius doing?"

Kalugal sighed. "He's fussy, and we don't get much sleep, but he's the joy of our lives. I love him so much that I'm in a constant state of anxiety that something might happen to him before he reaches puberty and can transition. You're lucky to have a daughter who will transition much sooner."

"I'm lucky indeed." Kian clapped him on the back. "But so are you. You have a healthy baby boy, and Fates willing, he will grow up to be as smart as his father and as wise as his mother."

That brought a smile to Kalugal's lips. "You couldn't have said it better."

"Let's go outside."

"Yes, please. I've missed our chats over whiskey and cigars."

Surprisingly, Kian had too.

"It has been too long." He opened the sliding door and motioned for Kalugal to go ahead. "I'll tell you why I need to borrow your plane, and you'll tell me what you've been up to lately."

Kian had a feeling that curiosity wasn't the only reason Kalugal had said he would come over to hear the full story. The guy probably needed a break, and Kian could empathize. Babies were incredibly demanding, and as much as he and Syssi loved Allegra and would do anything for her, sometimes parents needed a short break to retain their sanity.

When he and Kalugal got comfortable on the lounge chairs, each with a glass of whiskey in hand, Kian opened the cigar box. "Which one would you like?"

"I'll take a Short Story. I promised Jacki to be back in an hour, so I don't have time for a full-sized cigar."

"That's a shame. I have a few Behikes."

Kalugal arched a brow. "Are you sure they are not counterfeit?"

"I'm sure."

"Oh, well. Then I have to try it." Kalugal pulled one out. "That's a special treat."

"I can give you the name of my supplier."

Kalugal smirked. "I only enjoy cigars in your company." He lit his cigar. "So, tell me why you need to borrow my plane when you have two and a helicopter."

"The helicopter is only good locally. And I need both planes for other things."

Kalugal puffed out. "I assume it has to do with the Kra-ell threat."

"Why am I not surprised that you know about it?"

Kalugal rolled his eyes. "You talked about it on Callie's opening night. Did you forget that I was there?"

"I didn't forget. It's just that we didn't discuss our plans. Hell, we didn't have a plan back then."

"And you have one now?"

"Well, it's an if-this-then-that sort of plan. Each stage depends on the results of the previous step."

While Kian explained Turner's proposed mission plan, Kalugal listened and puffed on his cigar but didn't comment or offer suggestions. When Kian was finished, he took a sip of his whiskey. "You need my men. I can't join in because Jacki would never forgive me if I left her alone, but Phinas can lead them."

That was an offer that Kian hadn't expected.

"Thank you for the offer, but your men haven't seen battle in decades, and from what I've seen, they don't train as often as they should to maintain their skills." A grimace twisted his lips when he thought about where they had learned those skills.

"It's true that my men haven't seen battle in a very long time, and it's also true that they don't train much, but they keep in good shape, and you need bodies to fill the exoskeletons for a show of force. Do you have enough of those suits for them?"

"I have plenty."

"Then it's settled. You'll need to charter a large plane to deliver the men and the suits to Karelia. Where are you going to land it?"

"So far, we have used St. Petersburg International Airport, but Turner is negotiating with his local contact to use an old Russian Air Force base an hour and a half away from Igor's compound. Some officials need to be bribed."

"This operation must be costing you a bundle."

"It is. I hope we can pay ourselves back from the funds Igor stole from Jade's tribe. He cleaned out their bank accounts, and according to Vrog, there was a lot of money in them. Regrettably, it's worth much less twenty-two years later."

"Maybe he invested it."

"Perhaps." Kian took a puff of his cigar. "We will find out when we take over the compound and catch the scumbag."

"Until then, I can help out with the expenses."

Kalugal wasn't usually that generous. He was still contributing monthly to the clan's charity, but that was the extent of his philanthropy. Maybe he'd changed his mind.

"Are you having second thoughts about lending me your men and your plane?"

"Not at all. The money will be in addition to that."

Kian narrowed his eyes at his cousin. "Why are you being so generous all of a sudden?"

"The Kra-ell are a potential threat to me as well. I want to know their plans and how many of them were on that ship." He took another sip of whiskey. "Most importantly, I want to know if more of them are coming."

That was a legitimate concern, but it wasn't typical of Kalugal. His cousin preferred to remain in the shadows and leave the work of protecting him and his men to the clan. He and his men had also been very busy for the past year, working long hours and even on weekends.

"What about that super-secret project you've been pushing forward? Are you done with that?"

"It's done." Kalugal smiled like a Cheshire Cat. "Have you heard about the new social media phenomenon that's sweeping over the world's teenagers?"

"Instatock? No way, it's yours?"

"It is."

"Wow." Kian leaned back. "I'm impressed. Cheryl is obsessed with it, but as far as I know, it's not monetized yet. What do you plan to do with it?"

"Take over the world." Kalugal puffed out a plume of smoke. "I'm not in a rush, though. For now, the app is just collecting information and subtly manipulating those youngsters' opinions to nudge them in the direction I choose, but soon, I'll start monetizing it by launching an advertising platform. After that, I'll launch a slew of games that will require tokens to play, which will bring in even more money, and when those teenagers grow up, their information will grow more valuable with them." He smiled. "Information, influence, and money equal power. You can never have enough of any."

That was absolutely brilliant and terrifying. Why was Kalugal telling him about it? Just to boast?

"You scare me, cousin."

"You have nothing to worry about. My intentions are to do good for humanity." Kalugal let out a sigh. "You must be wondering why I'm sharing this with you."

"I am."

"It's Jacki's fault. She managed to convince me that no one should hold so much power and that it would corrupt me. In her words, absolute power corrupts absolutely."

"Actually, the quote is attributed to Lord Acton, a nineteenth-century English historian."

"I didn't know that." Kalugal took another puff of his cigar. "I tried to convince her that my intentions were good and that I was only doing it for the betterment of humanity." He smiled. "And for a profit, of course. But she wouldn't budge. Her suggestion was to nominate Annani, you, and your council as a supervising board to ensure I don't run amok with it. Naturally, I want an equal number of board members to be my people, starting with myself, Jacki, Rufsur, and Phinas. I don't want you and yours to have all the power. The money goes to me, though."

"That's fair. Thank the Fates for Jacki and her wisdom, and thank you for listening to her. Having checks and balances on power is crucial. It reminds me that I need to call a council meeting and update them about the new developments with the Kra-ell."

Kalugal smirked. "You keep forgetting to meet with your council. Maybe you need someone monitoring you as well."

Marcel

"Goodnight." Roxana hugged Sofia. "Will I see you tomorrow at class?"

"I'm not sure." Sofia looked at Marcel. "I might be needed for that special project I can't talk about."

Roxana pouted. "There are only four days left in the retreat."

"I know." Sofia sighed. "I'll have to visit you in Washington."

The woman's face brightened. "That would be awesome. And if you are still with this scoundrel, bring him along."

"I will."

"Thank you for the roundabout invitation." Marcel offered the woman his hand.

"Nothing roundabout about it. You are invited." She pulled him into her arms, squashing him against her ample bosom. "I'm counting on you to bring Sofia to me. A friendship like this doesn't happen often." She wiped a tear from her eye and waved them off. "Just go before I start crying."

Sofia hesitated, but when Roxana walked back into her room and closed the door, she let out a breath and took Marcel's hand. "She's right. We did form a great friendship in a very short time."

"Maybe it's the affinity at work." He led her toward the back door of the lodge.

"Do you really think so?"

He shrugged. "Who knows? If her talent was real, I would be more inclined to believe that she might be a Dormant, but she might just be likable."

"She is." Sofia leaned her head against his shoulder. "I'm so tired. Do you have a bathtub in your bungalow? I could use a long soak."

The image of her in his tub was enough to harden him instantly. "I have a very nice tub. I hope you are not too tired."

Her lips lifted on one corner. "I am, but I can handle some lazy love."

"I can work with that." He slid his hand down to her tight ass and gave it a light squeeze.

Sofia slowed her steps. "Maybe we should stop by the nurse's office and get some condoms."

"What for?"

"The transition didn't start yet, and frankly, I hope it won't until this knotted mess unravels. I'd rather wait."

Marcel was disappointed, but he could understand why Sofia wanted to wait. Besides, it might be better for her to attempt transition without the added stress of what was about to happen in Karelia.

"We can get some on the way. They have them at the clinic."

"Thank you." She kissed his cheek.

"Nothing to thank me for. Kian wanted us to wait until we faked your death, and I haven't told him yet that we got carried away."

She arched a brow. "Why didn't you tell me?"

It had happened right after he'd told her about his crime, and when she'd accepted him unconditionally despite it, he couldn't deny her anything.

"So the blame would be on me."

Sofia shook her head. "Don't do that. We are a team, and we do everything together, including defying Kian and getting in trouble for it."

His heart swelled in his chest, and he tightened his arm around her. "I love you so much."

"I love you, too." She leaned her head on his shoulder.

When they got to the clinic, there was no one there, and as they helped themselves to several boxes of condoms, Sofia giggled like a schoolgirl.

"Are you sure it's okay to raid their stash like that?" she asked.

"I'm sure." He opened her duffle bag and stuffed the boxes inside. "I'll tell Gertrude tomorrow so she will know to order more." He pushed the door open and stepped outside.

"It's getting really cold." Sofia rubbed her hands over her arms. "Where is your bungalow?"

He transferred her duffle bag to his other shoulder and wrapped his arm around her. "It's the fourth one up the hill."

The structures were so small and close to each other that it took them less than five minutes to cover the distance.

"Go ahead. The door is open." He waited for Sofia to open up and flip the lights on.

"It's very nice." She looked around his space. "And so tidy. I like that you are not a slob. My last boyfriend was so messy. His dirty clothes were all over the floor, and unless I collected the paper plates with food leftovers and threw them away, they just stayed there and stunk up the place."

The image in his head wasn't of the boyfriend's laundry strewn over his dwelling. It was of Sofia lounging on said boyfriend's bed, and it elicited a nasty growl that started deep in his throat.

Thankfully, Sofia's human ears didn't pick it up.

"Please don't mention past boyfriends." He carried her luggage to the bedroom.

She followed him inside. "It's a deal if you don't mention your past girlfriends either. What happened in the past should stay in the past."

"Wise words." He followed her to the bathroom.

"I love it. Everything is so well planned that even though the bungalow is small, it has all the amenities." She walked over to the tub and started the water. "I think we can both fit inside." She cast him a bright smile. "What do you think?"

He swallowed. "Perhaps. But first, I want to pamper you. Would you allow me to wash you?"

"I would love that." She toed off her sneakers and started to undress. "Do you have wine? I would love to unwind with a glass."

"Coming right up."

Sofia closed her eyes and rested her head on the lip of the tub. It felt heavenly to soak her aching muscles. It was ridiculous that a short climb had been such a strain for her. She walked and jogged nearly daily, but she'd always done it on flat terrain. Climbing used different muscles, and hers were out of shape.

After all, she wasn't an athlete. She was a linguist or used to be.

Did Marcel's people need a translator? What was she going to do in their secluded village? Would she even be invited?

Marcel walked into the bathroom carrying a tray with a bottle of wine, two wine glasses, and an assortment of cheese and fruit. "I'm sorry it took so long. My fridge was empty, so I raided the dining hall kitchen."

Sofia hadn't been hungry until she saw the plate of cheese. "If I ever transition and become a hybrid, I will miss this." She reached for a wedge of Brie. "Most of them can't tolerate dairy or grains."

"I wonder how much the transition will change you." He leaned over and kissed her lips. "You are perfect the way you are, and I don't want you to change too much."

She eyed him from under lowered lashes. "Would it turn you off if I grew fangs?"

"No." He plucked a grape and popped it into his mouth.

"Are you sure?"

"Uh huh." He swallowed what he'd been chewing on. "I think it will be a turn-on."

"You said that one of the hybrids from Jade's former tribe who joined your clan was a female. Does she have fangs?"

"She does. Her name is Aliya, and she looks very Kra-ell, but I find her beautiful despite her alien looks. She's also a nice person."

"What does she do? I mean for work?"

"She works in the village café, and before you ask, she and the other hybrid are a couple. He's a nice guy too. He has a son who is part Kra-ell and part immortal."

"How is that possible?"

Marcel's phone rang before he could answer.

Putting the tray down, he pulled out the phone from his pocket and frowned. "It's Kian."

Sofia's heart skipped a beat. If the boss was calling so late in the day, he must have bad news.

"Hello, Kian," Marcel answered. There was a brief pause, and then Marcel said, "Yes, I'm with Sofia." There was another brief pause. "I'll activate the speaker."

"Hello, Sofia," Kian said. "How are you doing?"

He sounded so gruff that she wondered whether he was using a voice changer.

If he thought to intimidate her with that voice, he would be disappointed. After dealing with Igor, the most intimidating male in the world, she could handle the son of a benevolent goddess.

"Hi. It's nice to finally hear the voice of the mysterious boss, and as for how I'm feeling, I'm soaking in a bathtub, so please don't ask Marcel to switch to video."

Kian barked out a laugh. "Thanks for the warning."

She smiled. "You're most welcome."

"I want to give you an update on our plan."

Sofia hadn't expected that. She was a pawn, a nobody, and yet the big boss himself was calling to tell her his plan? They probably needed her to do something.

"What do I need to do?"

"Nothing. You need to stay in Safe Haven and call Valstar every other day to keep up the appearance of everything as usual."

"So why are you telling me the plan?"

"Courtesy. We are decent people, Sofia."

She let out a breath. "I know. So what's the plan?"

By the time Kian was done talking, Sofia's heart was hammering against her ribcage, and her throat was tight. She didn't like that the entire liberation plan depended on Jade.

"What's the time frame?" Marcel asked.

"Probably a few days."

Sofia motioned for Marcel to pour her wine. "If you plan to liberate the compound in the next two weeks, there is no need to fake my death."

"Let's leave it as a contingency," Kian said. "Our plans might change after we get more information from the guards at the entrance to the tunnel and then change again after we talk with Jade. We might decide to pull back and leave things as they are until we figure out a solution. If that happens, you'll run out of time. If Igor commands you to return before we fake your death, and we do it then, he will suspect the truth, and he might retaliate against your family."

Everything Kian had said was true, but if she could avoid causing her father unnecessary heartache, she would.

"He will not command me to come back in the next two weeks because he thinks I'm collecting valuable information for him. Can we at least wait that long?"

"One week," Kian said.

"Is it possible to give Jade a message for my father? I don't think his heart could take the news of my death."

"No," Kian said. "After we free Jade from Igor's compulsion, she can deliver a message, but your father won't be free, and the compulsion would force him to report what Jade told him. It would expose your ruse, and it would expose Jade."

Marcel

When the call ended, Sofia closed her eyes and let out a breath. "I'm scared."

"I know." Marcel brushed the curve of her arm with the tips of his fingers.

As goosebumps rose where he'd touched her, he scooped warm water into his cupped palm and sloshed it over her arm. "Are you cold? Do you want me to add hot water?"

"I'm not cold." She moved her head, and the long strands of her hair floated in the tub around her.

"Do you want me to wash your hair?"

She chuckled softly. "The only one who has ever washed it for me was my Aunt Isla. Aunt Hannele didn't have the patience to deal with it. My cousin Helmi always wore hers shoulder length."

"Do you have other cousins?"

"I have two more, but they are much younger. Helmi is only two years younger than me." She groaned. "I pray to the Mother that nothing happens to them and all the others I care about. Heck, I care about everyone except for the murderers." She shivered. "I didn't know what they did. I didn't like the purebloods because of their superior attitudes and low regard for everyone who wasn't a pureblood. I forgave most of the restrictions they put on us because it was necessary to hide that aliens were living on Earth. I even understood their need for human females as breeders. They made it seem as if the women had a choice and that they did it because sex with a pureblood or even a hybrid male was such a mind-blowing experience that they were more than willing. I doubted that part, and I even doubted Helmi, who sang the praises of her hybrid boyfriend's sexual prowess. I thought they had no real choice, so they pretended to like it." Sofia opened her eyes and smiled at him. "But if a Kra-ell's bite has a similar effect to yours, then I believe it. If I get to see Helmi again, I'll tell her." She chuckled. "She will be happy that I finally believe her."

He went down to his knees, picked up the shampoo bottle, and squirted a dollop into his palms. "You will see her again, as well as your aunts, your father, and everyone else."

"I pray to the Mother that I will."

He lifted her hair and supported her head with his forearm. "Who do you think is best suited to run the compound once Igor and his cronies are eliminated?"

"Frankly, I don't know. After them, Jade would be the most influential, and if she kills Igor, she would be the natural successor. That's the Kra-ell way. But if I was to choose the next leader of the compound, it wouldn't be her. I don't like her attitude toward humans. She's not cruel or anything, but she's dismissive of us. Can your people free the humans?"

Still trying to figure out how to wash such a mass of hair, Marcel smoothed the shampoo over the lengths. "I don't know if that's possible. They know that aliens walk among humans, and when we get involved, they will also know about us. It's impossible to thrall away a lifetime of memories, but they can be compelled to never talk about it." He started massaging the shampoo into her scalp.

Sofia moaned. "That feels so good that it's hard for me to think."

He chuckled. "Do you think it's easy for me to think while staring at your ripe berries?"

A smile curved her lips. "I can help with that." She cupped her breasts, robbing him of the sight.

"Don't do that. I want to watch."

"If you wish." She removed her hands and arched her back, so more of her breasts were above the water. "Immortals don't look alien. You could pretend to be humans with extra powers. If I believed you, they would too."

"You suspected that there was more to me than that." He kept massaging.

"Only because I got close to you. Otherwise, I wouldn't have suspected a thing."

"That's an option."

If they wore the exoskeletons, they would look like an army of invading aliens, but once they controlled the compound and removed the suits, they could say that they were a special task force of whatever. The United Nations or NATO.

"The other problem is that most of these humans were born in the compound. The young ones can adapt to living outside of it like you did, but the older ones might prefer to stay."

"They should be allowed to leave if they want to."

Talking about what would happen after the liberation had the effect that Marcel had intended. Sofia was no longer anxious about her family's survival and was instead thinking about their future after being freed.

"I agree. Can you lean your head back so I can wash the suds off?"

As she rested her arms on the sides of the tub and tilted her head back, the elegant arch of her torso was a work of art that Marcel would have loved to capture in a painting or a sculpture, but regrettably he had no artistic talents.

"You're so beautiful, Sofia," he murmured.

Sofia

The way Marcel said those words sent a delicious shiver of desire down her spine. Or was it her front?

Yeah, definitely her front.

Starting with her nipples and going down to her core. No one had ever called her beautiful, let alone so beautiful, and definitely not with so much feeling, and never with her name at the end.

She'd been called pretty, slender, and graceful, but no one had ever called her beautiful.

It shouldn't feel so good, but coming from Marcel, who was usually so dry and laconic, it was special.

Twisting her hair, she wrung out the excess water and wrapped the thick rope around itself on the top of her head.

"Can you please hand me the towel?"

Marcel arched a brow. "Don't you want me to join you in the tub?"

Sofia hesitated. It could be nice to share a bath, but what she had in mind was better done on a bed, especially since they had resolved to use a condom.

Talk about a mood spoiler, but it was necessary.

The last thing she wanted was to start transitioning, lose consciousness, and regain it to find out that it was all over, and Mother forbid, her family didn't survive.

"What's wrong?" Marcel unfolded the towel and spread it, waiting for her to get out. "You suddenly lost your good mood."

Sofia stepped out of the tub and let him wrap her in the towel and pull her into his arms. "I thought about transitioning, and then I thought about waking up to find out that something had happened to my family."

"Don't think like that." He rubbed his hands over her towel-covered arms. "We need to stay positive and visualize the best possible outcome."

She chuckled. "I've heard of that method. What is it called?"

"I don't remember. The gist is that if you believe you will get everything you want and ask for it, the universe will manifest it for you."

"Do you actually believe that?" She leaned into him and lifted her face. "Did you ask the universe to give you a perfect mate?"

He chuckled. "I must have yearned for you subconsciously." He drew the towel along her arms, then her belly, and as he dragged it up between her breasts, his knuckles brushed against her nipples, seemingly unintentionally. "Did you yearn for me?"

"I did," she admitted, her arousal dimming as her guilt surged. "I dreamt about being free and finding a man who I could share my life with. I didn't anticipate the unintended consequences."

Marcel arched a brow. "Freeing your family might be an unintended consequence, but it's a good one."

She closed her eyes. "If anything happens to them, I will not be able to forgive myself."

He hooked a finger under her chin and tilted her head up. "You were the one who told me to forgive myself. You should follow your own advice."

"The circumstances are very different."

"I don't think so." He lifted her into his arms and carried her to the bedroom. "I was willing to do anything for the woman I thought I loved, and you are willing to do anything for the people you love."

Marcel's logic was a bit skewed, but what Sofia had heard loud and clear was, "the woman I thought I loved."

"When did you realize that you didn't love her?"

He laid her gently on the bed and sprawled on his side next to her. "When I fell in love with you, I knew that what I felt for her hadn't been real." He cupped her cheek. "This feels real. What I felt for Cordelia was what I imagined love should feel like." His thumb dragged over her lower lip. "It's ironic that you set out to manipulate me, and yet everything you showed me, every emotion, every moan, and every sigh, it was all genuine. I don't think that you are capable of faking love or even like, and certainly not lust."

"About that. Eleanor told me that immortal males can smell a woman's arousal. If Cordelia was faking her attraction to you, you would have known that."

"That was the only thing she didn't fake."

Darlene

Darlene pulled an outfit from the closet and carried it to the guest bedroom.

"How do you want your eggs this morning?" Eric asked from the kitchen.

"Scrambled, please."

She'd asked for sunny side up the morning before, and it had proven too difficult for Eric. She hadn't minded that the eggs had ended up scrambled, but it had frustrated him. It was better to ask for something that wouldn't mess up his mood first thing in the morning.

It occurred to her that she was falling back on her old habits, avoiding anything that could upset her partner like she used to do with Leo. In her need to keep things calm and smooth, she'd often allowed herself to become his doormat.

Funny how dormant and doormat sounded the same but were the exact opposite. She was the granddaughter of a god, an immortal in the making, and she was nobody's doormat.

"Do you want onions in your eggs?"

"Sure." She draped the outfit over the back of the footboard.

They were using the other bedroom in the house until their new bed arrived. Eric had insisted on ordering another four-poster, even though she'd told him that she was never doing the thing with Max again. The frame of the new bed was made from iron posts that were welded together, not screwed, and it looked like nothing could destroy it.

Looking at the skirt and blouse she'd pulled out, Darlene sighed. The skirt was a little tight in the waist, and she was too tired to deal with anything uncomfortable. Perhaps she should just wear a pair of leggings with a long blouse over them.

There was no dress code in the lab, and no one cared whether she looked professional or frumpy. She dressed up mainly to please herself, but today, being comfortable would please her more.

The tiredness was not surprising, given Eric's stamina since his transition.

Darlene chuckled softly. Her guy's new alter ego was a gorilla, but a rabbit in heat was more fitting. What was surprising, however, was that she wasn't sore. Given that Eric didn't have the healing venom yet, that she was still human, and that her lady parts had never been particularly resilient, the miracle could be attributed either to the composition of Eric's immortal semen or his saliva.

She needed more sleep, though. Five hours a night might be enough for Eric, but it wasn't for her.

With a sigh, Darlene hung the outfit she'd chosen back in the closet, pulled on a pair of black leggings, and finished with a colorful blouse. Makeup seemed like too much trouble as well, so she decided to skip it. Thankfully, the hair treatment she'd gotten guaranteed a perfect hairdo each morning, so she didn't need to worry about that.

"Breakfast is ready!" Eric called from the kitchen.

"Coming." She slid her feet into a pair of low-heeled mules and walked into the living room.

Eric lifted a brow. "Are you staying home with me today?"

"I'm not." She pulled out a stool next to the counter and sat down. "I just didn't have the energy to dress up this morning. You exhausted me." She lifted a hand to stop his pouting. "In the best possible way. I just need to catch up on some sleep."

Worry clouding his eyes, he finished scooping the scrambled eggs onto two plates, put the pan aside, and walked over to her. "You look a little pale. Are you feeling alright?" He put his hand on her forehead. "You're a little warm."

Her heart skipped a beat. "Could it be the transition?"

"Fever is one of the first signs. We should go to the clinic." He untied the apron and pulled it over his head. "Let's go."

Darlene chuckled. "Relax. It might be allergies, or I might have caught something in the supermarket yesterday. Remember that woman who kept sneezing? She didn't use her elbow and sprayed the entire aisle with viruses."

"She said it was allergies."

"She probably lied. I'll just pop a couple of vitamin C pills. Can you hand me the bottle?"

Looking skeptical, Eric did as she asked. "We will go after breakfast." He put the plates on the counter, poured coffee into two mugs, and joined her.

"I'll feel better after I have some caffeine in me." She took a sip from the mug. "You make great coffee."

He smirked. "As opposed to my cooking?"

"Are you fishing for compliments?"

"Yes."

"Your cooking has improved significantly." She took a piece of toast and smeared it with butter.

"Yeah, I can make toast." He sighed. "But seriously. It's the perfect timing for you to start transitioning. Two and a half days passed since we did it, which is when it usually starts if it worked."

"If it worked." She took another sip. "Let's see how I feel during the day. If it gets worse, I'll call you, and we can meet at the clinic."

"What if you lose consciousness in that tiny office of yours? No one would know."

"I'll leave the door open and ask Kaia to keep an eye on me. She's at William's desk all day."

Eric

Eric pulled a noodle out of the pot and put it in his mouth.

"Still too hard." He stood next to the pot and waited two more minutes before pulling out another one. "You'd better be ready now." He dipped the fork in the water and fished out another noodle.

It was almost perfect, but he didn't have the patience to keep checking. The noodles would soften in the sauce. Turning the burner off, he took the pot to the sink and drained the water.

Playing house had been nice for a while, but Eric was getting bored with it. He felt great, and it was time to get a real job. Kian had said that he needed another pilot, and with rumors flying about a possible rescue mission in Russia, he probably could use one now.

Except Eric couldn't go anywhere until Darlene transitioned, which could start today, tomorrow, or the day after.

Eric pulled out his phone and called her. It was only eleven o'clock, and this was his fifth call that morning.

"I'm still fine," she answered. "I might be a little late for lunch, though. William needs my help sorting the supplies and ordering what's missing."

"Is it for the mission?"

She laughed. "What mission?"

"The secret one that everyone is talking about."

"That's why I'm laughing. I'm supposed to say that there is no mission."

"You sound energetic, so perhaps what you felt this morning was just fatigue."

"I told you so. But just in case, I told Kaia to keep an eye on me. She took it very seriously and moved William's desk so she could see me from where she was working."

"Awesome. Do you want me to bring your lunch to the office? We can eat it together on your desk."

"Good idea. I'll see you later."

Perhaps he could stop by Kian's office on the way?

Nah. He should call first, or better yet, text. Kian was a busy guy, and Eric was no one important. Well, beyond being Darlene's mate and Toven's future grandson-in-law. Did that make him special?

Not likely.

Perhaps texting Shai was a better idea. After all, the guy was his future father-in-law.

On second thought, being Darlene's chosen made him a well-connected guy.

Scrolling through his contacts list, Eric found Kian's number and typed up a message. *Hello, Kian. You mentioned needing another pilot. As soon as Darlene transitions, I will be ready to serve. Who do I need to see about piloting for the clan?*

That was short, to the point, and wouldn't waste much of Kian's time.

His phone rang a moment later. "What planes can you fly?" Kian asked without preamble.

"Nearly all of them except for large passenger jets. I'm not certified to fly those." Eric rattled out a long list of jets, including those he'd flown while serving in the Air Force.

"Impressive. You're hired. I'll tell Onegus to put you in the training program."

As far as Eric was aware, he could teach the clan's two pilots, not the other way around.

"What kind of training are you talking about?"

"Guardian training. I assume that you got combat training in the Air Force, but that was long ago. You need a refresher, and you also need to learn to work with our Guardians. It's nonnegotiable."

"I'm not negotiating. I was just wondering about the kind of training you had in mind, and now that you've explained, I get it. Should I wait for Onegus to call me?"

"Just stop by his office whenever you can, and if he's busy, you can wait. We are not very formal here. I'll tell him to expect you."

"Thank you."

"No problem. He'll also tell you how much the job pays."

"The pay is secondary to me. I just need to be up in the air again."

"You still need to get paid. How is Darlene doing?"

Had Kian heard about their induction attempt?

Probably.

Darlene had asked Max not to tell anyone, but they had told Karen and Kaia, who had probably told Cheryl, who'd probably shared it with Lisa and Parker, and that was how a day later, the entire village had known about it.

"This morning, she felt a little under the weather, and I hoped it was the start of her transition, but I just spoke with her, and she sounded fine. Kaia is watching her in case she suddenly collapses."

"Darlene is a god's granddaughter, so her symptoms might be mild. Make sure to check on her frequently, and if her symptoms worsen, get her to the clinic."

"I will."

When Kian ended the call, Eric rose to his feet and headed back to the kitchen. It was still too early for lunch, but since he was going to see Onegus, and the chief's office was one level up from the lab, he could do that first and have lunch with Darlene right after.

Half an hour later, Eric was out of Onegus's office with a contract for a three-month trial period, a schedule of classes and, what he was most excited about, the one-on-one drone flying training with Charlie.

Eric preferred to be up in the sky and not down on the ground with a remote or inside a simulator, but it was something he hadn't tried before, and he was eager to learn. Turned out that the clan had military-grade drones, but they weren't going to use them in the upcoming mission and were getting a couple of drones locally. Eric wouldn't be ready in time to join the current mission, but he would be ready the next time the clan needed to fly them.

Carrying the bag with the pasta and salad he'd made, he got in front of the door to William's lab and looked up into the camera. "Open sesame."

As the door buzzed open, Kaia smiled at him. "Darlene told me that you're bringing lunch. Is there enough for me?"

"Sure. But aren't you having lunch at home with William?"

She shook her head. "Not today. It's a madhouse in here. William is leaving this evening, and he has been running around all day. Sadly, I don't think he has time to go home for lunch. He isn't even packed yet." She looked at him hopefully. "Did you make enough for him too?"

Not really, but he could let the three of them eat and skip lunch himself. "Of course. Are you going with William?"

"I can't. He needs me here."

"Will you be okay without him?"

"It's going to be tough, but I'll stay with Mom and help her with the little ones until Gilbert returns. That will keep me busy."

"She's going to love it. You flew the nest so suddenly that she didn't have time to prepare."

Kaia snorted. "We live a ten-minute walk away from each other. I still have one leg in the nest."

"True." He put the thermal bag on her desk and walked over to Darlene's office. "Are you hungry yet? Food is here."

She lifted her head and looked at him with glazed eyes. "I don't feel well. I think we should go to the clinic."

Toven

"Here are the suitcases." Shamash rolled two brand new pieces of luggage into Toven and Mia's living room. "Kalugal and Jacki say bon voyage."

"Thank you, Shamash."

"You could have used ours," Curtis said. "They are not as fancy as these, but they are still good."

"These are larger, Grandpa." Mia drove over and grabbed one handle. "I have everything ready. I just need to put it inside."

Toven followed her into the bedroom. "What I have wouldn't fill even half of that suitcase. I could've taken my trusty carry-on."

"Then you would have needed to buy luggage in St. Petersburg to fit the new stuff we are going to get."

When his phone rang, Toven wasn't surprised to see it was Kian.

"Hello," he answered. "Are there any changes to the timeline?"

"Darlene is transitioning," Kian said. "Kaia called Bridget to let her know that Darlene and Eric are heading to the clinic, and Bridget told me on her way out."

Toven tensed. That was such inconvenient timing. He was leaving, and he wouldn't be there to help Darlene with his blood.

"The timing could have been better, but it is what it is. Thank you for letting me know."

"You're welcome. I thought that you might want to visit her before you leave and give her your blessing."

"That is a good idea. I will need to ask your mother to continue the blessings in my absence."

"Indeed. Good luck and congratulations."

"Thanks." He turned to Mia. "Do you want to come with me?"

"Of course." She dropped an article of clothing into her suitcase. "I'll race you there."

He could run much faster than she could drive her chair, and when they'd played the racing game before, he hadn't used his full speed.

"We don't have time. I'll run ahead."

"I knew it." She wagged her finger at him. "You were holding back."

"Naturally." He leaned and kissed her cheek. "I'll see you in the clinic."

As Toven ran, he was a blur of motion, and the immortals he passed gaped, trying to figure out what they were seeing. Annani never ran, so they had never seen a god running at full speed.

When he reached the clinic, he found Eric pacing in the small waiting room. "What are you doing out here? Shouldn't you be with Darlene?"

"Bridget and Hildegard are hooking her up to the monitoring equipment, and they kicked me out."

"I see. What are her symptoms?"

"It started with fatigue, but Darlene went to work anyway. I called every half an hour, and she was fine, but when I came to visit her at lunch, she told me that she was feeling worse. She couldn't even stand up, so I carried her, and in the five minutes it took me to get from her office in the lab to the clinic, she lost consciousness."

Toven put a hand on Eric's shoulder. "I know how stressful it is. I came to give Darlene a blessing before I leave, and Annani will take over while I'm gone."

"Thank you." Eric let out a breath. "I was worried because you were leaving, and I know how important your blessing was to my transition."

"How did you know that I was leaving?"

"I was in Onegus's office this morning about piloting for the clan, and he told me that he could've used me for this mission, but that I needed to go through training with the Guardians first. I told him that I didn't need to train to fly a plane from one point to the next, but that was before Darlene started transitioning. Now, I'm not going anywhere."

When a knock sounded on the front door, Toven rushed to open it for Mia, who couldn't pull the heavy glass open while sitting in her chair. They should automate the thing for handicapped access.

"You're incredible." Mia drove in. "You can outrun a cheetah."

"I can."

"And you're not even sweaty."

He smiled. "When we are in Karelia, and you are on my back, I'll treat you to a speedy run."

She scrunched her nose. "I don't know if I want to try it. It's probably scary."

Eric shook his head. "Should I even ask what you are talking about?"

Toven was about to answer when the door to Darlene's room opened, and Bridget walked out with the nurse.

"Hello, people. Darlene is awake, but that's not going to last long, so if you want to say goodbye before you leave, I suggest you do it now and do it quickly."

That wasn't good. He needed Darlene asleep or unconscious, to give her a transfusion. He would have to thrall her.

"How is she doing?" Eric asked.

"It's too early to tell. So far, her vitals are strong."

"Excellent." Toven smiled and turned to Eric. "Mia and I will not take long. Is it okay if we go in first to say our goodbyes?"

"Sure. And don't forget the blessing."

"I won't."

Sofia

Once again, they were going to Sofia's spot on the beach, but this time they were doing it during lunch break.

Eleanor stroked Cecelia's back. "I don't know why I like this cat so much. Her temperament is the opposite of mine. I like to be active, while she likes to do as little as possible."

"She has a calming effect." Sofia scratched the cat under her chin, eliciting louder purring.

Marcel was quiet, contemplative. He didn't take part in their conversation, but his arm around her waist was warm and sure, and from time to time, his palm moved over her hip, reminding her of their morning lovemaking.

Those intimate moments were the only times she was distracted enough for her anxiety to subside so she could forget about the danger to her family.

She'd prayed to the Mother of All Life for Jade to succeed in eliminating Igor. If she did, Marcel's people wouldn't have to invade, there wouldn't be bloodshed beyond Igor's, and in her gratitude for their help, Jade would sign a treaty with the immortals.

Talk about wishful thinking.

But even that best-case scenario wouldn't be the end of her worries. Marcel still planned on confessing his crime to the clan's judge and accepting any punishment she saw fit. What if the judge sentenced him to entombment? It was such a horrible punishment that even a whipping seemed preferable to it.

"Do you want to hear something funny?" Eleanor said.

Marcel cast her a sidelong glance. "A good joke would be most welcome right now."

Was he tormented by the same thoughts that plagued Sofia?

"Syssi thinks that I might be of Kra-ell descent."

Sofia chuckled. "The thought crossed my mind when I started noticing peculiarities about Marcel, and I wondered about your and Emmett's compulsion abilities."

"What does she base that on?" Marcel asked.

"Mainly my looks and my ability to compel. If I am of Kra-ell descent, it's good news for Sofia because it means that Kra-ell Dormants can be induced the same way as immortal Dormants even many generations later. But I don't think that I'm Kra-ell. Toven is a compeller, and so were his brother and his uncle. We know that they are not Kra-ell."

"Who is Toven?" Sofia asked.

Marcel and Eleanor exchanged looks, and then Marcel shrugged. "I guess it's okay to tell you. Toven uses the name Tom when he deals with humans."

"Why? I've never heard the name Toven. It doesn't mean anything to me."

"He has his reasons," Eleanor said. "Anyway, I wonder if Bridget can tell the difference between Kra-ell and immortal genes."

"Kaia might help with that." Marcel stopped next to Sofia's boulder and pulled the pendant from his left pocket and the special earpieces from the other. "Here you go."

Taking a deep breath, she draped the chain around her neck and turned to Eleanor. "I assume that you want to compel me before I put the earpieces in."

Eleanor nodded. "Repeat the story we rehearsed before."

After Sofia had done that, Eleanor compelled her to stick to the story, and then it was time to make the call.

She put the translating earpieces in and pulled the communication earpiece from the pendant and activated it.

"Sofia," Valstar responded immediately. "This is an unusual time for you to call."

"I couldn't get away last night, but I needed to tell you what I found out. I have a heart problem. I wasn't feeling well, and the retreat's doctor referred me to a cardiologist. I saw him yesterday, and I'm afraid that the bill was quite steep. I owe Safe Haven a lot of money. They paid for it, but I need to pay them back."

"You can pay them back in installments from your salary. What else do you have to report?"

She shouldn't have been surprised at his lack of concern for her health, but it still hurt. He hadn't even asked how severe her heart problem was and if it was life-threatening.

"After the doctor's visit, we went to a get-together hosted by a rich backer of the paranormal program. Turns out that they are running a candidate as a test for their future plans, which are at the national level. I think that the candidate they are backing is one of them."

"That's interesting. What's his name?"

"It's a woman. Her name is Katie Berlindor."

"Never heard of her, but then we don't care who the Governor of Oregon is."

"Normally, I would agree with you, but the paranormals might be just testing the waters in Oregon. Their next target might be the presidential race, and they could take over the country. I don't know what the impact of that would be on our community, but I'm sure Igor would want to know about it."

"I'll let him know. Anything else?"

"No, that's it for now."

"Keep up the good work. Goodbye, Sofia."

"I don't know how long I'll be able to do that. My health has deteriorated significantly."

"If you could attend a fancy get-together yesterday, you are not on your deathbed." The line went silent.

"Well, that was a slap in the face." Sofia deactivated the device and pulled the chain over her head.

"I'm sorry." Marcel took her into his arms.

"I'm not." Sofia rested her head on his shoulder. "I should not have expected any emotional response from him. I don't know what I was thinking."

"He's a jerk." Eleanor patted her shoulder. "And he's a lousy leader. Even if he didn't care, he should have at least pretended that he did."

Toven

"Over here." Okidu waved Toven and Mia over to the bus.

"I thought that we were taking the limo to the clan's airstrip." Mia drove her portable chair to where the butler stood.

"Master William has a lot of equipment that he's taking with him. There wasn't enough room in the limousine. Master Kian offered to send Onidu to drive you and Master Toven in the limousine, but Master Toven said that the bus was fine."

The Russian drones needed to be outfitted with advanced electronics, and if they got to stage three of the plan, William would need to scramble the compound's communications. He would also need to figure out how to remove the collars many of the hybrids and purebloods had been outfitted with, hopefully without blowing their heads off.

"I hope you don't mind," Toven said.

"Of course not." Mia looked at the stairs and winced. "But you'll need to carry me up."

He grinned. "You know I love doing that."

As Okidu took their luggage, Toven lifted Mia along with her compact wheelchair and carried her up the stairs. "Let's see if it can fit through the aisle."

They had purchased it for use on commercial flights, and it was supposed to be air travel approved, but they hadn't tested it yet.

"It does." Mia drove it to the end of the bus. "But I can't turn around."

"You're not supposed to." Toven pulled her out of the chair, set her down on the seat, and folded the chair. "It's supposed to be stored in the overhead compartment."

She sighed. "I'm glad that we are taking a private jet. It would have been so embarrassing to have you carry me to the bathroom."

"Hello." William climbed into the bus, followed by Roni's mate.

Her name had come up when they had been talking about disabling the cameras on the dirt road leading to the first tunnel entrance, but Toven had forgotten about her part in the plan.

He walked over to them and offered his hand to Sylvia first. "Hello."

"Hi." She shook his hand and then ducked around him to give Mia a hug. "You and I are going shopping together. I don't have any proper winter clothes."

As the two started chatting, Toven shook William's hand. "Okidu told us that you are bringing a lot of equipment with us. Are we going to use the noise cannon after all?"

"We are not. The damage it might do to the children's ears precludes us from using it." William slid into the seat across from the one Mia and Sylvia were seated in. "I'm preparing stage three. If Jade takes care of the problem for us, we might not need to get there, but if we do, I need to be ready. The Russian military drones that Turner's supplier got for us need to be fortified with more advanced electronics and hooked up to our satellite communication protocol. I don't know if the amphibian needs any modifications, but I brought some components in case it does. I also brought equipment to disrupt their communication capabilities."

"How does that work?"

William waved a dismissive hand. "It's involved, but the gist of it is that everyone in a ten-mile radius around the compound and inside of it won't be able to send or receive a cellular or satellite signal, except for us, of course. My disruptor is calibrated not to affect our connection to the clan's satellite."

"What about landlines?"

"I assume that there aren't any in such a remote area, but I will check once we get there." He smiled. "I have the equipment for that as well."

"I'm impressed." Toven gave William an approving nod. "Modern technology can do much more than a god or even several gods ever could. If my people had survived, they would have been obsolete in this world."

William pursed his lips. "If they had survived, the world would be a very different place today."

"Indeed."

Toven tried to imagine a world in which the gods were still running things. He doubted that humanity would have advanced as much as it had, or that its population would have grown to eight billion people. Ahn wouldn't have allowed humans to multiply the way they had. He would have engineered global culling events to thin out human populations so he could maintain control over it.

"How come Roni is not coming with you?" Mia asked Sylvia.

"He can't. With both William and Marcel gone, he's the only one left to run the lab."

"What about Kaia? Is she coming with us?" Toven asked.

William shook his head. "I'll miss her, but I didn't want to endanger her." He glanced at Mia.

"I can protect my mate." Toven crossed his arms over his chest. "Besides, Mia is crucial to the success of this operation. She enhances my compulsion power and, at the same time, makes it easier on the compelled."

"I know. Kian told me." William turned to look at Mia and gave her the thumbs up. "You have a very cool talent."

"Thank you."

"Go, Mia." Sylvia lifted her hand for Mia to high-five her.

"Go, Sylvia." Mia clapped her hand. "Your talent is one of a kind as well."

Sylvia could disable electronics, but regrettably, she could only do that in close proximity. She couldn't disable the compound's electricity grid or its cellular tower.

"How do they get power?" Toven asked William. "Are they connected to the grid?"

William nodded. "They are. Power is fed via pole-suspended conductors, which makes for an easy target to take it down, but I prefer not to touch it. That would trigger an investigation from the Russian electric company, and it wouldn't do us much good to take it down anyway."

"What about the exoskeletons?" Toven asked. "Are we taking those as well?"

William laughed. "Do you have any idea how big and heavy they are? As it is, we are already maxing out the jet's cargo capacity. We will need a big plane to carry the suits, the Guardians, and Kalugal's men. I hope that Jade will eliminate Igor and that they won't be needed."

Sofia

"I hope you don't want to return to the retreat." Marcel stopped at the gate to the private enclave where his bungalow was located.

"I don't have a choice," Eleanor said, even though his question hadn't been directed at her. "I have a class to teach." She winked. "I'll see you two when I see you." She hugged Cecilia to her chest and kept on walking.

After talking with Valstar, Sofia was too distraught to pay attention in class, and the distraction that Marcel offered with his skillful lovemaking was very appealing.

She wound her arms around his neck. "What do you want me to do instead?"

He smiled. "I have a few ideas."

She'd noticed that he'd been smiling a lot more lately, and she wondered whether it was because he'd finally shared his guilty secret with someone or because he was in love with her.

It was probably both, and knowing that she was responsible for his newfound happiness made her heart swell with gratitude and love.

What would happen if she didn't transition, though?

"Think positive," she murmured. "Ask, and you shall receive."

"What's the matter?" Marcel opened the door to his bungalow. "Bad thoughts again?"

She didn't want to spoil his mood. Meeting his gaze with a coy smile, she tilted her head. "Why do you assume that I was thinking bad thoughts? Maybe I was asking the universe for orgasms?"

His eyes blazed with an inner light. "You can ask me, and I shall deliver." He picked her up by the waist and deposited her on the kitchen counter.

The thing was small, no more than five feet across, and that included a sink.

"What are you doing?"

"Answering a request." His lips feathered over her neck. "I never told you this before, but you have a beautiful neck. And even though your hair is magnificent, I like that you keep it up, exposing this graceful column. I get hard imagining my fangs grazing your smooth skin right here." He kissed the spot.

As she opened her legs wider, making room for him between them, her hands found the back of his neck, and she drew him closer. "Kiss me."

The hard ridge of his arousal pressed against her sensitive tissues through the fabric of his slacks and her leggings, both of them made of thin material that did little to take away from the sensation.

As his tongue tangled with hers, his hands slid down from her waist to her ass, and as he pulled her harder against that straining erection, she lifted her legs and hooked them around his hips.

The moment his hands left her bottom, she mourned the loss of his touch, but then he was tugging at her T-shirt and pulling it over her head.

When she was left with only her push-up bra, she reached for his turtleneck and pulled it out of the waistband of his slacks. "Take it off."

When he pulled away to do as she commanded, she leaned back, propping herself on her forearms to watch him expose his magnificent chest. Lean muscle with a light smattering of blond hair that was barely visible against his pale skin.

Leaning over her, Marcel pushed his fingers under the elastic of her leggings, and as he pulled them down, she toed off her sneakers.

He tossed the leggings on the floor and then removed her right sock but didn't let go of her foot. He kissed her ankle, then her calf, then the inside of her knee, and just as she thought that he would keep going to where her panties were soaked through, he lifted her left foot and repeated what he had done with her right.

"You're such a tease."

His nostrils flaring, he smiled with a mouthful of fangs. "Ask, and you shall receive. What's your pleasure, love?"

He called her love, and it made her giddy because it wasn't just a term of endearment for him. Marcel loved her. It was in his glowing eyes, the gentle way he held her, and in the patience and restraint he practiced because she was human and fragile compared to him.

Arching her back, she lifted her bottom an inch off the counter. "Kiss me there."

That was such a wanton thing to say, and she loved that she could do that with Marcel and feel good about it. There was no judgment in his eyes, only desire.

He pressed a kiss to the front of her panties and then hooked his thumbs in the elastic and dragged them down her legs.

She expected him to come back and kiss her flesh, but when he gripped her feet and propped them onto the counter, she'd never felt so exposed or so turned on.

When his head lowered between her splayed thighs, he rested his cheek on one side and just breathed her in. "I want to bottle this scent and carry it with me all day long."

Normally, she wouldn't have found the idea sexy, but she was so turned on that his words just added fuel to the fire.

"You're teasing me again."

He kissed her inner thigh, then the other side, and then his tongue made contact with her clit, and it was as if an electrical current zapped her.

"Marcel," she groaned.

He didn't answer. Instead, his tongue flicked over her clit, once, twice, and then he pushed it inside of her.

A guttural moan left her throat, and as she arched up to get more of his tongue, he slid his hands under her ass and gripped it hard.

It was as if her moan had unleashed his beast. Driving his tongue in and out of her, he alternated with flicks over that sensitive bundle of nerves, and when he released one butt cheek and drove two fingers inside of her, Sofia exploded with a scream that must have been heard all over the enclave.

Marcel

Marcel licked and pumped his fingers until Sofia went limp, and her head dropped against the backsplash. When all of her shudders subsided, and she let out a breath, he pressed a gentle kiss to her petals and lifted his gaze to her flushed face.

"You're the most beautiful after you climax."

She smiled. "I love you, too."

Upon hearing those words, something shifted in his chest. Something eased. He felt lighter, almost buoyant, and as he pushed to his feet and embraced the woman he loved, he felt complete like he'd never felt before.

"I love you, my Sofia," he murmured into her tangled hair.

It had come undone, and he collected it in his hands and twisted it up to expose her neck. Brushing his lips over the long column, he suppressed the urge to sink his fangs into her skin. The time for that would be later when he was deep inside of her, and she was climaxing again.

"I still have my bra on," she murmured.

"I'll take care of it." He lifted her off the counter, carried her to the bedroom, and laid her down on the bed.

"You keep carrying me around." She sprawled lazily on the bed, her legs parted in invitation.

"Because I know that you like it."

"I do." She reached behind her and unclasped her bra.

He pulled her hand out and kissed her fingers. "I said that I'll take care of it."

"Then do it." She pouted. "My poor nipples are hungry for your attention."

He was on her before she'd finished the sentence, ripping the bra off and sucking one turgid peak into his mouth.

"Oh, yeah. Just like that." Sofia arched her back, pushing more of her small breast into his mouth. "More."

He lightly pinched her other nipple, drawing a moan from her lips, and then he switched, tonguing the other one, and sometime during all that, he'd gotten rid of his slacks.

"Kiss me," Sofia breathed.

He pushed up her body and took her mouth, sweeping in with his tongue that still carried her taste, and as she nipped his lip, stars exploded behind his eyelids.

He needed to be inside of her.

Getting on top of her, he slicked his shaft with her wetness, and she surprised him by joining her hand with his and guiding him toward her entrance.

"I love you." She lifted her lips to his and let go of his shaft.

He took her mouth and surged inside of her, but not all at once. He halted and waited for her to signal that she was ready for more. By now, he knew her body and its responses so well that he didn't need to guess when to be gentle and when to be rough.

Right now, Sofia needed tender loving, and he was going to give her precisely that, even though it was torturous to hold his beast back.

When she pulled her lips away and smiled, he pushed in another inch, and when she cupped his ass and arched up, he slammed all the way home.

Sofia's fingers clawed at his ass, spurring him on, and he gave her what she wanted, going faster and harder until her body stiffened and a release blasted through her. Only then did he flick his tongue over the spot on her neck and, with a hiss, sank his fangs into her.

Marcel's climax erupted along with the venom he released into her system, and only when he was all spent and retracted his fangs did he remember that they had forgotten to use a condom once again.

Not that he believed a single condom could have contained all that he'd spilled into her.

It hadn't been regular lovemaking.

For some reason that he wasn't clear on, this time, it had felt like a claiming.

It had been mutual.

Sofia had claimed him as surely as he had claimed her.

Perhaps it had been the finality she'd felt after talking with Valstar. By giving up on her grandfather, she'd finally unraveled the last of her ties to the Kra-ell community and fully embraced her new life with Marcel.

"I'm sorry, my love." He licked the two tiny wounds. "I know that you wanted to wait."

Sofia didn't respond.

With a dreamy expression on her beautiful face, she was out, and he hoped she was experiencing wonderful adventures on her euphoric postorgasmic trip.

He brushed a strand of hair off her forehead. "I love you."

Gazing at her flushed cheeks and her puffy lips, he realized that loving her no longer scared him.

She wasn't an unhealthy obsession like Cordelia had been. She wasn't dangerous or manipulative or demanding.

Sofia was his home, his safe place.

"My beautiful, courageous mate." He kissed her lips.

Toven

Sylvia walked about thirty feet in front of the van and waved her hand this way and that, but Toven couldn't see the cameras even with his godly eyesight.

"How does she know where they are?" he asked Yamanu.

The Guardian shrugged. "I think she can sense the devices. The neat thing about her ability is that she can disable them one at a time, just long enough for our van to pass through. Whoever is watching the feed would assume that the cameras are glitching."

"Is it common for surveillance cameras to glitch?" Mia asked.

"They can lag," Morris said. "It depends on their quality and the quality of the network they are connected to. They can experience latency due to the speed of the decoding and encoding process or the data's travel time over the network."

Mia pursed her lips. "That went straight over my head."

Yamanu grinned. "Mine too. Morris is just parroting what William told him."

The pilot snorted. "Don't assume that everyone is as ignorant about technology as you are."

Yamanu and Morris kept at it as if they were on a field trip and not about to abduct a dangerous pureblood, and even Mia joined in as if nothing dangerous was about to happen.

It had been decided that the Guardians who were coming at the Kra-ell through the woods would tranquilize all three but leave the hybrids inside the tunnel. They would stage them so they wouldn't look asleep in the camera's view and only take the pureblood to the van. Two Guardians would remain with the hybrids to make sure that they didn't wake up too soon, and another two would bring the tranquilized pureblood to the van for interrogation.

From the outside the vehicle appeared like an old, beat-up Russian make from the eighties, but on the inside it was kitted out with modern equipment. If Sylvia failed to disable any of the cameras, the van wouldn't look too suspicious.

They needed to stop the van far away from the tunnel's entrance so the guards wouldn't hear the engine, and as they veered off the path into the woods, Sylvia continued walking straight ahead.

She still had to disable the camera right at the entrance.

The maneuver required precise coordination and was probably the most dangerous part of the operation.

The snipers hiding in the woods would have to fire the tranquilizer darts a moment after Sylvia took care of the camera, and then they had to stage the two sleeping hybrids in a way that would just show their backs.

The Guardians had been observing the three guards for two days, and they had behaved like any other guards who didn't expect anyone to inspect them or any enemy to suddenly appear. They were complacent. They sat on foldable chairs, watched movies on their phones, played card games, drank booze, and smoked what was probably weed.

The Guardians hadn't gotten close enough to smell it.

Twenty minutes or so passed when Yamanu said, "On my mark, Sylvia. Now."

Mia squeezed Toven's hand as they waited for the Guardians to report.

"It's done," Yamanu said. "Bobbie and Drake are on their way with the pureblood."

They were communicating via earpieces, but Toven hadn't been given one, and he hadn't asked for it. The men knew what they were doing, and they didn't need his input. His job was to remove the compulsion and interrogate the pureblood.

"Is Sylvia coming back with Bobbie and Drake?" Mia asked.

"No," Yamanu said. "She's staying with the two Guardians at the tunnel. The one carrying the pureblood is running through the woods to avoid the cameras."

Yamanu collected the titanium chains, opened the door, and stepped out of the van.

The Guardian carrying the Kra-ell male appeared at a dead run mere minutes later. "Son of a bitch is already waking up." He dropped him on the ground. "Hurry up."

"No worries, buddy." Yamanu knelt next to the Kra-ell. "I've got him."

Toven stepped out of the van, ready to assist if needed, but Yamanu had the pureblood hogtied and propped against the van in seconds.

The male's eyelashes fluttered for a split second, and then he opened his enormous eyes and hissed, *"Kto ti?"*

"My name is Tom," Toven answered in English. He could conduct the interrogation in Russian, but if the guard spoke English, the others could take part in it too. "What's yours?" Toven used the full power of his compulsion, and with Mia in the van right behind him, she was enhancing it further.

The pureblood's black eyes flickered red.

Was red a sign of aggression or of fear?

Toven had forgotten.

"My name is Pavel," he answered in heavily accented English. "Who are you?"

Eric

After Geraldine and Roni left and Eric was left alone with Darlene, he picked up the romance book Geraldine had brought for him. Leafing through it, he searched for a hot sex scene.

Darlene had read to him when he'd been transitioning, and she believed that hearing the steamy descriptions had helped pull him out of the coma. He didn't remember being aware of her reading to him, but just in case she was right, he was going to do the same for her.

It was unnerving watching her lying so still on the hospital bed.

To someone else's eyes she would appear asleep, but he knew her sleeping habits, and she never slept on her back or remained in the same position for more than half an hour.

Darlene wasn't a peaceful sleeper, and he was used to her turning from side to side, reaching for the blanket and tucking it between her thighs, or punching the pillow to mold it into a shape that was comfortable for her.

With a sigh, he returned to the book. "Let's see what we've got here."

It was a billionaire romance about a tech mogul who falls in love with his housemaid. A classic *Cinderella* story with a modern twist. The guy was a little kinky, and the girl was young and virginal. Skipping over her first time, which Eric didn't find sexy in the least, he searched for steamier scenes further into the book.

"Here we go." He leaned back. "Rachel was on her knees, scrubbing the baseboards like Edward had asked her to, the short skirt of her uniform riding up and exposing the back of her thighs. A week ago, she would have been tugging on it to cover her ass, but she was no longer shy. The world of pleasure that Edward had introduced her to had changed her, and all she could think about was him coming in, kneeling behind her, and pushing her thong aside."

"What the hell are you reading?" Max stood at the doorway.

Eric looked at him over his shoulder. "Grab a chair and join the reading club. You might learn a thing or two about women's fantasies. Let me tell you this, though, they are much kinkier than men's."

Max lifted one of the chairs in the waiting room, brought it over next to Eric's, and went back to close the door behind him.

"Why did you close the door?"

"If Bridget can't see me, she can't kick me out." He pulled out a bottle of whiskey from the inner pocket of his bomber jacket. "I thought you could use some."

"I can." Eric put the book on the bed and took the bottle. "You're the best."

"I know." Max grinned. "Not too long ago, I was sitting here with Darlene and watching you lying in that bed still like a mummy."

Eric twisted the cap off and took a long swig, letting the whiskey coat his throat. "Was she freaking out like I am?" He handed the bottle to Max.

"Pretty much." He took a swig and glanced at the book. "Do you want to keep reading?"

"Sure. Let me bring you up to speed." Eric lifted the book and showed Max the cover. "This is Rachel, she's nineteen, broke, and she works as a maid for an agency. They send her to clean the house of a young and very handsome tech billionaire. This dude." He tapped the cover. "His name is Edward, and he likes control. A few chapters ago, he took her virginity, but I skipped that part. This is a week later, and she's already addicted to his kinky style."

Max took the book from him. "Is that what Darlene is into?"

As rage bubbled hot and quick, Eric wrestled it down. At least now he was prepared for the irrational possessiveness of his new immortal instincts, and he did his best not to let them turn him into a caveman.

"Give it back." He pulled the paperback from Max's hand. "I'm grateful for what you have done for Darlene and me, but I'd appreciate it if you didn't put Darlene and sex in the same sentence."

Max lifted his hands, one still gripping the whiskey bottle. "Forgive me. I will never do that again. It's just that I would have never guessed. She's so mild." Laughing, he ducked as Eric tried to swat him over the head. "Okay, I'll stop. I promise." He was still laughing.

"Wait until you have a mate. I'll pay you back for this."

"You know that I was just joking." He waved at the book. "Keep reading."

"I think I'd better not." Eric closed the book and put it on the bed. "How about a nice fairytale?" He pulled out his phone and typed fairytales into the search field.

"Sure. What did you find?"

Eric shook his head. "Goldie and the Three Bear Shifters, Beauty and the Sexy Beast, Wendy and the Bully Lost Boys." He lifted his gaze to Max. "What the hell is that? What happened to all the nice fairytales?"

"They were never nice." Max handed him the bottle. "Personally, I prefer the new sexy versions. Give me that phone."

Toven

Toven wondered why Igor had chosen two low-level hybrids to trail Sofia when he had a pureblood who spoke English. It seemed that their command of the language hadn't been the only reason they had been chosen. Igor hadn't wanted to send this one for some reason.

The pureblood struggled against the chains, and when he realized that his struggles were futile, he looked at Toven with eyes that were filled with fear mingled with curiosity. "Who are you? What do you want from me? What did you do with my friends?"

"I told you. My name is Tom, and I want to ask you a few questions. But first, we need to free you from Igor's compulsion."

"How do you know about Igor?"

"Stop asking questions," Toven commanded.

The Kra-ell opened his mouth, tried to speak, and closed it. Evidently, he could be compelled as long as it didn't contradict Igor's compulsion.

"You can tell me everything you were ever told to keep a secret." Toven slammed his power of compulsion into the guy.

Pavel's eyelids twitched, and he hissed, revealing two very long, sharp fangs. They looked exactly the same as any male god or immortal's when fully elongated. Also, his huge bug-like eyes were fully red now and glowing from the inside. But despite the alien features and the aggression, the male didn't look like a monster.

He was just different.

"Tell me about the weapons in your compound's arsenal."

Pavel repeated the same information Dima and Anton had provided, but Toven had a feeling that he wasn't telling him everything.

As someone who had dealt with compulsion probably since birth, Pavel had no doubt figured out that there were ways to resist it as long as it wasn't phrased tightly enough.

"Are the weapons you told me about the compound's only defense against intruders?"

Pavel shook his head as much as the chains allowed.

"What other defenses does the compound have?"

"Everything is rigged with explosives. If we are invaded, Igor blows everything and everyone up."

Toven frowned. "Who knows about this?"

"Everyone who needs to know."

"You mean the purebloods?"

Pavel's big eyes widened even further. "Yes. You know about us." He couldn't ask a question because of Toven's command, so he circumvented it by stating what he wanted to ask.

"Is he going to blow up the compound with you in it?" Toven asked.

Pavel nodded. "No one is to be taken alive."

"I bet Igor has an escape tunnel. He's not the type of guy who would go down with the ship."

The Kra-ell looked puzzled. "I don't understand."

"He will not die with his people."

"I don't know about an escape tunnel." The guy couldn't hide the telltale grimace.

"But you suspect that he has one."

"Maybe. I didn't think much about it. No one knows that we are here." He glanced at Yamanu. "But you do."

The question was burning in the guy's eyes, but he couldn't ask it. The red color had faded a little, and the inner light had turned green, but Toven didn't remember what that meant either.

Not that it mattered.

If Jade killed Igor, the explosives wouldn't be a problem unless someone else could press the button.

"Is Igor the only one who can detonate the explosives?"

"I don't know."

"What do you suspect?"

"Maybe his second-in-command can do that. His third might do it too."

"Can Jade?"

The pureblood's eyes bugged out. "No."

"Any of the other females?"

"No."

"Where did the Kra-ell come from?"

Toven had a few minutes to spare, and it wouldn't hurt to find out a little more while he was at it.

"I don't know."

Toven let out a breath. "Were you born on Earth?"

"Yes."

"Where do you suspect they came from?"

"Somewhere hundreds of light years away."

"That's not very helpful."

Yamanu cleared his throat. "We are running out of time. Let's try the shrouding and thralling."

"Right." Toven cast an illusion of an attacking beast.

Yamanu and Bobbie flinched, Mia gasped, but the Kra-ell didn't even blink.

"I assume that you don't see anything."

The guy opened his mouth and closed it. "I still can't ask questions."

"You can ask questions now."

"What was I supposed to see?"

"Never mind. I want you to deliver a message to Jade, and you have to do it in a way that will seem as if you are inviting her to a tryst."

"Why would I want to do that? She's Igor's prime."

"Does he forbid her to have sex with other males?"

"I don't know. His other females are allowed to accept invitations from pureblooded males when they are not in their fertile cycle, and they do. But Jade doesn't. I never invited her, so I don't know for sure, but I never saw her with other males."

"If he allows the other females to have sex with other males, he probably allows her too. Besides, you just need to issue the invitation. She doesn't have to accept. Your job is only to deliver the message in a way that will seem as if you are offering sex. You are to invite her to hunt for

Veskars on Friday at two in the afternoon, where the three rivers intersect."

"What are Veskars?" Pavel asked.

Toven smiled. "Magical rats on your home world that grant wishes to those who can catch them. They are very difficult to hunt. It's part of the sexual innuendo. Do you understand?"

"I do."

"Repeat the instructions."

Pavel parroted what Toven had told him.

"Good. I just need to do one more thing." Toven tried to reach into the guy's mind, but it was like trying to thrall another god. He had no access.

Damn. That wasn't good. The explosives were no good, and their entire plan resting on Jade's ability to eliminate Igor wasn't good either.

"You will deliver the message to Jade. You will not tell anyone, and you will not make a note or communicate in any form, verbal or nonverbal, that you were captured and interrogated. You will act as if nothing unusual has happened. Repeat what I told you to do."

After the pureblood repeated the instructions word for word, Toven shifted his gaze to Yamanu. "He's all yours."

Kian

"Any news from the field?" Turner asked as he walked into Kian's office.

"Not yet."

"It's after four in the afternoon over there." He put his coffee cup down on Kian's desk. "Toven should be done."

"He'll call when they are on their way back."

The abduction of the guard had been scheduled for two in the afternoon, right at the start of their shift. At night, sound carried much farther, and they would've been forced to leave the van on the main road and traverse the dirt path on foot, which presented more problems than a daytime operation.

Ten more minutes of tense anticipation passed before the call finally came in.

"Toven." Kian activated the speaker. "Is everyone okay?"

"Good morning, Kian," Toven said with a condescending tone that reminded Kian of his mother. "Everyone is fine."

She would've sounded the same if he'd failed to precede his inquiry with a socially acceptable greeting.

Kian couldn't care less what most people thought about his manners or lack thereof, but Toven was a god, and he needed to be addressed with the same respect as Annani.

"Forgive my impatience. I've been worried."

"That's understandable. We are on our way back to St. Petersburg."

"How did it go?"

"The operation went without a hitch. The Guardians tranquilized the guards and brought the pureblood to the van. After I overrode Igor's compulsion, he confirmed everything that the two hybrids had told us. However, he added a crucial piece of information that only the purebloods are privy to, and it is a game changer. Igor has the entire compound rigged. If he's attacked, and he thinks that he's going to lose, he'll blow the place up along with everyone in it."

Turner released a breath. "That requires a change of plans."

Kian didn't buy that. "Despots don't go down with the sinking ship. He's either lying to the purebloods about the explosives, or he has an escape tunnel or some other means of getting out of there. He's also not going to escape alone. He needs his inner circle, and I bet they all know where that escape tunnel is."

"If there is one, it would be in the office building," Turner said. "That's where they spend most of their time. The question is, where's the exit point? My bet is that it's somewhere in their hunting grounds, which means that he must have a vehicle hidden nearby. If I were him, I would have a boat and a car or an amphibian stashed where I can get to them. When the rivers freeze, they turn into roads and can be driven over, but in the summer, he will need a boat. An amphibian combines the two, but it's a slow-moving vehicle. A helicopter would be better, but Sofia would have heard or seen it taking off or landing, and she didn't."

"There are pluses and minuses for both ground and airborne vehicles," Kian said.

"None of the three guards I interrogated mentioned a helicopter or an amphibian," Toven said. "But then none of them mentioned a tunnel either. It's possible that the tunnel is known only to Igor's inner circle, and if he has a helicopter, it is stashed deep inside the hunting grounds where it's not visible from the compound."

"What about the message to Jade?" Turner asked. "Did you compel him to deliver it after you learned about the explosives?"

"I scheduled the meeting for Friday at two o'clock local time."

"I hope you're not walking into a trap."

"I hope so too." Toven sighed. "There is more bad news. The pureblood was immune to thralling and to shrouding, which means that I can't seize the purebloods' minds."

Kian shook his head. "This is progressing from bad to worse, and I'm inclined to abort the whole thing. I don't want you there, and I don't want Mia and William there either. Without your mind manipulation ability, you can't protect them."

"I still have my compulsion power, and with Mia enhancing it, I can command the attackers to stand down. I ordered the pureblood to stop asking questions before I removed Igor's compulsion, and he obeyed immediately."

"That's good," Turner said. "Freeing Jade from Igor's compulsion is still our best chance of eliminating him without committing fully to taking on his entire force."

Kian drummed his fingers on the desk. "She might know about the explosives and where the detonation switch or switches are. If she can disable them, we can still proceed with stage three of our plan to free the compound."

Turner huffed out a breath. "Aborting the plan is also a viable option. Sofia can meet up with Tim, and he can draw a portrait of Igor that we can feed to the facial recognition software. Igor must leave the compound from time to time, and he can't fool cameras with his compulsion powers. If he goes through an airport, we might catch his trail and eliminate him when he's not behind the protective shield of his compound." Turner crossed his arms over his chest. "He might be able to detonate the explosives remotely before we manage to disarm him. I don't think he would, but it's a possibility that we need to account for."

Kian frowned. "Why would he do that? The compound wouldn't be under siege, and he would hope that his cronies would rescue him. He's not going to blow them up along with everyone else, and he wouldn't have time to give them a warning to use the escape tunnel. We can liberate the place after capturing him."

"Instead of detonating immediately, Igor's signal could initiate a sequence," Turner said. "The inner circle pure-bloods would know to evacuate, and the rest wouldn't know that anything was going on and would stay."

Sofia

When Marcel's phone rang, Sofia knew it was news from Karelia.

It didn't require intuition or precognition.

Marcel was on an enforced vacation, so he didn't receive calls about work, and it seemed that he didn't have friends because his phone never rang with personal calls either. He'd told her that his mother lived in Scotland and that they spoke on the phone about once a week, but she hadn't heard him talking to his mother even once.

They didn't seem to be close.

If Sofia could call her father, Helmi, and her aunts, she would be calling them daily, but no one was allowed phones in the compound. Every time she'd returned home, she'd had to deposit her cell phone in the security office.

"Thanks for the update. I'll let Sofia know." Marcel ended the call and regarded her with a frown.

Her gut squeezed. "Bad news?"

"They caught a pureblood guard, and he told them that Igor has the entire compound rigged with explosives."

Sofia felt the blood drain from her face. "Dear Mother of All Life. Why?"

"So no one is caught alive, I guess. Kian thinks that Igor has an escape tunnel. It doesn't fit his profile to go down with his people."

"The mission has to be aborted." She waved at his phone. "Call your boss and tell him to pull his people out of there."

"Toven already sent a message with the guard to Jade. They hope she will have a plan. In fact, she might know about Igor's secret tunnel. The fable she wrote to Emmett talked about the rats digging a tunnel to save the lions, so maybe it was a hint for him to find the tunnel and use it to infiltrate the compound."

She frowned. "What are you talking about? What fable?"

Marcel smoothed his hand over the back of his head. "In all the commotion, I forgot that I didn't tell you how Jade had contacted Emmett. She wrote a fable for a writing competition. It was written very cleverly so only he would understand that it was from her. Even if Igor saw it, which I'm sure he did, he wouldn't have known that it contained a secret message. I can show it to you."

He sat on the couch next to her and scrolled on his phone. "I saved it in my notes." He handed her the device.

The fable read like a children's story, and the moral was not to underestimate those who appear weaker, but where was the secret message?

"How did Emmett know that she was talking about herself and that she was trapped?"

"Emmett's Kra-ell name is Veskar, which is the name of a rodent resembling a rat in the Kra-ell home world. He hates that name, and no one outside his tribe knew him as Veskar. Jade must have recognized him from his pictures on the Safe Haven website, or she might have seen it in one of the advertisements for the paranormal retreat. She entered the competition to send him a message, hoping that he could help her. The numbers of the lions and cubs represent coordinates." Marcel showed her how they had arrived at the combinations that produced the longitude and latitude.

"Jade is a genius." Sofia looked at that paragraph again. "How did Emmett figure that out? It would have never occurred to me."

Marcel smiled shyly. "Emmett only figured out that the email was from Jade. I deciphered the meaning of the numbers. She gave us the approximate coordinates of the compound."

"But you couldn't find it anyway. Not until you got me to tell you where it was."

"We would have found it sooner or later. You just saved us some time."

That didn't help her feel any less guilty or anxious.

"Can I speak with Kian? I have to convince him to abort the mission. As much as I feel sorry for Jade and the other females, their freedom is not worth the lives of everyone in the compound."

She didn't wish them harm, but they weren't the nicest people, and her family and the other humans came first.

Marcel hesitated. "I'll text Shai and ask him to tell Kian that you wish to speak with him."

"Thank you. Do you think he'll call me?"

"He will." Marcel typed up the message. "Kian has a short temper and no patience, but he's a good guy, and if approached correctly, he tries to accommodate the needs and wishes of his people."

"I'm not his people."

"Of course you are. You're my mate, and you're part of the clan now."

Sofia knew what that term meant for immortals, and it was a big deal.

"What if I don't transition?"

Marcel cupped her cheek. "Human or long-lived, you are still my mate." He dipped his head and took her lips in a loving kiss. "I hope you live to be at least a thousand years old, but I'll take whatever time with you the Fates grant us."

It was so sweet, but it wasn't true. "Truelove mates are only possible between immortals or immortals and

Dormants. Even if I transition, it would be as a Kra-ell Dormant, and so I can't be your fated one and only."

"What was true yesterday might be proven wrong tomorrow. None of it is an exact science." He put his hand over his chest. "I know in here that you are my one and only. I feel it in every fiber of my being. For the first time in three hundred years, I'm not afraid to love. On the contrary, being with you feels like home to me. Safe."

Sofia swallowed. "Loving you feels the same to me." Tears stung the back of her eyes. "But in my case, it comes with a dose of guilt. I abandoned my family for you."

Marcel

Marcel clasped her hand. "You didn't abandon your family. None of what you have done was voluntary. You were put in this situation by Igor, and you didn't choose to be with me."

She smiled. "I chose to love you, and I'm free." She winced. "Sort of. I'm exchanging one restrictive existence for another, but at least this one comes with the man I love, so it's a sweeter deal. But if I lose my family...." She shook her head. "I can't let it happen. How can I have my happily-ever-after with them gone? If I hadn't told you where the entrance to the tunnel was, you might not have found it."

"Not true. First of all, Toven could have compelled it out of you. And secondly, we could have found out where it was from the two hybrids we caught. Besides, you are thinking about it all wrong. We are trying to liberate your family and everyone else who has no choice but to serve

Igor. If we can't do that without causing major casualties, we won't engage."

"You said that you are not in charge. I want to hear it from Kian."

"Fair enough." Marcel looked at the phone, willing it to ring.

When it did, he was surprised it had worked. He hadn't really believed in the wishing and visualizing and the universe responding.

"Hi, Kian. Thank you for calling. I'm activating the speaker so Sofia can join the conversation."

"How can I help you, Sofia?" Kian asked.

She swallowed. "I want to convince you to abort the mission. Freedom is great, but not if it's achieved by death, and that's what will happen if you attack the compound. Igor will see a superior force, and instead of running like you predicted, he will destroy everyone so they don't get captured. It's not worth the risk."

"I agree. If we can't find a way to ensure the detonation doesn't happen, we will not proceed with stage three of the plan. Tom is going to meet with Jade, and we will take it from there. She's been Igor's prime for a reason, and it was probably to learn as much as she could about his weaknesses and plan a rebellion. She can't do anything while under his compulsion, but once she's free and she has us for backup, she might have a plan of her own that she can launch to eliminate Igor while making sure that he doesn't trigger the explosives."

"He's not the only one that can do that. If Jade kills Igor, my grandfather will take over."

"Is he a strong compeller?"

"I don't know. I don't even know if Jade is. None of the other purebloods compelled anyone. It was all Igor."

"We know that Jade is strong, and she's ruthless. By the way, how do you feel about her taking over control of the compound?"

"I don't know her all that well. She's just as stuck-up as the other purebloods, and she doesn't interact with humans."

"Who do you think would be best for the job?"

Kian asked her? Sofia had fantasized about it so often, and she had plenty of ideas for how the compound should be run so everyone's needs were met, but she'd never thought that it could happen.

"They should have an election and choose three representatives. One pureblood, one hybrid, and one human. Or maybe two of each. The three should have an equal say on all major decisions, and if they don't do their job well, they need to be replaced with other elected representatives. But it would never work. The purebloods are too powerful, so they are at the top of the food chain, then the hybrids, and lastly, the humans. Unless someone from the outside enforces the democratic elections of representatives from all three groups, it's not going to happen."

Kian chuckled. "Are you suggesting that my clan should be that outside influence?"

"I was speaking hypothetically."

He let out a breath. "Let's take it one step at a time. Friday, Tom will meet Jade, and hopefully, she will have a plan."

Marcel cleared his throat. "Sofia knows that Tom's name is Toven. I hope it's okay that I told her."

"Toven prefers that his name is not known to outsiders. Sofia is with you, so she's no longer an outsider, but for the time being, Eleanor or Emmett should compel her to keep it a secret as well."

"Do you want me to call Valstar again?" Sofia asked.

"You called him yesterday, and he doesn't expect you to call him every day. Wait until tomorrow."

She chewed on her lower lip. "I thought to plead with him to let my father come here because I'm so sick, and I need open heart surgery."

"Do you think he'll do that?"

Sofia sighed. "Not really."

"Then why put yourself through the heartache?"

"Because if something happens to my father, I need to know that I did everything possible to save him."

"I promise you that nothing will happen to him."

He couldn't promise her that. Her father was human, and they had a family history of heart disease. He could have a stroke tomorrow.

"Thank you, but you can't guarantee that."

"True. But I can promise that I will do everything in my power to guarantee his safety. Do you believe me?"

"I do."

"I'm glad. Good day, Sofia." He ended the call.

"He meant it," Marcel said. "Kian never says things he doesn't mean just to make someone feel good. It's not his style."

"I know, and I appreciate it. I'm just afraid of the unintended consequences, and I don't even know whether they will be worse because of your clan's action or inaction."

Jade

When Pavel strode into Jade's classroom, she lifted an eyebrow. "Do you miss listening to my stories?"

He was young, only thirty-two, and when she'd started teaching twenty years ago, he'd been twelve, and she hadn't been his teacher. She preferred teaching the little ones who hadn't been corrupted by Igor's deviant spin on what it meant to be a Kra-ell, but Pavel had enjoyed hearing her stories and had wandered into her classroom from time to time.

He sat on the mat next to Moshun. "I want to hear the story about you hunting for Veskars."

Jade's heart stuttered. "Why would I be hunting for Veskars? They are not very tasty."

"What are Veskars?" Moshun asked.

"They are magical little rats," Pavel said. "If you catch one, it will grant you a wish."

Moshun's eyes brightened. "Any wish? If I catch one, will he give me a toy?"

Pavel smiled suggestively at Jade. "The Veskar only grants wishes to adults, and they are very difficult to catch, but there is a good chance of catching one at the junction of the three rivers this Friday at two in the afternoon."

Cold sweat slithered down Jade's back.

Pavel sounded as if he was flirting with her, going as far as scheduling a time and place for their assignation, but everyone in the compound knew that she didn't accept invitations from anyone other than Igor, and she only accepted his because she had no choice.

Besides, Pavel shouldn't even know what a Veskar was. The first time she'd included the rat in one of her stories was in the fable she'd sent to Safe Haven.

There could be only two reasons for Pavel to use the rat in his flirting. One was that Igor had figured out what she'd done and had sent him to taunt her or even trap her, and the other one was that the male called Veskar had sent Pavel to deliver the message and schedule a meeting with her in the hunting grounds.

Pavel was a guard, so he could have been approached outside of the compound, and whoever had approached him somehow managed to overcome Igor's compulsion. Could Veskar's power increase so much in two decades?

Impossible.

The only other compellers who were possibly more powerful than Igor were the royal twins, and they were most likely dead. Even if they'd somehow survived, they wouldn't be sending her a message with a guard. She was a nobody to them. They would just walk in and take over the compound.

Jade had spent many nights praying to the Mother for that to happen, even before she'd been captured by Igor and the males of her family had been slaughtered. Since then, she'd prayed twice as fervently, but the Mother hadn't answered her prayers.

The royals were dead.

"Are you offering to help me hunt for the magical Veskar?" Jade asked to maintain the pretense of sexual banter.

"I certainly am." Pavel pushed to his feet. "I'll be thinking of you, fair Jade." He blew her an air kiss, which was shockingly un-Kra-ell of him. "I'll meet you at the junction."

Pureblooded Kra-ell didn't blow kisses at each other, and they didn't whisper sweet endearments in each other's ears like humans. They fought for dominance, and if the male managed to subdue the female, he got to plant his seed in her womb.

It wasn't her fertile cycle, so Igor wouldn't mind that she accepted Pavel's invitation, but she had no intention of indulging the young male if it turned out that his intent had indeed been purely sexual and the mention of a Veskar coincidental.

For the males, sex was as much for pleasure as it was for procreation, and it used to be for her as well, but Jade hadn't done anything for her own enjoyment since she'd failed to protect her tribe, and she wasn't about to break that tradition with Pavel.

If the message was from the real Veskar, it had been very cleverly constructed not to trigger Igor's compulsion to report it. Still, it was possible that she was attaching meaning to what was a simple invitation to sex.

Friday, she would go hunting alone, and she would be at the junction of the three rivers at two in the afternoon. If Pavel showed up expecting sex, she would just turn him down.

Thankfully, Igor wasn't at the compound, and if she was lucky, he wouldn't be back by then.

He watched her like a hawk, and if he noticed any change in her behavior, he would try to compel her to tell him the reason behind it. Jade was already stretching her mental powers to hide her call for help, and she doubted that she could resist his compulsion when he commanded her to tell him what was making her edgier than usual.

What if it was a trap, though?

What if Igor was testing her?

If she showed up at the junction of the three rivers at two o'clock, it would be like an admission of guilt. But if she actually had sex with Pavel, she could claim that she'd accepted his invitation, and that was the only reason she'd shown up.

The Veskar element wasn't a factor in her decision at all.

The problem was that Igor rarely left the compound for longer than a couple of days, and he'd left yesterday.

He didn't share his plans with her, but she'd figured that the short trips were to compel local authorities to ignore the compound. They were secluded, but they were connected to the electrical grid, so someone was aware of their existence. Also, the supply trucks lumbering over a dirt path leading to nowhere could have been noticed.

The only times Igor had left for longer than a couple of days had been when he'd gone after other Kra-ell communities, and that hadn't happened in a long time.

He'd stopped either because he'd found all the survivors and all the rest were dead or because he didn't know how to find the others.

After her class ended and Borga took over, Jade strode to the office building in search of Valstar. He would know when Igor was due back, but the trick was to make him tell her.

No one searched her as she climbed the stairs to the second floor, and Igor's guard was absent from his station.

Evidently, Valstar's life was deemed less valuable than his master's.

She knocked on his door and then opened it without waiting for his response. "When is Igor coming back?"

He regarded her with a smirk. "Why? Do you miss him?"

"No, I hope he's dead. I want to know how long of a reprieve I have. I might choose to enjoy a virile, young male in his absence." She smiled evilly. "He says that he doesn't mind if I do, but I want to test it."

When the females did the choosing, it was considered bad form to horde males within the tribe. Unlike humans, there was never a question of paternity among the Kra-ell, and every adult in the tribe was free to engage with whomever they pleased. But Igor had adopted patriarchal attitudes, and his little harem of females suitable for breeding was forbidden to engage with other males during their fertile cycles. Lucky for him, their cycles weren't synchronized like they had been on the home planet.

Valstar's eyes gleamed with arousal. "That's a new twist. You haven't been with anyone but Igor. I was starting to think that your hatred for him was an act."

"Oh, believe me. It's not an act. It was self-inflicted punishment for my failure to protect my people, but over two decades of suffering is enough. I'm ready to start living again."

"Excellent." He rose to his feet and rounded the desk. "I'm not young, but I assure you that I'm virile."

She dragged her eyes over his body, pretending to consider it. "As tempting as it is, you don't want to be the first male I test Igor with."

His eyes blazed with purple light. "You are worth the risk."

She sauntered over and put her hand on his chest. "When is he coming back?"

"Monday."

"That's unusually long. Did he find more Kra-ell tribes to raid and slaughter?"

Igor's compulsion prevented her from talking about the murders and abductions with those who didn't know about what he had done, but it didn't include those who'd committed the crimes.

Even in the old days of the Kra-ell, before the queen outlawed tribal wars and duels to the death, the stealth attack would have been considered a travesty.

Warring tribes had faced each other on the battlefield and had followed a code of honor that the Mother of All Life herself had laid down. But Igor and his lackeys had followed none of the Mother's rules, and for that, they would forever walk the valley of the shamed. However, that was a paltry consolation for Jade's loss and the years of misery and subjugation, and if she failed to avenge her people, she would end up in the same place of shame as the murderers of her tribe.

"I don't think he found any more survivors," Valstar said. "But who knows? He doesn't tell me everything."

"He doesn't?" Jade dragged her fangs over his neck.

"He went to Moscow. He wants to expand his influence."

That was way too easy, and she was starting to think that the entire thing had been staged to trap her.

"I don't really care." She pushed Valstar away and pivoted on her heel.

"Come to my quarters tonight," he commanded.

She turned to look at him over her shoulder. "I'll consider it, but don't stay up waiting for me."

Toven

"That wasn't what I expected." Toven lowered Mia into Yamanu's outstretched arms.

The amphibian was an old Russian navy model that looked like a tank and could only be accessed from the top. Inside, two long benches lined the sides. Six Guardians were already seated in the fetid cabin, their equipment tucked under the benches.

Military vehicles were usually kept clean, but the amphibian was old, probably decommissioned, and belonged to a drug lord or a weapons smuggler.

As Yamanu put Mia on the bench, Toven jumped down and sat next to her. "They don't even have safety belts. Is this thing even operable?"

Yamanu shrugged. "We tested it yesterday, and it did what it was supposed to do. It's not a luxury vehicle."

"Did you get Mia's harness and Kevlar suit from the van?"

"It's right here." Yamanu motioned to the large duffel bag under his seat.

"Thank you."

"No need to thank me. It's my job to ensure that we have all the necessary equipment."

Toven leaned closer to Mia, intending to whisper in her ear, but with how everyone was sitting, the others would hear him no matter how quietly he did that. "I want you to sit on my lap so I can hold you. This is going to get bumpy, and your balance isn't as good as the others."

"Okay," she said, surprising him.

He'd expected an argument, but for once Mia had chosen safety over pride.

"That was easy." He wrapped his arms around her, and as he lifted her and sat her on his lap, she buried her nose in the crook of his neck.

"I'd rather smell you than this cabin."

So that was why she'd agreed so readily.

"The ride is about two hours long," Yamanu said. "Try to get comfortable."

"I'm very comfortable." Mia nuzzled Toven's neck. "After the day we had yesterday, I could use a little nap." She sighed and put her head on his chest. "Shopping is exhausting."

While the Guardians had tested the amphibian and scoped the hunting grounds, William had worked on the drones, and Toven, Mia, and Sylvia had spent the day shopping and sightseeing in St. Petersburg.

"I have a question," Toven turned his gaze to Yamanu. "How did you and your Guardians manage to stay hidden from the occasional Kra-ell patrol? The purebloods can smell and hear as well as the gods, which means that they can hear and smell the Guardians before the Guardians can hear and smell them unless the patrolmen are all hybrids. It makes sense that the task would be relegated to them, but I would expect at least one pureblood to command each patrolling unit."

Yamanu grinned. "We have the advantage of technology on our side. We no longer have to rely on our senses alone."

"I see." Toven nodded. "Perhaps I should join a few of your training sessions to acquaint myself with modern warfare."

Mia sighed. "I'm too anxious to fall asleep. I've never taken part in a military operation."

"That's not true," Yamanu said. "This is your fourth time. You helped Toven twice in Safe Haven, and two days ago, you helped him interrogate a Kra-ell. You're a veteran."

She chuckled. "The two hybrids in Safe Haven don't count. I was perfectly safe there. I was a little apprehensive the day before yesterday, but I never even left the van. Today I'm going to be strapped to Toven's back as he sprints through the woods with a team of immortal warriors at his side and with danger lurking all around. That's a real adventure."

"Don't worry, Mia. You have a god and seven immortal Guardians protecting you. We won't let harm come to you."

Yamanu's sing-song voice had a soothing effect, and as he started humming a tune, Mia let out a breath, and a moment later she was asleep.

Toven regarded the Guardian with even greater appreciation. "In addition to being an incredible thraller and shrouder, you can also sing people to sleep?"

Yamanu nodded. "I think it works the same way as compulsion does because I need to use my voice. Kri has a calming influence that works more like thralling. She helps calm down the trafficking victims we rescue."

"Do you do that as well?"

"I don't go out on rescue missions, but I volunteer in the halfway house once a week. I organize a karaoke night, which is the most popular activity in the house. The girls love it."

"I'm sure they do." Toven adjusted Mia on his lap. "Perhaps I could volunteer as well, and I know Mia would love to contribute too. I could teach a creative writing class, and Mia can teach children's book illustration." He gave the Guardian a sidelong glance. "If they are not intimidated by you, they probably won't be intimidated by me."

Yamanu pursed his fleshy lips. "No offense, Toven, but you lack my charming personality. I might be intimidating at first glance, but all it takes to break the ice is one smile." He flashed a toothy grin that was indeed disarming.

"I can smile too." Toven tried to imitate the Guardian.

Yamanu winced. "Again, no offense, but you need to work on that. You look like you're constipated."

Jade

Kagra trailed behind Jade to the security office. "Why are you refusing to take me hunting with you today?"

Jade was tempted to share Pavel's strange invitation with her second and tell her what it could possibly mean. Kagra was strong, and she could resist the compulsion to report suspicious activity to the security office, but if Jade was walking into a trap, she didn't want to take Kagra down with her.

"I told you. I'm restless. I need some time alone."

Kagra stopped and turned to face her. "What's going on? I know you too well to buy that."

She didn't want to lie, especially about something like this, but Kagra left her no choice. "I'm meeting Pavel. I accepted his invitation."

Kagra's brows shot up. "What happened to the vow you made never to enjoy yourself sexually again?"

"I never took a vow. I just wasn't in the right state of mind to seek pleasure." She affected a grin and leaned closer to Kagra. "I'm still not. Igor is out of the compound, and when he returns, I'm going to rub it in his face that Pavel is a better lover."

Her second looked doubtful. "Pavel is a kid, and I doubt he can overpower you. You know that you can't lie to Igor."

Jade shrugged. "So I need to make sure that I enjoy it. I don't detest Pavel, and maybe I can enjoy myself without fighting for dominance. You said that I should try it."

"I did, but I never believed that you would actually listen to me. You are as prime as they come. Can you even get turned on without it?"

"You are as much prime material as I am, and yet you said that you sometimes skipped the fighting stage and enjoyed softer touches."

"Once in a while, it's nice to try something different. I still find fighting for dominance arousing." She smiled wickedly. "Even when the males don't win."

"You're not a traditionalist, that's for sure."

Back in the day, telling a pureblood that she was abandoning tradition would have been considered an insult. They prided themselves on being traditionalists. But after two decades with Igor, adhering to the old rules of conduct seemed like a futile attempt to cling to what had been lost.

"No, I'm not." Kagra clapped her on the back. "I'm a progressive like the Wise Queen, and I'm willing to try new things."

The Wise Queen had been the one who had outlawed the tribal wars and duels to the death, but Jade wasn't sure it had been such a wise move. It had stopped the bloodshed, but it had created a slew of other problems.

"We wouldn't be here if the Wise Queen had left things the way they were."

Kagra shrugged. "There is no point engaging in what ifs. Tell me how it goes with Pavel."

As her second walked away, Jade expelled a breath. If Kagra had bought her story, everyone else would as well. No one knew her better than her second, not even her own daughter.

At the security office, the guard on duty didn't ask why she was going hunting alone, and as she walked to the gate with the clearance badge attached to her chest, the guard opened it up for her and waved her through.

"Good hunting," he called after her.

Surprised, she looked over her shoulder and nodded her thank you.

Did he know that she was meeting Pavel? Was that why the guard had wished her good hunting?

Pavel might have spread the rumor about their assignation. Getting her to accept his invitation was something to boast about.

But was she meeting Pavel? Or was she meeting Veskar?

The junction of the three rivers was an hour away by walking, and half of that if she ran. Curiosity urged her to run, but prudence convinced her to walk. It was one o'clock in the afternoon, and if she ran, she would arrive at the meeting spot ahead of time and could scope the area. But running would deplete her energy, and she needed to preserve it. She didn't know what was awaiting her at the meeting location and whether Veskar might bring reinforcements.

Tugging at the collar around her neck, she wondered for the umpteenth time whether it was true that it contained explosives and would go off if she left the area.

Knowing Igor as well as she did, the thing was rigged. Every so often, he would replace the collars, sending the ones that had been taken off to maintenance and putting others on. Rodof, who was in charge of that, probably checked that the wiring still worked and that the explosives hadn't expired.

Did explosives go bad and expire?

She didn't know, and it didn't matter.

Even if Veskar had come to rescue her, and even if he knew to bring an explosives expert with him, she wouldn't flee and leave the others behind. She had a responsibility to her people, not only those from her former tribe, but also to others who had no one else to help them.

The only way she might be convinced to flee was if she could return with an army to free the rest or at least a compeller strong enough to squash Igor.

But no one knew whether the royals had survived or even where to find their remains to perform the ritual that would send their souls to the Mother.

Not that she believed the ritual was needed for that. The dead passed on whether the living prayed for them or not, but it provided closure for those left behind. It was just one more thing that Igor had robbed her and the other females of. One more thing for her to avenge.

Toven

Yamanu hummed a tune as he lifted Mia into the harness on Toven's back and adjusted the straps.

"Are you comfortable?" Toven asked Mia when Yamanu was done.

"The harness is okay, but I don't like the helmet. I'm afraid it's going to chafe my chin when you run."

"If it does, tell me, and I'll stop so you can adjust it. Your head and your heart are the two most vulnerable places on your immortal body, and they need to be protected."

The Guardians also wore Kevlar vests and helmets, and they were armed to the teeth with hot and cold weapons and tranquilizer darts.

"I know." She rested her chin on his shoulder. "Let's go."

They had gone to shore a couple of miles west of the meeting point and had hidden the amphibian. It hadn't been an easy choice between getting as close to the river junction as the vehicle could get them or stopping way before that and making the rest of the way on foot.

The amphibian was noisy, making a stealth approach impossible, but it was also secure and allowed for a quick retreat.

In the end, it had been Toven's decision to choose stealth over convenience and a better retreat option.

After two of the Guardians had sped ahead to check the meeting place and take care of Pavel when he got there, Toven hooked his arms around Mia's thighs and nodded at Yamanu and the other Guardians.

As they broke into a jog, Toven made sure to stay inside the protective circle the Guardians formed around him and Mia. When they neared the junction, the two Guardians who had gone ahead communicated that they had Pavel, the area was clear, and it was okay for them to close the rest of the distance.

The five remaining Guardians climbed the surrounding trees, leaving Toven and Mia alone on the riverbank but well protected.

Toven was worried that once Jade became aware of their presence, she might flee, but there was no way around it. He needed those Guardians to watch his and Mia's backs.

When a female emerged from the thicket, he activated the portable signal disrupter William had given him and affected a bright smile. "Jade, I presume?"

Her whole body swelling with aggression, she bared her fangs and hissed. "Who are you?"

"I'm here to help. Veskar sent me."

"Where is he?"

Lifting his hands to show her that he wasn't armed, Toven smiled again. "Veskar, i.e., Emmett, is a spiritual guy, not a fighter."

Jade narrowed her eyes at him. "That face of yours is too pretty to be human. What are you? And why do you carry a child on your back?"

"I'm not a child," Mia said. "I'm his mate."

Jade's eyes didn't shift from Toven's. "You're a god," she stated.

How did she know that just from looking at him?

"What makes you think that?"

She snorted. "I know one when I see one. I wondered what had happened to the gods. I thought that you either had left and gone home or that the humans had killed you all. Regrettably, I see that they didn't. Where have you been hiding?"

Toven had been prepared for Jade to be fearful and suspicious but not hateful.

"I came to help you, and you're spouting venom at me. I didn't do anything to hurt you or your people, so I don't know where that's coming from."

She tilted her head. "Were you born on Earth?"

"Why does it matter?"

"Because you are obviously ignorant about your history. Your parents either didn't tell you anything or they lied about their past. The gods like to rewrite history to make themselves look good."

Excitement rose in his chest. Could Jade finally shed light on his ancestors' history and where they'd come from?

But now was not the time for a history lesson.

"You're very fortunate that some of us survived. I'm here to free you from Igor's compulsion, and I'm the only one who can do that."

"Why would you do that for me?"

"He's a threat to us, and we want him eliminated, but if we attack, there would be many casualties, and we want to avoid that. We hope that once you're free from his compulsion, you can eliminate him for us."

Jade didn't look excited. She looked suspicious. "How do I know that I can trust you? Maybe you need me to get rid of him so you can take over? I prefer a rotten Kra-ell to a god in charge of my people and me."

"Is she for real?" Mia murmured. "She's nasty."

There was no way Jade hadn't heard Mia, but she didn't acknowledge her.

"You don't need to trust me," Toven said. "You contacted Veskar and asked for his help, but he doesn't have what it takes to help you. Fortunately, he has the support of my people. He asked us to do what we could for you and the other females Igor had abducted and subjugated. I'm here to free your mind. What you do with that is up to you. If you don't want to take out the one who ordered the slaughter of every male in your tribe, that's your choice. We will find another way to mitigate the risk he represents."

Jade dropped her aggressive stance. "How do you know all that about me?" she asked in a much more amicable tone. "Veskar wasn't there when that happened, and I didn't include any of it in the fable."

"Three of your former tribe members joined our community. That's how we knew what happened to you."

"Who?"

"Veskar, who is mated to one of our females, and Vrog and Aliya, who found love in each other's arms."

He could have sworn that Jade's huge eyes misted with tears, but a blink later, it was gone.

"Thank the Mother that they survived." She frowned. "How do I know that you are telling me the truth? Maybe they are your prisoners?"

"You can talk with one of them if you wish. I can call either one."

Jade

Jade didn't trust the gods. They were liars and manipulators.

If not for the child-like woman with no legs strapped to the god's back, she would have attacked him first and talked later while holding him in a chokehold.

It had taken her a couple of moments to realize who he was, and when she had, she'd also noticed the woman who she'd mistaken for a child.

The trouble with the fuckers was that they seemed human if one didn't know what to look for, like the too-perfect features, the smooth alabaster skin, and their preference to stay in the shade because of their sensitive eyes.

They were like rats who only came out at night.

"If you can make a call from here," she said. "I would like to speak to Veskar."

He was clever enough to convey a message even if he was being held captive. Vrog had never been much for subterfuge, and she had no idea what kind of person Aliya had grown up to be. She would love to know how they ended up with the gods, though.

The god pulled a phone out of his pocket. "It's a satellite phone that can be used from anywhere, and the communication is secure."

"What's your name, god?" She shook her head. "I really don't like how you assholes refer to yourselves. We both know that there is nothing godly about you."

"Why are you so mean to him?" asked the woman named Mia. "He's risking himself and me to help you."

"That is true." She should dial back her hatred for the gods and give him a chance. "Are you human?" She looked pointedly at the missing legs. "Gods can regrow limbs."

"I'm not a goddess, but I'm not human either."

The god lifted his hand to silence the woman. "Mia is none of your business. I go by Tom."

He sounded so protective of the female with no legs, which was atypical of the gods who worshiped perfection. Maybe he was indeed different.

"That's a human name," she said.

"So is Jade."

"True." She let out a breath. "I apologize. You are not to blame for the deeds of your forefathers. I will give you the benefit of the doubt that you are a different breed." She forced a smile. "New and improved."

He lifted his hand again, this time to shush her as he put the phone to his ear.

"Did she come?" She heard a male's voice on the other side.

"I'm with her. She wants to talk to you." He handed her the phone. "Make it quick. We don't have much time."

She nodded. "Veskar?"

"It is me," he answered in Kra-ell. "Are you well?"

"As well as a captive can be. Can I trust Tom?"

"Yes, you can. Remember the story you told the children about the pompalo and the dorga?"

She'd known Veskar would find a way to tell her whether she could trust the god. He was using a fable they both knew.

A pompalo was a fearsome tiger-like animal, and a dorga was a large bird that was quite rare and a symbol of good luck. The story was that the bird was injured, and the pompalo saved her instead of eating her. When she asked him why, he said that she wasn't his enemy, nor was she his food source, and saving her would bring him luck.

"Who is the pompalo, and who is the dorga?"

Veskar chuckled. "Tom is the pompalo, and you are the dorga. He's a good guy. You can trust him."

"One last thing. Why does he carry a woman on his back?"

Perhaps it wasn't the most important question to ask, but it was so unusual and so un-god-like that she had to know the reason.

"She's his mate, but that's not why he brought her along. He is a powerful compeller, and she enhances his power. Together, they can free your mind from Igor's compulsion and with no adverse side effects. Without her, it will take longer and be more painful."

Compulsion was a rare talent among the gods. They had other mind manipulation powers that were even more impressive than compulsion, but the gods' ruling family had it in addition to the other talents, which was what had probably made them the rulers from time immemorial.

Tom must be related to them, one of the thousands of descendants of the Eternal King.

Things might have changed over the many centuries that had passed since she'd left, and perhaps the Eternal King was no more, or maybe he'd been long gone even before that and they had a new king who had assumed the same title. It was impossible to know the truth about the gods. They were masters of misinformation, shaping it in any which way that benefited them and their self-image.

Tom might be full of bluster.

If he was more powerful than Igor, he wouldn't have to convince her to cooperate with him. He could just compel her to kill Igor and skip over the pretense of being her people's savior.

"Thank you, Veskar, and may the Mother bless you. I knew that you'd find a clever way to tell me whether I could trust Tom even if you were their captive or under compulsion. You've earned your place in the fields of the brave."

"May the Mother help you fight for your freedom. Be well, Jade."

Jade ended the call and handed the device back to the god. "Veskar assured me that you are a good guy. Let's talk." She sat on the ground and assumed the lotus position.

When he did the same, Mia tapped his shoulder. "Can you put me down? I'd rather sit next to you."

"Sorry, love, but I can't. We need to be ready to flee."

Jade nodded. "No one is patrolling right now, and other hunters usually don't venture this far, but you never know."

"Fine." Mia let out a breath. "What did Emmett tell you that convinced you?"

"It was an old Kra-ell proverb. It conveyed that I can trust Tom. Veskar is a smart male."

The thing was, she still didn't trust the god. Veskar was a hybrid who was born on Earth. He didn't know their history and didn't realize how duplicitous the gods were.

"Let's assume that I can kill Igor once I'm free. What's next?"

"You can take over as the head of the compound, and we will enter negotiations for peaceful coexistence between our people and hopefully cooperation as well."

"Sounds good to me, provided that you can actually release me."

"Let's do it." Tom looked into her eyes. "You no longer have to obey Igor's commands in any way. You are free to act and talk as you will."

Jade felt the easing in her mind, the lightness in her chest, but she didn't trust the feeling. She'd resisted Igor's compulsion over the years. She'd talked freely and done things that he didn't allow, but what she couldn't do was run away or kill him.

Tom smiled. "Give it a try."

"He didn't have complete control over me, and I talked freely before. But I couldn't leave, and I couldn't kill him."

"Can you kill him now?" Tom asked.

She shook her head. "He can freeze me with one word."

"I have a solution for that." Tom pulled a small box from his pocket and opened it. "Those are translating earpieces, but they have been modified so they completely block outside voices. The machine voice you'll hear will repeat whatever Igor says, but it will filter the compulsion. If you wear your hair down, it will be invisible."

When she reached for the box, Tom shook his head. "Not yet. I'll give it to you when we part."

She really wanted those devices, but wearing them in Igor's presence was a death sentence, even if she managed to sneak them past the guards, which wasn't likely. They conducted very thorough searches.

"His guards will find the devices, and that will be the end of it. But even if I somehow manage to sneak them in, he's physically stronger than me."

"We can give you a weapon. A syringe filled with something that will stop his heart."

She smiled. "Your venom?"

"Regrettably, it can't be bottled. It deteriorates immediately."

"It wouldn't help. I can't sneak anything past his guards. Not the earpieces nor a weapon. On top of that, they are always primed to defend him."

Toven

Toven had expected Jade to say that, but it was still a disappointment.

"Can you think of any way that can be done? Is there anyone you can trust to assist you?" He pushed compulsion into his voice to make her answer truthfully.

"My second, Kagra. But even if you free her from Igor's compulsion, his guards wouldn't let us past them. If we show up together, they will know that something is up."

"You could pretend that you want a ménage with her and Igor," Mia suggested.

Jade cast her an indulgent smile. "Kra-ell females are not into ménages with other females. No one will buy it."

"You are a compeller, correct?" Toven asked. "Can't you compel the guards to let you and Kagra through?"

"Igor's compulsion is stronger than mine, and I can't override it even when I'm free of it. I can't compel the guards to do anything that will endanger him. I'm glad that he's not in the compound right now, or I would be more apprehensive about being here. He's not going to be back until Monday, so I have a few days to come up with something." She rubbed her temple. "The guards are not as careful when he's not here. So maybe I can hide something in his personal quarters now and use it when he returns."

Toven's mind jumped into action. "Are you sure he won't be back before Monday?"

"That's what his second told me. But Igor could change his plans, so that is not set in stone."

"Do you know that the entire compound is rigged with explosives?"

She nodded. "Igor doesn't take any chances. None of us are to be taken alive."

"Who can blow it up in his absence?"

"His second-in-command, probably his third as well. Also, I wouldn't be surprised if Igor has a way to do it remotely."

Toven smiled. "He can't do it remotely if he has no connection. We can block all communications in and out of the compound."

"That's good."

He could see the wheels in her mind working, but she didn't offer to share her thoughts.

"Would Igor's second-in-command actually pull the trigger?" Mia asked. "Knowing that he will die too?"

Jade regarded Mia with her too-big, dark eyes. "Valstar will do what Igor compelled him to do. The will of everyone in the community is not their own. I can mouth off to Igor and tell him that I hate him, because he allows it, and he doesn't compel me to stop. But I can't tell anyone about what he did to my tribe because the compulsion to keep it a secret is so strong." She took a deep breath. "He killed all the males of my tribe. He killed my sons." She took in another breath. "It's such a relief to finally be able to tell someone."

Toven nodded. "My condolences on your loss. They say that time heals all wounds, but I know that some wounds keep bleeding forever."

Jade nodded. "Maybe mine will heal once I kill Igor and avenge my people. But unless you have an army of gods you can summon, I don't know how that's possible."

"I can summon an army, not of gods but of immortals, what you call hybrids. But we can't attack knowing that there is a chance Igor or his second will blow everyone up."

She tilted her head. "Why would you bring an army?"

"I told you. Igor is a threat that needs to be eliminated before he finds out about us."

"Who are 'us'? How come I couldn't find anything in human history about gods in the modern era?"

He didn't want to share with her what happened to the other gods until he got her to tell him the gods' history. He might not be able to hide his ignorance, but he knew how to phrase things in a way that could be interpreted in different ways.

"Only a few of us remain, and we were born on Earth. We know next to nothing about our history, where the gods came from, and why. That's another reason we offer our help. You have information that's valuable to us, which makes you an asset."

"What I know is what I was told, and I realized a long time ago that most of it was fabricated for one reason or another. I don't trust any of it to be true unless I witnessed it myself."

That was cynical but smart.

"How old are you?" he asked.

She laughed. "Humans consider that a rude question to ask a lady. You're lucky that I'm not."

"A lady or a human?"

"Neither, and to answer your question, I'm very old, but I wasn't awake for most of that time."

"You traveled here in stasis?"

She nodded.

That confirmed his suspicion that the gods gave themselves the ability to go into stasis so they could traverse the universe, and evidently, they gave the same ability to the Kra-ell.

"We are running out of time," Mia reminded them. "We need to come up with a plan to liberate Jade and her people. You can talk about your history once she's free."

Toven nodded. "Mia is right. How long do we have before they notice that you've been gone longer than usual?"

"When I go hunting alone, I usually return in about two hours, sometimes three. I've been gone out longer a few times, but that was when I was leading a group of youngsters." She looked up at the sky. "It took me about an hour to get here, and I can make it back in half the time if I run, so we still have about an hour left."

"Will they know that you didn't get blood?" Mia asked. "Do you get paler or something?"

"Why, are you offering yours?"

Mia shuddered. "Of course not."

"I'm good," Jade said. "I don't need to get blood every day. Besides, I was supposed to meet Pavel here and engage in other activities, but since he didn't show up, I assume that he wasn't actually supposed to come?"

"As you probably guessed, we grabbed him from his guard duty, released him from Igor's compulsion, and put him under mine. He was instructed to follow through with the pretense and come out to meet you, so it would look legit to you. My companions intercepted him and kept him busy so we could talk in privacy."

Jade

Jade wasn't surprised that Tom and Mia had backup. She would have been surprised if they hadn't. She'd felt the others, but by the time their presence had registered, it had been too late to turn back.

She narrowed her eyes at him. "What do you mean, busy?"

"Nothing nefarious. He's being restrained, and once we are done, I'll compel him to support your version of the story, whatever you choose it to be. I knew that you were Igor's prime, and I didn't know if it was okay for you to get intimate with another male, so I didn't do it ahead of time. I can compel him to say that you met him, but nothing happened, or the exact opposite."

"As long as I'm not in my fertile cycle, Igor doesn't care who I have sex with. He keeps me as his prime because he wants me to produce a son for him, not because he cares for me." She smirked. "Traditionally, a female child is the most desirable because females are so rare, but Igor wants males to be in charge. Unlucky for him, the Mother has a wicked sense of humor, and she blessed me with a daughter. He has plenty of sons by other females, but he wants one from me because our child will be the most powerful."

"How old is your daughter?" Mia asked.

"She's sixteen."

Jade wanted a better future for her daughter. Drova was indoctrinated into Igor's philosophy, and it would be difficult to undo, but she was a smart female, so there was still hope.

"Let's get back to devising a plan," Tom said. "We need to come up with a way to free the compound, and if there is any time left after we find a doable solution, I would love to hear a little bit more about the gods' history, of which I'm ignorant."

More than Veskar's reassurances and anything else Tom had said, that convinced her that he wanted to help. It was obvious that he was desperate to learn more about his people, but he was willing to potentially lose his chance to do it in favor of helping liberate her.

"I might be able to eliminate Valstar. With Igor away, the guards won't bother to search me as thoroughly, and I might be able to sneak in a weapon or a drug. Valstar is probably not a strong compeller, so he can't compel me to stand down, and if I drug him, I can overpower him physically. Kagra can take down the third, but the two of us can't overcome every pureblood and hybrid in the compound."

"Maybe they would submit to your authority," Mia said. "With the second and the third gone, you'll be the natural leader. You could open the gates and walk out with whoever wants to be free."

Jade smiled indulgently. "If it was that simple, Igor would have never left the compound. He has everyone compelled to follow his orders even in his absence."

"Is there a chance that you can detain Valstar without killing him?" Toven asked.

She frowned. "Why would you want to spare him? He's a murderer."

"He's also Sofia's grandfather."

She'd forgotten about the human female Igor had sent to spy on Safe Haven.

"Ah, Sofia. You must have freed her mind as well. That's how you knew where to find Pavel."

Was the human stupid enough to plead for leniency for her grandfather? Didn't she know that he would feed her to a pompalo if it served him or Igor in any way?

Tom nodded. "I freed Sofia, and then we caught the two hybrids Igor sent to follow the tracker he put inside of her, and we questioned them as well. We learned a lot from them, but they didn't know about the compound being rigged. We learned about the explosives from Pavel."

"Is he also free of Igor's compulsion?"

"He's under mine."

"Excellent. Then he can help me."

"Indeed."

"If you had access to the compound, could you free everyone at once?"

Tom shook his head. "I might be able to do that with the humans, but the pureblooded Kra-ell are a different story. I can't thrall them. I can't even make them see illusions. The hybrids are easier, but I don't think I can free them from Igor's compulsion in one fell swoop. I'd need to do it one at a time."

That made sense, and she appreciated that he wasn't trying to make himself seem more powerful than he was.

"If you can bring your army of hybrids within a day or two, I can eliminate Valstar and the third and get everyone out of the office building. That's where the detonation button or lever or whatever it is must be. Igor lives in that building. His and Valstar's quarters are there."

"We can block the communications at the same time, so no one can notify Igor. By the way, do you know if he has an escape tunnel?"

"If there is one, he didn't tell me about it. He and his lackeys always leave and return by the front gate, but that doesn't mean that they don't have some secret tunnel somewhere."

"I thought that you hinted at it in your fable."

She shook her head. "It was just something that the crafty rat could do. It had no other meaning besides that."

"Igor is not the type who would die with his people," Tom said. "If he planned to destroy everyone if the compound was invaded by a superior force, he must have planned for a way to escape."

Jade wasn't sure about that. If the royals ever surfaced and came for Igor, he would prefer to die rather than suffer their wrath for betraying them.

But she wasn't going to tell Tom about the royal twins. To let a god know about them was a worse betrayal than what Igor had done.

"We don't have time to look for the tunnel," she said. "Once I eliminate Igor's lieutenants and take control of the office building, I'll give you the all-clear signal, and you will come in with your army. There will be some casualties, but that's unavoidable. When we have the entire compound under our control, we will wait for Igor to return and capture him." She pinned Tom with a hard stare. "He's mine to kill. Dreaming about doing that is what kept me from running away and detonating this damn collar to end my suffering."

Tom dipped his head. "I'll do my best to save him for you. But speaking of the collar, did Igor or any of his lackeys ever do anything to control people with it? Can it deliver pain?"

"It was never used to do that, so I assume it can't. It's supposed to explode and take my head off if I try to leave the hunting grounds, so in addition to explosives, it must have a location tracker as well."

Toven

"If the collar emits a signal, it's not going anywhere. I'm disrupting it." Toven pulled the device from a pocket in his vest and showed it to her. "That's a miniature version of the big one we will use to disrupt all communications to the compound. The guy who gave it to me can also remove the collars without causing them to explode, but we didn't bring him with us this time."

Jade tilted her head. "Why? Were you afraid that I would run and you would lose your assassin?"

"It never occurred to me that you would leave without your people. Everyone who knows you says that you are an honorable person."

That got a small smile out of her. "They probably also say that I'm a colossal bitch, and when applying human standards to females, they are right. As a Kra-ell leader, though, I've been considered fair. I took good care of my tribe, but in the end, I failed them."

She was obviously riddled with guilt, and Toven could empathize. He'd failed so many times that he'd lost count.

"We didn't bring our tech guy because we knew we weren't taking you. You need to return to the compound and keep up the pretense that you are still under Igor's compulsion and nothing has changed."

She put her hand over the metal band. "You'd better activate your big disrupter before I make my first move. What if Valstar or one of the others has the remote to my collar and can cause it to explode? And not just mine. Except for those in Igor's inner circle, all the purebloods and hybrids are forced to wear collars, but the humans are not."

Jade was right. It was a possibility that they needed to account for.

"The hybrids he sent to follow Sofia had their collars removed, but I'm sure they had trackers embedded in their bodies. Sofia had one, and we removed it."

"Makes sense. He couldn't send them into the human world wearing collars, but he needed to retain control over them."

"You'll need to signal when you are ready for us to proceed."

"What kind of signal? The only thing I can think of is starting a fire, but given that there are explosives hidden, the Mother knows where, that's not a good idea."

"What about the roof of the office building? If you can put a metal trash can up there and set a small fire inside of it, we will see the smoke rise above the trees."

She nodded. "I can put the trash can near the building, and after I secure it, I'll get it to the roof and light the fire. Or I can get Pavel to do that for me."

"That can work," Mia said. "But what if you and Kagra eliminate Igor's second and third, but you are discovered before you can light the fire? The coast will be clear for us to commence with the plan, but without the signal, we won't know that."

"Good point." Jade drummed her fingers on her knees. "Do you have a better idea? Perhaps you can give me your phone."

"Do they search you when you return from a hunt?" Toven asked.

"Regrettably, they do, and I can't bring anything into the compound. I was just joking about your phone."

"What about waving a flag or blasting music on loudspeakers?" Mia asked.

Jade shook her head. "I can't do any of that. I might be able to use Valstar's laptop to send an email to Safe Haven after I kill him, but only if it's unlocked, which I'm sure it won't be. Valstar is not stupid, and even with lust clouding his judgment, he will be suspicious when I accept his invitation."

"You can't send an email even if he leaves the laptop open," Toven said. "We will be disrupting the signal, remember?"

"I forgot. It has to be the fire, then. What about you? How will you let me know if you can't make it?"

"We can fly a military drone low over the compound. It's hard to miss."

"You'll give yourself away."

"Not necessarily. It's a Russian drone, and there is a base two hundred miles or so south of here. A drone could malfunction and veer off its course."

She nodded. "It will take me time to get everything in place, and I don't think I can be ready tomorrow, but it has to happen before Igor returns, so it has to be on Sunday."

Kian wouldn't be able to send the rest of the force earlier than that, either. Even Sunday was pushing it, but they didn't have much choice.

"Sunday will work. By the way, how many men did Igor take with him?"

"I don't know for sure, but he usually takes three. Two purebloods and one hybrid. He can compel the humans not to see his and the two purebloods' alien features, but he needs a hybrid who looks human to send on errands."

"So his compulsion has an element of shrouding," Toven said. "Interesting. My shrouding and thralling didn't work on Pavel."

Jade pursed her lips. "We can only do that to humans. It doesn't work on us. Igor can't make me see what's not there, but he can force me to act as if I'm seeing it. Speaking of Pavel, I could also use his help. Can you compel him to obey my commands?"

Toven nodded. "I will do that. What time should I expect your signal?"

"I can't give you a precise hour, but it won't be in the morning." She winced. "To get to Valstar, I need to pretend to be interested in him sexually, and it will look suspicious if I do that first thing in the morning."

"We will do our best to get everyone in position by midday," Toven said. "If we can't have everything ready in time, we will grab one of the guards at the entrance to the tunnel and send a message with him."

Jade's eyes emitted a reddish glow. "If you free tomorrow's guard from Igor's compulsion and send him to me, I can use him to send a message back." She looked around. "I'll leave a note under that tree. Would you be able to retrieve it?"

"I'd rather that you came out again. Someone can meet you here tomorrow at the same time."

She nodded. "I'll send my second. Her name is Kagra, and I will need her help. You need to remove Igor's compulsion from her as well, and if you can do it early in the morning, it would be best so I can share my plan with her."

"You need to come with her. Can you make it here at eight in the morning?"

She tilted her head. "The hour is not a problem, but why do you need me to come with her?"

"You can't tell Kagra why you're sending her, and she will wonder why you want her to go to this precise spot. Furthermore, after I confer with my team, I might have updates that you need to know about. Igor's absence changes everything."

"You have a point. And since today I was supposed to be here with Pavel, I can say that I didn't get to hunt and that I'm famished after today's activities."

"Would they buy it?"

Jade smiled. "I'm a great actress, but after two decades of denying myself, this is atypical behavior for me. They might get suspicious. That's why I suggested that Kagra come alone. And like me, she has a strong mind and can resist the compulsion to some degree. After you free her, you can tell her about your team's suggestions."

"That's not good enough. We can't take the risk of her telling someone. You have to come with her."

"You don't trust me, do you?"

"Why would you say that? I'm risking myself and my mate to help free you, and all I have to base my trust on is your people's respect for you."

She nodded. "You can trust me. I vow not to betray you, and since you claim to know so much about me, you should also know that I take my vows very seriously."

"I heard it mentioned that the Kra-ell believe in the power of vows."

"Not all Kra-ell. Igor and his misfits do not take our traditions to heart, but I do." She smiled. "I also vow that after you rescue my people, I'll tell you what I know about the history of yours."

"It's a deal." He rose to his feet and offered her his hand.

They hadn't discussed what would happen after the liberation, but it was too early for that. Toven's objective was to ensure that the Kra-ell were not a threat to the clan, and with Igor out of the way, he could compel Jade or whoever else took over the compound to cooperate with Kian and Sari.

Jade shook his offered hand. "Before I go, I'll give you a little taste of history, so you will crave more. Long before the gods learned how to traverse space, they learned how to manipulate genetics, and they turned themselves immortal. Later, that allowed them to travel to distant planets and create slave species to serve them. They combined their genetic material with that of a local animal that was advanced enough to be suitable, and at first, they made many mistakes, but they learned from them. There is a reason you can't manipulate purebloods' minds, but you can do it to hybrids and humans. The gods designed human minds to be easily manipulated, and the hybrids inherited that from their human parents." She smiled. "The rest will come after my people are free."

Kian

The call from Toven came at six-thirty in the morning, and after Kian put Turner and Onegus on the line, the god told them about the plan he'd hatched with Jade.

Kian groaned. "We have forty hours to get everyone in position on the other side of the globe, which includes about sixteen hours in transit. I don't think it's possible. We will have to wait for Igor to leave the compound again. I like Turner's idea of catching him with the help of facial recognition."

On the other side of the line, Turner huffed out a breath. "In Igor's absence, Valstar would take over, and we will be back to square one. We still need to invade the compound and ensure that no one blows it apart, get Toven to release everyone from Igor's compulsion, and reach a cooperation agreement with Jade. We've already sent the equipment to Russia, got an amphibian, and two drones, and we have twelve Guardians, including Yamanu and Bhathian, in place. We can make it."

"How are we going to transport everyone at once?" Kian asked. "Together with Kalugal's men, we need a plane that can carry seventy-one warriors and eighty-four exoskeletons."

"I was already working on chartering a Boeing 737. Let me get on it, and I'll have it ready for us in under six hours, and by the time they land, I will have a place for them to camp that's close to the compound."

"I need to let the men know so they get ready," Onegus said. "We will need to load supplies for field accommodations, which means that I need to raid our emergency storage."

"Go," Kian said. "Tell Kalugal to get his men ready and keep me updated."

"I will." The chief ended the call on his side.

"There are two problems with Jade's plan," Turner said. "She can't kill Valstar, and the attack needs to be at night."

"Why can't she kill Valstar?" Toven asked. "Because of Sofia?"

Kian knew that wasn't the reason because Turner wouldn't concern himself with that. "We need him alive."

"Correct," Turner said. "If Igor calls, which I'm sure he does every so often when he's away, he will expect Valstar to answer. If the communication is down for more than a few hours, or if his second is not available to answer him, he will know that something is up, and he won't show up. Jade needs to incapacitate Valstar, but not kill him. After we take control of the compound, you need to compel him to sing the tune we want him to sing, and he will await Igor's call with our special earpiece glued to his ears and someone standing over him with an ax."

Toven groaned. "Jade is not going to like it."

"She's going to like Igor escaping even less," Turner said. "She can kill Valstar later, along with Igor. When you meet her again tomorrow, make sure she understands."

"What about the timing?" Toven said. "Does it need to happen at night because we can't get everyone in position in time?"

"Although giving ourselves a few more hours to get ready is a definite plus, that's not the reason. At night, the office building will be vacant, the humans will be asleep, and so will most of the purebloods and hybrids, except for those on guard and patrol duty. It will make the task easier."

"The problem is Igor," Toven said. "He's supposed to return Monday, but Jade says that he might come back earlier. That's why she wanted to do it Sunday at two in the afternoon. Also, after we take over, I will need to compel everyone in the compound before we restore communications, and we are talking about over three hundred people. That might take all night."

"Only about two hundred and fifty are adults, and about a third of them are human. After you free them from

Igor's compulsion, we can delegate the task of compelling the humans, the hybrids, and the children to say what we need them to say to our four other compellers. They can do that remotely from here. You will only have to compel the adult purebloods."

"You can't seriously suggest that we use Parker," Kian said.

"He'll be less intimidating to the children."

He had a point. "I'll have to get Vivian and Magnus's permission, but since most of the children probably don't speak English, I doubt Parker would be able to compel them."

"That could be an issue," Turner said.

"What time at night should we schedule the attack for?" Toven asked.

"Two o'clock Monday morning, " Turner said. "The humans will be out of the way in their quarters, and most of the hybrids and purebloods will be asleep as well. Another advantage of doing it then is that Igor probably won't call his second in the middle of the night. It simplifies the entire operation."

Kian had to agree. "Anything else that you wish to add?" he asked.

"For now, that's it. You can continue without me, and if I think of anything else, I'll let you know." Turner terminated the call on his side.

Left only with Toven, Kian let out a breath. "What's your impression of Jade? Can we forge an alliance with her?"

"She's tough and abrasive, but she's honorable and cares for her people. Unlike Igor, she's precisely the type that would go down with the ship, which makes her a much better option as the leader of that community. She also knows our history."

Kian's breath caught. "What did she tell you?"

"Jade hates the gods passionately. It took her a while to trust me, and she did only after she spoke to Emmett. She says that the gods twist the truth and rewrite history as it suits them to make themselves look good. She didn't elaborate on whether they do that for interior consumption of their own population or to impress others. She also claims that the gods designed humans to be susceptible to thralling and compulsion so they could be easily controlled."

Kian had suspected that for a long time.

"Does that surprise you?"

"Frankly, it does. I guess the misinformation Jade mentioned was successfully employed by my father and uncle and the rest of the original gods. They convinced us that they were the good guys, spreading civilization, establishing just laws, and bringing prosperity to humans."

"You're too smart to have bought the lies."

Toven chuckled. "Those were not lies. The gods were actually striving to do that. The lie was that they had always been like that. But you are right. I was suspicious. I had an older brother who had been one of the original gods, and he taunted me, hinting about my naïveté left and right. I thought it was his way of tormenting me. Mortdh resented me for being our father's favorite son."

Ekin had been a scientist and an inventor, and Toven was a scholar, a philosopher, and an explorer. Mortdh had been the only one with political aspirations.

"You were more like Ekin than Mortdh was, in intellect as well as in temperament. Well, except for the womanizing. Ekin was legendary in his relentless pursuit of ladies regardless of their mated status."

Toven laughed. "He was, and most of those legends were true. The only one that was a total fabrication was that he wanted to get his half-sister pregnant. That never happened."

"My mother told me that it was common among the gods. As long as the mothers were not related, it was fine to mate a half-sister, even encouraged."

"Athor was a scientist herself, a geneticist, and for a goddess, she wasn't very attractive. She had her human servants to have fun with, and she wouldn't have allowed Ekin anywhere near her."

"Speaking of attractiveness, what does Jade look like?"

"She doesn't look significantly more alien than Aliya, and she could be considered attractive by those who like their women super bossy, abrasive, and intimidating." He chuckled. "She's you, just prettier."

"I don't know what's more offensive, your insinuation that I'm bossy and abrasive or that I'm not good-looking enough."

For a moment, the god didn't respond, probably trying to figure out whether Kian had really been offended or was just teasing.

"I hope you're not serious," Toven said.

"I'm not. Have you spoken with William?"

"Not yet. I called you first."

"I'll call him. A lot depends on whether he can have his equipment ready in time for Sunday."

Sofia

"Sofia." Marcel put his hand on her shoulder. "Wake up, love."

She bolted upright. "What's happening? Did they talk to Jade?"

Worried about the meeting between Toven and Jade, she'd spent most of the night tossing and turning, finally falling asleep when it was already light outside.

The worry was not only about the outcome. It was also about whether it would even happen and whether Toven was walking into a trap.

Nevertheless, the rush of adrenaline burned through the grogginess, and she was instantly wide awake.

"They did. Shai is on the line with the details, and later Kian wants to talk to you."

"Okay." She pulled the blanket up to her chin.

Marcel turned the speaker on. "Go ahead, Shai."

"Good morning, Sofia. Kian is extremely busy organizing the mission, and he asked me to give you an update."

"I appreciate it."

"Here is what's going to happen over the next forty-eight hours."

When he was done, Sofia's chest felt so tight that she could barely breathe. "Jade is going to kill my grandfather?"

"Toven will try to convince her to hold off until after we take over the compound," Shai said. "We need him alive to capture Igor, but she's not going to show him mercy once Igor is caught. According to her, he's a murderer and doesn't deserve leniency."

"I don't get it," Marcel said. "With Igor out of the compound, Valstar is no doubt in charge of the trigger to detonate the explosives. We can't risk leaving him alive."

Sofia shuddered.

She understood the need to eliminate the threat to everyone in the compound but the callous way they talked about killing her grandfather was disturbing, to say the least.

"Toven will speak with Jade tomorrow and tell her about the change of plans," Shai said. "She will need to incapacitate Valstar until Toven can take control of his mind. The question is will she listen, and if she does, will she be able to incapacitate him without killing him. If the answer is no, we will not restore communications to the compound and hope that Igor will return despite not being able to contact anyone there. But in either case, Valstar's demise is imminent. Once everyone's minds are free, Jade will not be the only one who wants him to pay for his crimes."

As another cold shiver pulsed through Sofia's body, Marcel took her trembling hand and gave it a reassuring squeeze.

Valstar's impending demise wasn't the only reason for the tremor, though. He might have contributed his genetic material to her creation, but he wasn't real family to her.

Sofia was worried about the ones she couldn't contemplate losing, and she couldn't stay in Safe Haven while everyone she cared for was in mortal danger.

"I want to be there for my family. Once the compound is freed, they will be confused, and having me there will reassure them."

"Hold on one second. Kian wants to talk to you."

"I'm sorry about your grandfather," Kian said, surprising her. She had never met him, but he didn't sound like the empathic type, and yet he'd been the only one who'd bothered to say that.

"Yeah, me too. I wish things were different, but I can't change who he is."

"True. I'm also sorry about denying your request to go to Karelia. We need you to keep the pretense up."

"I can call him right now, I mean, after I get to my regular spot, so he won't expect me to call tomorrow, and by Sunday, it will all be over, one way or another. Please, I need to be there."

Kian didn't answer right away, and the second or two that it had taken him to respond seemed to last an eternity. "You have a valid point, but it's a logistic nightmare to get you and Marcel to St. Petersburg. The force leaves for the airstrip in three hours, so even if I send a jet to pick you up, you won't make it on time."

"We can fly commercial," Marcel said. "I'll book us a flight to St. Petersburg, and we will join the force there."

"They are going directly to the campsite Turner secured for them. They are not staying in a hotel, and good luck finding a flight that will get you there on time."

"Eric can fly them," Shai said in the background.

"Darlene is transitioning," Kian said. "Do you really think that he would leave her side?"

"Let me check with him. If he agrees to fly Sofia and Marcel, he can pick them up in Portland and continue from there."

"Thank you, Shai," Marcel said.

"Don't thank me yet. I didn't get Eric to agree yet, and Kian is probably right."

"I'm always right," Kian grumbled. "You should talk to Valstar as soon as you can and get ready to leave on a moment's notice." The line went silent.

Sofia jumped out of bed. "I'll get dressed and pack my bag. Do you have warm clothing? It's cold out there this time of year."

"Don't worry about me." Marcel pulled her into his arms for a quick hug. "I'll make us coffee and something to eat."

She lifted her lips to his. "You're the best."

"So are you."

Twenty minutes later, they met with Eleanor and Cecelia at the beach.

"Lots of excitement, eh?" Eleanor patted the cat. "Do you want to hold her?"

Sofia shook her head. "I'm too nervous."

"That's why you should pet her. It's relaxing."

"I don't think it will help this time. Who is Darlene?"

Eleanor glanced at Marcel. "Why are we talking about Darlene?"

"Shai told us that he would ask Eric if he could fly us to Russia, but since Darlene is transitioning, that's not likely." He turned to Sofia. "Darlene is Toven's granddaughter, but he didn't know that he had grandchildren until recently. She met a nice guy who's a pilot, and without bothering you with too many details, he induced her, and she's in the process of transitioning. But since she's older, it's not going as smoothly as yours will."

Apparently, she wasn't the only one with a lousy grandfather. Tom also didn't care much about his granddaughter if he was on the other side of the globe while she was transitioning.

"I see." Sofia wrapped her arms around herself. "Shouldn't Tom be with Darlene when she's fighting for her life?"

"I'm sure he wants to be there for her," Eleanor said. "But since he's the only one who can overcome Igor's compulsion, he doesn't have much choice. He felt that it was up to him to free Jade and the rest of your people. Besides, Darlene is in good hands. She has her mate with her, and the clan doctor is supervising her transition."

Marcel

Marcel had been expecting Shai to call back during their walk to Sofia's spot on the beach, but when they reached their destination and Shai still hadn't called, he turned the ringer off on his phone, and Eleanor did the same.

"Tell me what you are going to talk about with Valstar," Eleanor said as he handed Sofia the pendant to make the call.

Marcel listened with half an ear as Eleanor did her regular routine of compelling Sofia to stick to a pre-agreed script. When it was done, he and Eleanor put in their earpieces, which were in translation mode so they could understand Sofia's conversation with her grandfather.

Taking a deep breath, Sofia opened the pendant, pulled out the earpiece, and activated the device.

Valstar didn't answer right away like he usually did. "Sofia. I didn't expect a call from you today. Do you have news for me?"

"My condition is getting worse. The doctor says that I need an open heart surgery."

"That's very unfortunate, but it is not something that I can help you with."

Hearing the guy's answer spoken in a machine voice made him sound apathetic, and since Sofia heard the delivery in the same voice, her impression must also be the same.

"There is something you can do. It will help me tremendously to have my father with me. Can you let him know that I'm going to have an operation and send him here? I'll pay for his airfare, of course."

"I can't make a decision like that without Igor's permission, and he's not here at the moment. Call me again tomorrow."

Marcel tensed. Was Igor returning earlier than expected?

The panic in Sofia's eyes conveyed the same fear. "I might not be able to call tomorrow."

"Then call when you can. When is the operation?"

"Next week on Wednesday."

"Then you have plenty of time."

"Will Igor be back by tomorrow?" she asked.

"That's none of your business. I'll ask him when he calls, but I doubt he'll agree. Your father has never left the compound before, and it's not safe for him to travel alone."

As if Valstar was concerned with Sofia's father's safety.

The good news, though, was that Valstar had just confirmed that Igor wasn't returning to the compound the next day.

"Please, can you ask him anyway? Maybe he will show compassion for me. I might not make it through this operation."

"You are a strong girl, Sofia. You will survive. Be well." He ended the call on his side.

With a sigh, Sofia deactivated the device and put the tiny earpiece inside the pendant. "I got scared there for a moment. He sounded as if Igor was returning shortly."

Marcel wrapped his arms around her and ran small soothing circles on her back. "Valstar didn't sound like he didn't care. The machine voice eliminates the nuances of tonality, but what he said wasn't that bad. He called you strong and wished you well."

"Valstar was polite. Igor is polite as well. That doesn't make either of them any less of a monster." Sofia pulled out of his arms. "Check your phone. Shai might have tried to call you."

Marcel had put the device in vibrate mode, but he'd been distracted by Sofia's distress, and when he checked, there was indeed a missed call from Shai, and he returned it immediately.

"I'm sorry about not picking up before. Sofia was speaking with Valstar, and we needed to maintain silence. Did Eric agree?"

"I went to the clinic to speak with Eric, but Kian was right, and Eric doesn't want to leave Darlene's side unless it's a life and death situation, which it's not. But a better solution presented itself. The Clan Mother was visiting Darlene, and when she heard us talking, she offered her jet along with her pilot. He can pick you up from Eugene Airport and fly you to St. Petersburg."

"I don't know what to say. It's so incredibly generous of the Clan Mother. I need to call her and thank her in person."

"You should. Her Odu is already on his way to the airstrip. You also should hurry up and get a ride to the airport." He chuckled. "I have a feeling that you will get to Russia before the Guardians."

"Thank you, Shai."

"You're welcome." He ended the call.

"What did he say?" Sofia asked as Marcel returned the phone to his pocket.

"The Clan Mother is loaning us her private jet along with her pilot."

Sofia's eyes widened. "That's incredible. Why would she be so generous toward someone she's never met?"

"Because she has a huge heart." Marcel wrapped his arm around Sofia's waist. "Have you ever flown on a private jet?"

"Are you kidding me? The first time I flew was when I came here, and I sat in the middle seat in basic economy, squeezed between two large men. It wasn't fun."

Eleanor snorted. "From a virgin flyer to a member of the mile-high club. You sure move up quickly, doll."

"What's the mile-high club?"

"I'll let Marcel explain." Smirking, Eleanor scratched Cecilia's ear and kept walking.

Sofia

They made it to the airport almost an hour before the Clan Mother's plane landed, so they had time to grab a bite to eat in the coffee shop.

"I assume that there will be no food served on the flight." Sofia nibbled on the muffin Marcel had gotten for her.

"I don't know. I've never flown on the Clan Mother's jet." Marcel still looked a little shell-shocked. "I don't think she's let anyone other than her children use it before. You have no idea what an honor it is."

"I do." She stuffed another bite into her mouth. "I'm so hyped up that I don't know what I'm feeling. I'm terrified of what's going to happen, I'm excited about flying on an executive jet like some movie star, and I want to join the mile-high club, but I wouldn't dare do it on the Clan Mother's property."

That got a smile out of Marcel. "Yeah, the same thought crossed my mind."

As they walked onto the field, the door opened out, forming stairs, and a guy who looked like a butler rushed down to greet them.

"Good afternoon, Mistress Sofia, Master Marcel." He took their luggage and ran up the stairs with a suitcase in each hand as if they weighed nothing.

Sofia leaned closer to Marcel's ear. "You said that there was not going to be service on the plane, but it seems like your Clan Mother sent her butler along as well."

He chuckled. "Oshidu is the pilot. He's also a butler, but since he can't do both at the same time, he's only going to pilot the plane."

"Are you sure that he knows what he's doing?" She started up the stairs.

"Don't worry. He's been piloting this jet for many years. The Clan Mother travels extensively, and she doesn't fly commercial."

There were only four seats inside the small cabin, but they were wide and plush and could be turned into comfortable beds.

"There are pillows and blankets in the overhead compartments," said the pilot, who looked like a butler. "The middle console houses an assortment of drinks, and I took the liberty of collecting several sandwiches and pastries from the café so you wouldn't go hungry on the way."

"Thank you, Oshidu." Marcel smiled. "I appreciate your thoughtfulness."

The guy grinned, and it kind of looked fake. "You are very welcome, Master Marcel. The flight will take fourteen hours. I shall see you again after we land. Enjoy." He dipped his head and pivoted on his heel.

Sofia waited until the pilot was in his seat. "Are we stopping to refuel somewhere?" she whispered. "How is he going to stay focused for so long?"

"Don't worry about him." Marcel opened the center console and looked inside. "What's your pleasure?"

"Is there wine?"

"There is." He pulled out a bottle and two glasses.

"Please, buckle up," the pilot said. "We are starting to move."

Sofia found the seatbelt, secured it around her middle, and glanced at the pilot again. "I guess the mile-high club is not an option. There is no partition between Oshidu and us. By the way, is Oshidu Japanese?"

Marcel chuckled. "Does he look Japanese?"

"Not really, but he has the kind of features that could pass for anyone of mixed heritage."

"I guess he does, but he's not Japanese."

"So why does he have a Japanese name?"

"It's not Japanese." Marcel was starting to sound exasperated.

"I'm sorry. I know that I talk too much when I'm nervous."

He leaned and took her hand. "That's okay. I like hearing you talk. You are curious, and you get excited over the most mundane things. You're not reserved, and you're not pretending to be anyone other than yourself, and I find that endearing."

She huffed out a laugh. "I'm the progeny of aliens, I grew up in a secluded compound, and while attending university, which was throughout my entire adult life, I was pretending to be like the other humans around me."

"That's not the same. You had to hide those things, but you've always been genuine. You might hide who you are, but you don't hide your feelings, and you're not embarrassed about voicing your opinions. When you're mad, you are not trying to hide it, and when you fall in love, you have the courage to admit it. You show the world the real you at all times." He lifted her hand to his lips and brushed kisses over her knuckles. "In summary, you are wonderful, and I feel blessed to have you as my mate."

Sofia swallowed. It was still difficult for her to hear him say that without a smidgen of fear creeping into her heart.

Would he still call her his mate when she didn't transition? Or when she transitioned and grew a pair of fangs and became stronger than him?

Annani

"Good evening," Syssi said as she opened the door for Annani.

"Good evening, my dear." Annani motioned for her to dip her head so she could kiss her cheek. "I am so glad that we are still having our Friday night family dinner despite the stressful situation."

Syssi chuckled. "If I canceled it every time something came up, we would have it only on rare occasions."

A smile tugged on Annani's lips. "I knew that the Fates had chosen wisely for my son—a mate who is steadfast and does not crumble under pressure."

"Good evening, Mother." Kian walked up to her and dipped his head to touch his lips to her cheek. "Thank you again for loaning the use of your plane and Oshidu to Sofia and Marcel."

She nodded. "When I heard Shai tell Eric that she has a human family in the compound who she cares deeply about, I was moved." She sat down on the chair he pulled out for her and smiled at her granddaughter.

Seated in a high chair, Allegra was playing on a tablet with her little face scrunched in concentration.

"Should a child this young handle such a device?"

Kian smiled at his daughter. "Allegra gets bored playing with inanimate objects. If she has a playmate, she doesn't mind the old boring toys, but when she doesn't, they don't provide enough stimulation. Syssi has been hesitant to let her play with electronics at such a young age, but you know Allegra. When she wants something, she gets it."

Syssi affected an apologetic expression. "I downloaded an application that is designed for babies nine months and older. She loves it."

The little girl lifted her head and gave Annani a bright smile. "Na-na."

"Yes, my love. Nana is here."

"Da-da," Allegra said with a resolute tone and went back to her tablet.

Annani laughed. "She communicates very clearly. She said hello and then told me to talk to Daddy."

As Syssi went to open the door for more dinner guests, Kian sat down next to Annani and brought his chair closer. "Thank you for helping Darlene pull through. I'm sure that Toven is grateful."

"He is. He called me to ask about Darlene's progress, and he also called Geraldine and Eric. He is very concerned about his granddaughter."

Kian frowned. "Is there a reason for concern? I thought she was doing fine."

"Bridget assures us that Darlene is doing great, but Toven hoped that she would transition more easily. He is disappointed that the potent godly blood flowing in her veins is not giving her a more significant advantage over other transitioning Dormants."

As Amanda and Dalhu entered with Evie in a baby carrier, and Kian pushed to his feet and walked over to greet them, Annani shifted her attention back to Allegra.

She was not an ordinary child, and Annani was not the kind of grandmother who saw greatness in all of her grandchildren and great-grandchildren. She had hundreds, and she followed their lives as closely as she could. She loved them all, but that did not mean that she believed they all were destined for greatness.

Allegra would one day lead the clan. Not because she was Kian's daughter but because she was a natural leader.

After all the guests had arrived, everyone had greeted everyone else, and Okidu had served the first course, the topic of conversation had naturally moved to the mission in Karelia.

"I should have joined the force," Orion said.

Alena put her hand on his shoulder. "You can't leave your pregnant mate alone. Besides, someone needs to stay and defend the village, right?" She looked at Kian.

"Absolutely. The reserve Guardians and the remainder of Kalugal's men are meeting in the gym tomorrow morning at seven for a briefing with Onegus. You are welcome to join them."

"I will. Thank you for telling me."

No one around the table missed the note of sarcasm in Orion's voice, including Kian.

"I didn't tell you about the meeting before because you don't really need to join the training. If Fates forbid we are attacked, you will serve us best with your compulsion ability."

Orion nodded. "You are right. Perhaps I should practice with Kalugal combining our powers. Each of us has a slightly different aspect of the ability."

"That's an interesting observation," Kian said. "You and Kalugal can compel people to forget things, but Toven, who is much more powerful than both of you, cannot."

"I didn't know that." Orion rubbed a hand over his jaw. "I'm immune, so I didn't experience his compulsion."

Annani smiled. "It reminds me of something Kaia told me about gene expression. I did not understand most of what she said, but I understood that the same genetic combination can produce different results under different conditions. You might have inherited compulsion ability from a common ancestor, but it expresses itself differently in each of you."

"The same is true for you, Mother," Amanda said. "You share the same common ancestor. Your paternal grandfather must have been a powerful compeller." She sighed. "It's a shame that none of your children inherited the ability. I would have loved to be able to compel."

Jade

"Why do we need to go hunting so early?" Kagra walked beside Jade toward the security office.

"Because I'm hungry, and yesterday you seemed eager to go."

"That was noon, now it's six in the morning, and it's Saturday. I don't get up at dawn on weekends."

"You don't get up at dawn on weekdays either, but the early hours of the morning are the best for training, which I decided to step up for you."

"What's the point? It's not as if I'm going to lead my own tribe one day."

Jade cast her a sidelong glance. "You never know what the future will bring, and it's best to be prepared for the best possible outcome."

Weekends were nothing special in the compound, and everyone continued performing their duties, but there were no classes for the children, so Jade's time was free, and she usually spent it training with Kagra, but today it wasn't about that.

Today, Kagra would be set free.

"Good morning." The hybrid on duty gave her a once-over. "Going hunting so early?"

The rumor about her so-called hunting with Pavel had spread, probably thanks to Pavel himself, and the result was much more attention from all the purebloods that she could do without.

The hybrids knew that they had no chance with her, so they just gave her covetous looks, but this one was more daring than the others.

She looked down her nose at him. "I don't waste time on more sleep than is absolutely necessary to maintain my health."

The guard looked at the schedule. "I see that you went hunting yesterday."

She narrowed her eyes at him. "Yesterday's hunt was about fresh blood, but not the kind that fills my belly."

"So I've heard." He gave her a suggestive look as he handed her two badges. "Good hunting."

Nodding, she handed Kagra one of the badges, affixed the other one to her jacket, and turned on her booted heel.

"It wouldn't kill you to say thank you from time to time," Kagra grumbled.

Today, it actually might, but Jade said nothing. The dismissive behavior was what everyone expected from her, and she'd already acted out of character by accepting Pavel's invitation.

Halfway to the gate they were intercepted by Valstar, and he didn't look happy.

"I heard that you met up with Pavel yesterday," he said as if she owed him an explanation. "While I waited for you."

"It wasn't while you waited for me." She sauntered over to him and put her hand on his chest. "It was in the afternoon. I prefer to sleep at night and perform strenuous activities while my energy levels are high. Besides, I figured I'd spare you Igor's wrath. Are you really brave enough to issue an invitation to his prime?"

Hopefully, Valstar would take the bait.

"Igor doesn't care who you fuck when you're not fertile. Come to my room this afternoon."

He was so predictable that it was pathetic.

She smiled to bare her fangs at him. "I have plans for today. But if you are free tomorrow, I might accept your invitation."

His eyes blazed red. "Two o'clock. Be there this time."

"Noon. I have a training session with Drova at four, and I don't want to rush." She trailed her hand down his stomach, halting just above his bulge.

"Noon works too." Valstar looked her over with lust clouding his eyes. "Wear something nice."

When he walked away, Kagra gaped at her. "What's going on, Jade? You detest Valstar almost as much as you abhor Igor."

"Actually, I detest him more." She waited for the guard to check her badge and open the gate for her. "Igor is a sociopath, which means that he doesn't feel anything, and he doesn't take pleasure in killing. Valstar enjoys it."

"So why did you accept his invitation?"

"I have my reasons." Jade walked out the gate.

She was going to kill him, and he'd just made it easier for her.

"Which you usually share with me. Yesterday you met Pavel, and you promised to tell me how it was, but all I got was one word. And today, you accepted an invitation from Valstar of all people. Was Pavel that bad?"

She hadn't seen Pavel until later that day, and he could barely speak with the power of Tom's compulsion acting like a gag. But he managed to communicate that she could count on him and that it wasn't only because he was forced to aid her.

Perhaps once he'd been freed from Igor's compulsion, the young male's natural Kra-ell instincts had come back online, and he'd accepted her authority over him.

They were still within sight of the guard tower though, and if she told Kagra the truth now, her second might do something that would betray her. It was better to save all the explanations for when they reached the meeting place with Tom. That was why she planned on arriving there half an hour early.

In the meantime, she needed to perpetuate the lie for Kagra's ears and possibly for the ears of the guards in the tower.

"Pavel was fine, but I should have known better than to accept a kid's invitation. I need someone more mature and stronger."

"And Valstar is it? Almost any of the other purebloods would have been better."

Jade shrugged. "I know him well, and I know that it will irk Igor despite what he says about me being free to fuck whoever I want when I'm not fertile."

Kagra shook her head. "I think that you finally snapped. This is not you."

"Maybe I am losing my mind." She cast Kagra a sidelong smile. "A good run will clear my head." She broke into an easy jog. "Are you up for a race this early in the morning? Or do you concede defeat before we even start?"

Kagra grinned. "What do I get if I win?"

"The satisfaction of finally besting me, but you're not going to win."

"We will see about that." Kagra sprinted ahead.

Toven

The preparations for today's meeting had been just as extensive as the day before, with Yamanu flying a small surveillance drone over the area where the three rivers crossed and a group of Guardians scoping it on foot ahead of time.

Yamanu had reported that Jade and another female had arrived half an hour or so earlier and that it didn't seem as if anyone had followed them to the remote spot.

Still, as Toven ran through the woods with Mia strapped on his back, he was more apprehensive than he had been yesterday.

The drone was limited in what it could see under the canopy of trees, and the Guardians could be overwhelmed by a large force. Jade could have been caught doing something out of character that raised suspicion, and Pavel could have talked despite the compulsion, although that was highly unlikely.

Toven's powers of compulsion seemed to work just fine on the purebloods, which meant that he could freeze attackers with a command to stand down, but he didn't know how many Kra-ell minds he could seize at once.

Jade and her second were already there when he arrived, and given that the other female wasn't panicking, Jade had warned her about his arrival.

"Hello." He stopped right in front of them and activated the disrupter.

"Hi." The female named Kagra looked at him with her enormous eyes. "I've never seen a god before. You look human, just prettier." She shifted her gaze to Mia. "Are you a goddess?"

"I'm just an immortal." She extended her hand to Kagra. "My name is Mia."

"What happened to your legs?" Kagra said as she shook it. "Did you lose them in battle?"

There had been no pity in her voice, just curiosity.

"In a way, yes. It was done to save my life. I'm regrowing them."

Kagra tilted her head in puzzlement. "Only gods can do that."

"Immortals can do it as well." Toven shifted his gaze to Jade. "What did you tell her so far?"

"I couldn't risk telling Kagra anything until we got here, and when I told her the plan, she had so many questions that I didn't have time to tell her about your sidekick."

"I'm not his sidekick," Mia grumbled. "I'm his mate."

"I meant no disrespect." Jade dipped her head. "I thought that was what humans called their assistants."

"No harm done," Toven interrupted. "Well, that's only true about the sidekick comment. You shouldn't have told Kagra anything without the disrupter, but that's my fault. I failed to warn you not to say anything without me being present."

Toven was starting to realize that he wasn't well-suited for this modern-day style of battle with listening devices, trackers, and collars that could explode. His power of compulsion was necessary for this mission, but they should have given him a tech-savvy sidekick.

Jade didn't look concerned. "The collars are not transmitting or recording our conversations. I told Kagra about contacting Veskar, or Emmett as you call him, long before I actually did it, and Igor never confronted me about it until I entered the writing competition."

"I hope you're right about that."

"I am." She turned to Kagra. "This is the moment you've been waiting for since we were captured. Tom is going to release you from Igor's compulsion."

The woman nodded and stepped forward. "I'm ready."

Toven looked into her eyes. "You no longer have to obey Igor's commands in any way. You are free to act and talk as you will." He gave her an encouraging smile. "Go ahead. Say something that you couldn't say before."

She put her hand on her chest. "I feel it in here. The oily feeling is gone." She took in a deep breath. "I want to tear Igor and his cohorts limb from limb for killing most of my tribe and enslaving the rest of us." She smiled brilliantly. "It's the oddest thing to feel happy about, but you have no idea how liberating it is to actually say that to someone who doesn't already know about it. Thank you."

"You're welcome."

He had known about her tribe, but she hadn't known that he had.

Jade clapped Kagra on her back. "Now, you can help me bring Igor and the rest of them down." She turned to Toven. "Valstar is waiting for me to come to his quarters at noon tomorrow. He expects sex, but he's only going to get the fight for dominance part, and I'm going to end him. Kagra is going to take care of the third, and Pavel is going to help secure the office building."

"About that." Toven sat down on the ground. "You can't kill Valstar before we capture Igor. He probably calls his second every so often, and if he gets no answer, he's not going to return. We also have to change the time of the attack to two o'clock at night instead of two in the afternoon."

When Jade bared her fangs, he lifted his hand to stop her from arguing. "You have to incapacitate Valstar so he can't trigger the explosives when we attack, and that needs to hold until I can get to him. Once we capture Igor, you can do with him as you please."

"I don't like it, but I can understand the logic of leaving Valstar alive until we capture Igor. Why the change of time, though? It's really pushing it too close for comfort." She sat on the ground, and Kagra followed her example.

"With most of the compound population asleep, and the children and humans out of the way, our task will be much easier."

Jade let out a breath. "I'll have to change my plans with Valstar."

"Is that a problem?" Mia asked.

"It is, but I'll come up with some excuse. He's so eager to get me in his bed that he will overlook the warning signs." She looked at Toven. "I assume that you plan to compel Valstar to tell Igor that everything is okay."

He nodded.

"You will have to restore the compound's communication."

"Correct. Once we have the compound secure and I'm done compelling everyone, we will stop disrupting the signal, and when Igor calls, Valstar will tell him that there was a malfunction. But since it will all happen at night, Igor might not call at all."

Jade's enormous smart eyes bored into him. "It's not going to work unless you can compel the entire population of the compound all at once, and even Igor can't do that. Perhaps the humans can be compelled as a group, but I wouldn't risk it. I think that Igor compels each person individually and then reinforces it with his public speeches."

"You think, or you know?" Mia asked.

"I think. He doesn't share his methods with me, and I don't spend that much time around him."

"I was led to believe that the community has limited access to phones and computers," Toven said. "Why do we need to compel everyone at once? Perhaps I can compel just the key players, and we can lock the rest of them up somewhere secure until we trap Igor."

"It's true that the only phones and computers inside the compound are in the office building, but I'm sure that Igor has snitches who have a way to contact him, and I don't know who they are. They might be hybrid, human, and pureblood. Probably a couple of each."

Toven let out a breath. "It means that we will have to keep the disrupter running until I compel them all."

"It will take all night, and if Igor calls and can't get through, he will get suspicious. Even if it takes you only one minute to compel each person, and you don't take any rests in between, that's over three hundred minutes."

It would have taken him much longer than that if not for Turner's idea of delegating the second half of the process to the clan's other compellers. His tasks would be to free them from Igor's compulsion and compel them to listen to the instructions of the other compellers.

"I can make it work," Toven said. "As long as Igor can get to Valstar before heading back to the compound, and he is told the communication disruption was just a malfunction, he will be reassured that everything is back to normal."

Jade shook her head. "He will know that something is up. Igor is very thorough. He probably has a contingency for such an event, like sending someone to a nearby town to call him and let him know about the malfunction. That's what I would have done, and I'm not nearly as paranoid as Igor."

Toven shifted to a more comfortable position. "If there is a contingency plan like that, it's even more important to keep Valstar alive. I can get him to tell me what the plan is, and we can do that. In fact, I hope that they have that contingency. Igor will not suspect that someone found a way to use it against him."

Jade let out a breath. "Everything you say makes sense, but I know in my gut that I need to kill Valstar and not just incapacitate him."

Kagra frowned at Jade. "How are you even going to overpower him? Can you compel him?"

"I'm not sure. I've never had the chance to try, but being Igor's second, Valstar must be a strong compeller. That being said, I don't need to compel him to overpower him." Jade's savage grin was chilling. "I'm going to drug him. Pavel already got me a large dose from the human chemist. It's not going to kill Valstar, but it will weaken him and slow his reflexes. I'm going to drain him until his heart stops and watch the horror in his eyes as he realizes what's happening."

Bile rose in Toven's throat, but he forced it down and swallowed.

Jade noticed. "What's the matter, pretty boy? Too savage for you? Would you prefer that I used a more civilized weapon to end the bastard who murdered my sons?"

"Not at all. It's your kill, and you have the right to end him any way you please. He doesn't deserve mercy from you. But if you want to capture Igor, you'll need to postpone your revenge by one more day. Can you half-drain him? Would that incapacitate him?"

Jade nodded.

"I can do the same to his third," Kagra said. "In case Igor wants to verify that what Valstar is telling him is true, you should also compel Durmar, Igor's third."

Darlene

As Darlene became aware of the subtle sounds the medical equipment was making, she knew where she was and why, but not how long. She had been slipping in and out of consciousness, but she had no concept of time.

Had it been a day? Two? Maybe more?

She remembered waking up and talking to Eric, her mother, her son, and her sister, and she also remembered the goddess standing next to her bed and smiling down at her, but that could have been a dream.

Toven had promised to give her his blessings to help her along, but she hadn't even dreamt about him.

As Darlene's mind became more focused, she remembered Eric reminding her about a mission that Toven had accepted. Annani had taken his place, which explained the memory of the goddess being in her room. The Clan

Mother had come to bless her because Toven wasn't there.

Forcing her eyelids to lift, Darlene was greeted by her mother's smiling face. "Good morning, my sweet girl." Geraldine leaned over and kissed Darlene's forehead. "I hope that today you will stay awake for longer than a few minutes."

"How long have I been here?" Darlene whispered.

Geraldine smiled. "You ask the same question every time you wake up. Your transition started on Tuesday, and today is Saturday." Her mother wetted her lips with an ice cube. "Bridget doesn't allow me to give you water to drink. She says that you need to be awake for longer than a few moments."

Darlene licked the droplets of water from her lips. "Can you do it again?"

"Sure."

When she was done licking the scant moisture from her lips, she asked, "Where is Eric?"

"He went to the cafeteria to get us something to eat. He'll be sorry to have missed you being awake. I should call him."

"Don't. He needs a break."

Geraldine nodded. "He's with you twenty-four-seven. Shai tried to convince him to help out with the mission the whole village is buzzing about and fly some people over, but Eric declined. Luckily, the Clan Mother overheard them talking and volunteered her own jet with one of her Odus."

"That's nice of her." Darlene closed her eyes. "I remember Eric reading a steamy romance to me, but it wasn't one of mine. Did I dream it?"

Her mother giggled. "It's mine. He asked me to bring him a book to read to you, and he wanted it to be hot. He said that you read him a steamy romance when he was in a coma."

"I did, but he doesn't actually remember me doing that. I'm sure that it helped, though."

"Do you want me to read to you?" Geraldine asked.

"Tell me about the mission. What's the news on that?"

Her mother smiled indulgently. "It's still very hush-hush, and I'm not supposed to know anything, but Shai tells me bits and pieces. You'll probably slip away before I'm done, but fine."

Since the story sounded somewhat familiar, Darlene assumed that she'd heard it before. Maybe Eric and Annani had talked about it next to her, and she'd retained some of it.

Geraldine was nearing the end of the story when the door opened, and Eric walked in with a big brown bag and a tray with two cups of coffee.

"You're awake." He cast Geraldine an accusing glance. "Why didn't you call me?"

"I told her not to," Darlene said. "Come and give me a kiss."

As he handed her mother the bag and the tray and leaned over the bed, Darlene managed to lift her arms and embrace him. "I love you so much."

He looked into her eyes and smiled. "I love you more."

"Uh-uh. I love you more."

He caressed her cheek. "You seem to have more energy than you had the other times you woke up. You're more focused too."

Darlene frowned. "I feel good, and that coffee smells divine. Do you think you can give me some and not tell Bridget?"

He turned his head and looked at the open door. "She'll have my head. But there is nothing I won't do for you."

Darlene licked her lips again, this time in anticipation of a taste of coffee.

Her mother gave Eric a reproachful look, but she didn't argue when he took one of the paper cups off the tray, added cream and sugar, and stirred.

"Maybe that's the magic potion that will keep you awake."

He pressed a button on the remote, and the back of the bed lifted, bringing Darlene to a semi-reclining position.

"No wonder I was unconscious for four and a half days. I didn't have my morning coffee."

Eric brought the cup to her lips. "It's not too hot, but drink carefully and only a little. I'm sure that water would have been better, but you and I are rebels, right?" He winked at her.

Her heart swelled with so much love for him that it felt too big for her ribcage.

Taking a small sip, she sighed in bliss and then took two more before Eric took the cup away. "That's enough for now. If you stay awake for the next fifteen minutes, I'll give you more."

"That's an excellent incentive to stay awake."

Sofia

Sofia hadn't known what to expect when they'd landed in St. Petersburg, and neither had Marcel.

He'd made several phone calls during the long flight, but no one could give him a straight answer because everything had still been in flux.

Things hadn't improved much when they'd met up with the Guardians who'd arrived on a large plane straight from wherever Marcel's village was.

Nearly an hour passed before the convoy of trucks arrived to pick them up. They must have used mind tricks that encompassed the entire private section of the airport because no one was paying them any attention.

"Is Toven doing this?" she asked Marcel as he helped her climb to the back of one of the trucks. "Is he somehow compelling everyone in the airport not to notice a convoy of army trucks collecting soldiers that arrived on a private plane from the United States?"

They sat on one of the two long benches lining the sides of the truck.

"Toven's abilities are not limited to compulsion," Marcel said. "He can shroud the entire city if he wants, but he is not the only ace we have. We have a guy that can do it nearly as well, and I suspect this is his work."

"It's Yamanu's doing," one of the soldiers said. "He came with the convoy." The guy chuckled. "I wonder where he got these trucks."

"Probably from Turner's supplier," another Guardian said while his eyes roved over Sofia.

He was a handsome guy who looked a little like that famous British soccer player whose name she couldn't recall.

Marcel wrapped one arm around her shoulders and put a hand on her thigh. "Let me introduce you to my mate. This is Sofia. Sofia, this is Jay, and that's Elliot."

"Hi." Elliot smiled. "Nice to meet you."

As all sixteen Guardians introduced themselves, Sofia tried to memorize their names, but it was futile. She had a good memory for languages, probably because her brain had been trained for it, but names had always been a problem. When she taught classes at the university, she asked the students to wear name tags for the first week.

"Where are we going?" she asked.

The Guardian sitting on her other side shrugged. "Somewhere in the countryside. We brought field equipment with us, so I guess we are camping." He closed his eyes and leaned his head against the side of the truck.

"I'll check with Yamanu." Marcel pulled out his phone and typed a text.

When he got no response, he put the phone in his lap. "He must be busy."

As the truck trundled along the bumpy road, Sofia regretted the lack of windows, but she could understand the need to hide what was under the green tarp. It was cold, there was no heating in the cabin, and her puffer coat was in her suitcase that was somewhere among the boxes of equipment occupying the center of the truck. With the Guardians stretching their legs and propping them on the boxes, she couldn't go looking for it.

Instead, she cuddled closer to Marcel. "Aren't you cold?"

"Immortals are not as sensitive to the elements." He rubbed her arm.

"Here." The Guardian who looked like the British soccer player handed her his coat. "You can use mine."

"What about you?"

He flashed her a charming smile. "I'm an immortal. I don't get cold."

She chuckled. "In two weeks, even you'll be cold. Winters here are not for the fainthearted."

He looked offended. "First of all, I hope we will be out of here in a few days, and secondly, none of the Guardians are fainthearted."

"Of course not." She draped his coat over her front. "You are all manly men."

"You'd better believe it." He crossed his arms over his chest and closed his eyes again.

As Marcel's phone vibrated, he lifted it, read the message, and put it back down. "We are staying on a farm. The ladies will stay in the house, and the Guardians will erect tents in the field."

"I hope there's enough room in the house for you to join me."

He looked conflicted. "I'm glad that you will get to sleep in a warm bed. I should stay with the men."

"Don't be an idiot," the one who looked like the soccer player said. "Stay with your mate. No one will begrudge you that."

Eric

Darlene hadn't slipped back into unconsciousness. Except for a couple of short naps, she'd been awake since morning.

"Bridget should have checked on you instead of leaving Julian and the nurse in charge." Eric rose to his feet. "I'll go talk to him."

"I wouldn't bother Bridget today," Geraldine said. "Shai told me that she's helping with the preparation for the mission."

"The Guardians shipped out already. What else is there to do?"

Geraldine shrugged. "I don't know. Kian and Shai are still in the office, so there must be things that still need to be done."

"If Darlene is over the initial stage of her transition, I would like to take her home, but Julian told me that Bridget needs to approve it."

"I don't know why." Geraldine looked at Darlene and smiled. "None of us is a doctor, but we can all see that you are doing so much better. The color's returned to your cheeks, and you even drank coffee."

Darlene laughed. "Just don't tell Julian or Bridget that I did that."

Her mother affected an innocent expression. "Julian said that you can have liquids, including soup, so why not coffee?"

Eric agreed wholeheartedly.

It wasn't that he minded staying one more night in the clinic. What he needed was confirmation that the worst was behind them and that Darlene was out of danger.

Ever since she'd lost consciousness, he hadn't been able to take a full breath.

"I'll ask, and if Bridget can't come and Julian can't take responsibility for releasing you, we will have to spend another night here. But if Bridget can hop over for a few minutes and give her okay, I would really like to sleep in my own bed tonight with you in my arms."

Darlene sighed. "That sounds so lovely. But I really don't want to bother Bridget if she's busy."

"It doesn't hurt to check." Eric walked out of the room and into the doctor's office.

"She's coming," Julian said before Eric could open his mouth. "My mother loves welcoming transitioned

Dormants into immortality, and I didn't want to rob her of the experience by releasing Darlene myself."

Eric frowned. "Are you saying that you could have released her but kept her here for Bridget to do the honors?"

Julian smiled sheepishly. "It wasn't a big delay. Bridget wouldn't have released her immediately, either. In fact, she might insist that Darlene stays another night because of how long she's been in a coma."

Eric rolled his eyes. "Can you make up your mind? One moment you say that you can release Darlene, and the next, you say that she should stay another night. Are you just saying it to excuse the wait?"

Julian gave him one of those condescending smiles that doctors worldwide must have all practiced during their residencies. "There is a reason what physicians do is collectively called practicing medicine. Opinions vary, and decisions are highly subjective. If you want to be sure about a diagnosis, always ask for a second opinion."

"I hope never to need it again."

The front door opened, and Bridget walked in. Wearing a tight skirt and high heels, she looked like a pinup girl, not a doctor.

"Congratulations." She offered him her hand.

"Thank you, but you haven't seen Darlene yet."

"Let's do it together." She grabbed a white coat from a peg by the door and put it over her clothes.

"How is the mission going?" he asked.

She let out a breath. "It was one hell of an organizational effort to have everything in place in time."

Darlene grinned as they entered the room. "Hi, Bridget. That was fast."

"It was?" The doctor walked up to her.

"Bridget was already on her way," Eric explained. "I didn't need to call her."

"Are you in a hurry to go home?" The doctor checked the readouts on the various machines.

"I am. But I want the test done first."

Bridget tilted her head. "You don't really need to do that."

"I want to. Is that okay?"

"Of course."

"I'm calling Roni and Cassandra," Geraldine said. "Is there anyone else you want to witness the test?"

Darlene shifted her gaze to Eric. "Orion and Alena, Kaia, maybe Karen if she can. And the Clan Mother if she so wishes. You told me that she came to give me her blessing every day."

"She did." Eric pulled out his phone. "I'll call Alena and ask her if it's appropriate to invite the Clan Mother."

"I don't think it is," Geraldine said.

"It doesn't hurt to ask." Eric started texting.

"In the meantime, let's remove all the wires." Bridget shooed Eric and Geraldine out of the room and called the nurse in.

"Tell everyone to be here in an hour," Darlene called after them. "I want to shower first."

An hour later, the clinic was packed with people, and for a change, Bridget didn't make a fuss about them lining the walls of the small patient room.

"It is my honor and my pleasure to welcome Darlene into immortality. Toven couldn't be here in person, but that's what video calls are for." She waved at Julian, who had been standing in the doorway.

"That was part of the reason for the delay." He held up a tablet with Toven and Mia's faces occupying the screen.

"Congratulations!" they said at the same time.

"Not yet." Darlene pushed up on the pillows. "Wait until the cut test."

"You're awake," Toven said. "That's reason enough to celebrate." He lifted a bottle of vodka. "We wanted to toast your successful transition with a glass of champagne, but this is Russia, so vodka will have to do."

Tears glistened in Darlene's eyes as she offered her hand to Bridget, but Eric knew it wasn't because she was scared of a little pain. Underneath her soft exterior, Darlene was a fighter.

Nevertheless, he clasped her other hand for support.

"Bring the tablet closer," Bridget instructed Julian. "So Toven and Mia can see the test."

Roni grumbled as he had to move to give Julian access. "She's my mother. I have the right to be the closest."

"You can sit on the bed," Darlene offered.

Bridget turned to look around the room. "Everyone ready?"

When no one else complained about not being able to see, she lifted her surgical knife off the tray and made the cut so quickly that Darlene didn't have a chance to flinch.

Eric squeezed her other hand. "Are you okay?"

"Perfect," Bridget answered for Darlene. "Look at this. It's already closing." She turned her head and smiled at the tablet. "Being a god's granddaughter comes with great perks."

Darlene leaned over the hand that Bridget was still holding. "Where is it? I can't see the cut."

The doctor took a square of gauze from her tray and wiped the small smear of blood away. "It's already gone."

"That's amazing." Darlene shifted her gaze to her mother. "Did yours heal as fast?"

"Even faster. I made the cut myself to test whether what they'd told me was true. I couldn't believe that I was immortal." She chuckled. "A demigoddess. It closed incredibly fast."

Cassandra started clapping, and then others joined in, and as the word 'congratulations' echoed from the walls, Darlene smiled and wiped tears from her eyes.

"Thank you, everyone," she said once her family and friends quieted down. "I never expected to find such a warm home or such great love." She looked at Eric. "I wish Max was here to celebrate with us, but he's in Russia with the Guardian force." She looked at the tablet. "Keep him safe, will you?"

"I'll do my best," Toven said. "Goodnight, everyone." The transmission ended.

A few more minutes passed as Darlene was hugged and kissed on her cheeks, and then it was the four of them in the room. Him and Darlene, Geraldine, and Roni.

"Come, my grandson," Geraldine said. "Your mom needs to get dressed and go home."

Roni leaned over Darlene and pulled her into a fierce embrace. "Could you have ever imagined a day like this when you were still with Leo?"

"Not in my wildest fantasies."

"Welcome to forever, Mom."

Sofia

"You need to get some sleep." Marcel rubbed Sofia's arm.

He was spooning her on the narrow bed in the children's room, which was too small for both of them and not long enough either. But it was better than sleeping in a tent out in the cold. Sylvia got the other bed, and the only other room was occupied by Toven and Mia.

Marcel had offered to sleep on the couch in the living room, but Sofia needed him near her.

"I'm too anxious to sleep."

He nuzzled her neck. "I can provide a distraction."

She would have loved to get distracted, but they weren't alone, and Sylvia had probably heard Marcel's whispers.

"We are not alone," she whispered as quietly as she could.

"Sylvia is asleep."

"How do you know? She might be pretending."

"I can hear her breathing. It's slow and deep." As he trailed kisses down her throat, his hand skimmed her hip, circled over her belly, and snaked under the elastic of her pajama pants. "If you remain very quiet, she won't hear you." His fingers brushed over the top of her slit but didn't reach where she needed them. "Is that distracting enough?" He nipped her earlobe.

Swallowing the moan rising in her throat, Sofia pushed her bottom against his hard length, and his answering muffled groan was most satisfying.

His hand moved lower, the pads of his two longest fingers finally making contact with the bundle of nerves and drawing circles around it. "Is that enough?" He blew hot air into her ear.

"More," she whispered.

If Sylvia heard them and was pretending to sleep, Sofia was fine with that. She needed this.

He slipped his finger into her wet heat and then added another. "Good?" he whispered.

"Yes."

Pulling her pajama pants down with his other hand, Marcel added another long finger, and as he thrust in and out of her, he pulled down his own sweatpants and pressed his shaft to her ass.

For several long moments, he rubbed himself against her bottom in sync with his fingers moving inside of her, and as another moan rose in her throat, he clamped his hand over her mouth and replaced his fingers with his erection.

That was more than she'd bargained for, and Sylvia would no doubt wake up from their activity, but Sofia was beyond caring.

Licking at Marcel's fingers, she concentrated on the feel of him thrusting in and out of her so gently that the bed didn't make a sound. It was a delicious slow burn, and she knew she would climax the moment he added his fingers to the play, but would he be able to reach his own release at such a slow and gentle pace?

Turning her head back as far as she could, she offered him her lips, and he took them with a savage need.

When he pressed the tops of his fingers to that most sensitive spot, the tension inside of her curled until her body went taut and then snapped.

As pleasure consumed her, Marcel's hand muffled her cry of release, and his fingers kept their light circling until he wrung the last tremor out of her and stilled.

"Why did you stop?" she murmured.

"This was about you, not me. Now, go to sleep." He kissed her neck and pulled her pajama pants up.

She was too tired to argue. The orgasm left her boneless and relaxed, her head empty of disturbing thoughts, and as she drifted off to sleep, she murmured, "Thank you. I'll return the favor tomorrow."

He chuckled next to her neck. "You're welcome, my love. It was my pleasure."

Toven

The river was starting to ice over, but it was just the beginning, and the amphibian's progress hadn't been slowed down because of it. Nevertheless, the vehicle's speed was painfully slow.

Mia had protested when Toven had informed her that she needed to stay behind in the farmhouse with Sofia, but he'd been adamant about not bringing her into the battle. When they had control of the compound, she would be brought over by the Guardians he'd left with her.

She'd tried to argue that the men were needed in battle and that it was a waste to leave them behind just because of her and Sofia, and she'd even tried to pull the Sylvia card. If Roni's mate was going with William in the van that was leading half the force through the tunnels' side, then why weren't she and Sofia allowed to join the force that was attacking from the hunting grounds?

It was a valid point, and he hadn't had the heart to tell her that Sylvia's help was crucial because the cameras in the tunnels could be wired to the compound, and William's disrupter might not work on them, but she and Sofia weren't needed until they secured the compound.

The problem was that Toven wasn't at all sure that they would succeed. They had the element of surprise on their side, help from Jade and Kagra, and superior equipment and weaponry, but the Kra-ell were incredibly strong, and they would be defending their home and their children. They had no way of knowing that it was a liberation and not an impending annihilation.

"You haven't practiced wearing the exoskeleton," Yamanu said. "I know that you plan to fight with your mind and not your muscles, but the suit also provides superior protection. Unless they fire an RPG at you, which we know they don't have, you're not going to get hurt while inside of it."

Across from him, Merlin tried to stifle a smile and failed. The doctor was a strange choice for this mission, and Toven wondered why Julian hadn't been assigned to accompany the Guardians.

"What's funny?" Yamanu asked Merlin.

"Nothing. I'm not wearing a suit either."

"You are staying behind in the amphibian until we secure the compound, so you don't have to, but I would have felt better if you wore one."

Toven patted his Kevlar vest. "This, the helmet, and the goggles will do. As long as my head, my eyes, and my heart are protected, and the Kra-ell don't have anything stronger than grenades to throw at me, I'm good."

Yamanu shook his head. "As strong as they are, they can grab you and tear you limb from limb, reach into your ribcage and pull your heart out, or twist your head off."

"You forget that I can compel them to freeze. I don't expect any of them to be immune. Igor wouldn't have allowed an immune to live."

Yamanu didn't look impressed with his reasoning. "You might be able to seize the mind of one, maybe two attackers, but what if there are more?

Toven winced. "Then I guess you and your fellow Guardians will need to shield me."

"We will be busy with the rest of the Kra-ell."

"Then I guess I need to wear the suit."

Yamanu grinned as if he'd won an argument.

Toven frowned. "What part of what we were talking about amused you?"

"Bhathian and I made a bet, and he just lost. He said that you were going to play the haughty 'I'm an indestructible god' card, but I said that you were a reasonable dude, and you would understand that you couldn't join the attacking force without the suit. You'll have to stay behind in the amphibian and wait until we secure the compound."

"How difficult are those exoskeletons to operate?"

"They are cumbersome." He gave Toven a once-over. "But you're a god, which I assume makes you stronger than most immortals, and you are also a smart fellow. If you want to give it a try, you're welcome to a suit."

Toven had a feeling that he'd just been outmaneuvered by the Head Guardian. "You planned this entire conversation to convince me to wear the damn suit, didn't you?"

Yamanu shrugged. "It was a last-minute thing. Since we left two Guardians with Mia and Sofia, I had two extra exoskeletons. Besides, Kalugal's men didn't have a chance to practice wearing them either, so you won't be the only one who will look like an astronaut trying to walk on the moon."

"You could have started with that, you know. I was under the impression that everyone had practiced walking with them."

"The exoskeletons are our design, and this is our first joint mission with Kalugal's men, which was decided on about forty hours ago. When and where would Kalugal's men have had a chance to practice fighting with the suits on?"

"I'm new to the clan, remember? I didn't know that you've never fought side by side with them before."

"Right." Yamanu nodded. "You seem such an integral part of the clan that it is easy to forget you are a newcomer."

"Thank you." Toven smiled at the Guardian. "That was actually a nice compliment."

"You're welcome."

"By the way, do you know how William is going to disrupt the communications? It occurred to me that the compound might use landlines or a satellite like the clan does."

"There are no landlines," Yamanu said. "William checked, and there are no landlines anywhere in the vicinity of the compound. The Kra-ell have a huge antenna that's very cleverly camouflaged to look like an enormous tree. According to William, all wireless devices are susceptible to radio frequency interference, and he will scramble them with his gadget." Yamanu flashed him a smile. "Don't ask me to explain the how and why. I'm just repeating what he told me."

"I know how it works." Toven leaned his head against the vehicle's side wall. "Because of that, he can isolate the signal going to the clan's satellite so we will retain the ability to communicate while the Kra-ell will not."

"I'll take your word for it." Yamanu crossed his arms over his chest. "Let's just hope that our drone spots smoke coming from the roof of the office building. It will be a shame if we have to fold after making all this effort."

"Not to mention the expense," Toven said. "Kian might need my help to cover the costs."

Yamanu cast him a sidelong glance. "That's very generous of you to offer. What will you ask for in return?"

"I already have all I need, but I might negotiate with Syssi for full ownership of Perfect Match."

Yamanu pursed his lips. "I don't know what all the fuss is about. I can understand why people with mobility issues can benefit from it, but I prefer my adventures to be real, not virtual."

"That's because you already have your perfect match. But perhaps you and Mey would like to spend a romantic vacation that neither of you has the time for. You can experience up to three weeks of curated adventure in the span of three hours, and it can be the wildest thing either of you has ever imagined. Not only that, but artificial intelligence might also surprise you with more than you've bargained for. The adventure that Mia and I shared was only loosely based on what we both asked for, and it was incredible."

The Guardian looked intrigued. "I'll have to talk it over with Mey."

Jade

"Wear something nice, he said." Jade smoothed her hand over her leather pants. "I'll show him nice."

The truth was that she looked hot, and the covetous glances she got from males as she strode toward the office building confirmed that.

Valstar hadn't been too upset about the change in their appointment time. In fact, he'd looked relieved. Jade doubted that he'd been concerned with losing work time to accommodate her request for an afternoon assignation, and when she'd moved the appointment, he'd been glad that it would be after hours.

His obvious preference for the nighttime probably had more to do with Igor not checking in and interrupting their session.

The downside was that she needed to spend more time with Valstar than she'd originally planned. The attack was scheduled for two at night, but she couldn't justify showing up at his place later than ten, and she had to keep him incapacitated during all that time, which meant repeatedly draining him.

At the thought, bile rose in her throat.

That alone should be enough of a punishment to atone for all her sins and failures, of which there were many.

The drug was already mixed inside the vodka that the humans distilled from potatoes in their section of the compound, and she'd brought cranberry juice to mix with the vodka so Valstar wouldn't taste the powder.

The guard at the door lifted his hand to stop her. "What do you have there?"

"What does it look like?"

"Is it vodka?"

"No, it's water." She rolled her eyes. "Valstar must have told you that I'm coming to see him tonight."

"He did," Boris said. "He also told me to thoroughly search you."

He licked his fangs as he gave her outfit an appreciative once-over.

The tight leather pants couldn't even hide a thin wire to cut someone's throat with, she'd checked, and the shirt was made from a mesh fabric that left her back, her arms, and her midriff exposed. A three-inch opaque panel covered her breasts, but her nipples were clearly outlined.

It was a bit chilly for such an outfit, but she was a Kra-ell warrior, and she didn't let trivial things like that bother her.

"Go ahead." She lifted her arms, a bottle in each hand, and turned in a circle. "The only place I can hide something is in my boots. You're welcome to take them off for me."

"Right. So you can smash one of those bottles over my head."

Jade snorted. "I wouldn't waste good vodka on you."

He pointed to his chair. "Sit there and take the boots off."

She sat down and handed him the two bottles. "Go ahead, take a sip. I know you want to."

She pulled a boot off and stretched her long legs in front of her.

"I'm on duty." Boris handed her the bottles back.

"Don't you want to check that there is no poison inside?"

"What would be the point of that?" He lifted one boot, peeked inside, examined the sole and the heel, and put it down next to her leg before lifting the other. "Maybe you want to poison me and save the rest for Valstar. This visit is highly uncharacteristic of you."

"You know nothing about me, boy." She uncorked the vodka and took a swig, swishing it in her mouth for him to see before swallowing. "See? No poison. Do you want me to drink from the cranberry juice too?"

Checking her other boot, he nodded.

"It's not tasty on its own." She opened the bottle, took a sip, and swished it in her mouth before swallowing.

The purebloods enjoyed alcohol just as much as the hybrids and the humans did, and they could even tolerate mixing it with a limited selection of juices. Orange juice was not one of them.

She still remembered the cramps that had given her.

A few drops landed on her chin, and as she handed Boris the bottles to hold, she wiped them off with her fingers, and then licked them clean.

He watched her, transfixed.

"Don't drop these bottles," she warned as she pulled her boots back on. "The humans don't just give them away."

She might need a few swigs from the drug-infused vodka to be able to get through what she needed to do with Valstar, and even if she didn't, she would need to drink it if she wanted him to drink. It was harmless in small doses, so if she sipped slowly and kept refilling his glass, she should be okay.

"Why are you doing this?" Boris seemed unable to stop himself from asking.

She grinned evilly. "I figured that I'll get a rise out of Igor if I accept his second's invitation, and what's even better, I'll get Valstar in trouble."

His eyes flared red for a moment. "You are either stupidly brave or crazy."

"A little bit of both." She took the bottles from him and turned to walk away.

"Hold on," Boris called after her. "I need to check your hair."

She'd left it unbound, so that was unnecessary, but she stopped and turned back to him. "Go ahead."

He lifted the curtain of her hair almost reverently, and as his fingers brushed over her nape, she felt them tremble.

A small smile curved her lips. She could do that to any Kra-ell male even when she wasn't in her fertile cycle. The males drooled after her not because she was the greatest beauty but because she was a natural prime.

The male's nature was to prove himself worthy to the most powerful female and to outdo other males. Those whose Kra-ell souls hadn't been corrupted to their very core by Igor still possessed that instinct.

When Boris let go of her hair, she turned around, walked into the building, and headed up the stairs.

With the second floor hosting Igor and Valstar's offices and personal lodging, there was always another guard at the entry to their hallway, but with Igor gone, security seemed laxer than usual. Or perhaps Valstar had dismissed the guard so he could have more privacy with Igor's prime female.

The first floor housed the administrative offices, but no one was there this time of night. Tom had been right about it being an advantage. Once the communications went down and Pavel took care of Boris to bring her the titanium chains, there would be no witnesses.

When Jade got to Valstar's office, she knocked to let him know that she was coming in and opened the door. She'd never been to his private quarters before, but they were probably similar to Igor's, which meant that to get there, she needed to pass through the office.

"It's me." She knocked on the only other door.

Valstar pulled it open and gave her a once-over. "That's not what I had in mind when I told you to dress nicely, but it will do." He reached for her waist.

"I brought something for the mood." Jade sidestepped his hand and walked over to the sitting area. "Do you have glasses?"

"Of course."

He didn't look happy about her not being ready to play, but he was being cautious. Valstar was a murderer but not a rapist, and even if he was, he wouldn't dare force himself on Igor's prime. If he offended her, he knew that she would walk away, and he would have to let her go.

Pulling two glasses from a sideboard, he brought them to the coffee table. "Boris told me that you were bringing vodka and that you drank it in front of him to prove that you are not going to poison me."

"Why would I want to do that?" She poured the cranberry juice first. "I'm here to scratch an itch and to annoy Igor. Killing you is not on the menu."

Regrettably, that was true. She needed to keep him alive until Igor was caught.

Marcel

Toven had left more than two hours ago with the Guardians who formed the wing that would attack from the hunting grounds. Their journey through the river was much longer than Marcel's group's, and the amphibian they were traversing the distance in was much slower than the trucks his group was using.

Marcel utilized that time to practice wearing the exoskeleton suit along with Kalugal's men.

Not to deplete their energy before the battle, they weren't doing anything more strenuous than walking and aiming their weapons, but he was already tired, and it had been less than an hour.

"That's good enough," Bhathian said. "Take the suits off, but do it carefully so nothing gets damaged, and return them to their crates. Make sure that your name is on the crate so you can find it later. Bring it with you when we move out." He pointed to his watch. "You have half an hour."

The suits were going with them in the trucks, and they were going to put them on right before the battle.

As Marcel turned toward the farmhouse porch, he met Sofia's eyes, which were wide with wonder. She and the two other ladies were sitting on a bench, watching him and Kalugal's men test the exoskeletons.

Taking the helmet off, he smiled at her. "Impressed?"

She nodded. "You look like an alien. The purebloods will be so shocked when they see you that they might surrender without a fight."

"I wish, but I doubt it." He carefully removed the suit's sleeves. "In any case, you shouldn't worry. Our guns are loaded with tranquilizing darts, and we will take down as many as we can without killing them."

Instead of looking reassured, Mia looked more worried after what he'd said. "But you have regular guns as well, right?"

"Of course, we do."

"What if the humans join the fight?" Mia asked. "Those darts are calibrated to take down Kra-ell. They can kill a human."

Marcel looked at Sofia. "Will they fight?"

She shook her head. "They would just get in the way. No one ever talked about the possibility of the compound being attacked, but we had fire drills. In the case of fire, the humans are supposed to get the animals out of the barns and then assemble in the playground. Maybe the protocol is the same in the case of an invasion." She sighed. "I hope that they just stay in their rooms."

Sylvia crossed her arms over her chest. "I should just join the Guardian force. They keep recruiting me for these jobs, and I don't know how to even hold a gun."

"Do you want to be a Guardian?" Marcel asked.

"Not really. But there is nothing I'm passionate about, and the idea of having a job that I need to show up for every day doesn't appeal to me. I like to learn new things, and I like to take on interesting projects that are not too long. Otherwise, I get bored."

"Then Guardian training is not for you." Marcel finished folding the suit and put it in its crate.

When Sylvia pushed to her feet, Sofia followed her up. "I'll walk with you to the truck."

"Good luck," Mia said.

"Thank you." Sylvia bent to give Mia a hug. "Don't worry. With these suits, they are invincible."

"What about you? Are you going to wear one?"

Sylvia shook her head. "I'm staying in the van with William." She let go of Mia and stretched, then turned to Marcel. "You should stay in the van with us. It's the best seat in the house. We get to see the entire battle on the screen. The drones film everything on their path and transmit it to William's computer."

"Yeah." Sofia wrapped her arm around his middle. "You should stay in the van where it's safe, and let me know what's going on. You haven't been on active duty in centuries."

"I'll be fine. I train with the reserves."

Lifting his crate was no small effort. The suits weighed over two hundred pounds each, and they weren't the only thing in the crate. The rest of his weapons were there as well.

When they got to his designated truck, he climbed in, pushed the crate under the bench, and then got back down to say goodbye.

He pulled Sofia into his arms. "I'll ask Sylvia to give you updates."

"I prefer for you to do it. That way, I will know that you're safe."

"I am safe. These suits are not just for protection. They make me ten times stronger. I can take on a pureblood while wearing them and win."

She closed her eyes. "Things happen in battle, and I can't lose you. Promise me not to do anything stupid."

He arched a brow. "When did I ever give you the impression that I'm the reckless type?"

"Good point. Just be safe, and don't do anything overly heroic."

"I won't."

He kissed her, and as she wrapped her arms around his neck and kissed him back, he got so lost in the sensation that he didn't hear Bhathian calling his name until the Guardian clapped him on the back.

"Time to go. Save your kisses for later."

Jade

"Enough." Valstar swiped both glasses off the table, sending them flying to the concrete floor and shattering on impact.

Jade lifted a brow. "Impatient?"

His eyes were fully red, in part because of lust and in part because of the combination of alcohol and drugs, but he wasn't nearly as weakened as she'd hoped for.

A trickle of apprehension slithered down her spine.

She hadn't fed earlier in order to leave room in her digestive system for the copious amounts of blood she was about to suck from him, and that meant she wasn't at her maximum strength either.

The hatred and rage would have to be fuel enough.

"Get rid of your clothes if you don't want them ruined." He tore his shirt off, sending the buttons flying. One hit her face, and the rest tumbled harmlessly to the floor, landing among the shards of broken glass.

As a last resort, she could use the glass as a weapon and cut his carotid artery, but his body would repair the wound too fast for the loss of blood to weaken him. Her best chance was to get her fangs in his neck.

He would let her drink, thinking it was part of the sexual game, and when he realized that she was taking too much, he would be too weak to fight her off.

Jade rose to her feet, gripped Valstar by the throat, and tossed him on the bed.

Caught by surprise, he hadn't offered any resistance, and since she was still pretending to play the game, he didn't rise to attack her.

"I'm waiting to see that magnificent body of yours." He kicked his boots off. "Take off that thing that passes for a shirt."

She looked down at the floor. "Look what you have done. How am I supposed to walk on this without my boots?"

His gaze roamed over her. "If you can't remove the pants without removing the boots first, I can tear them off you."

"Impatient much?"

As he pulled his pants down and his shaft jutted from his hips, she wished she could have smuggled a knife into the building so she could cut it off. The blood loss from that might be enough, and if not that, the pain and horror would have been.

"They are not the kind that rips at the seams." She pretended to appreciate his size as she pulled the flimsy shirt over her head and tossed it on the couch.

He sucked in a breath. "Beautiful."

She faked an appreciative look-over. "You're not too bad yourself."

There was nothing wrong with his body, and if he wasn't a murderer, she might have found him attractive, but all she saw in front of her was a twisted monster.

Climbing on the bed with her knees, she put her hands on his chest and pushed him down. "If you want me, you'll have to prove your worth."

He smiled, revealing a pair of long fangs. "Oh, I will." He gripped her waist and twisted them around, pinning her under him. "I want a taste of you."

He lowered his mouth to her breast, but she bucked him off before his fangs touched her skin, and as he landed on the glass-strewn floor, he let out a hiss.

She was straddling him before he could process what was happening, her hands pushing on his shoulders and forcing him to stay down.

"A little pain fuels the lust." She stroked his neck with her fangs, sinking them into his carotid.

Valstar moaned, his hips shooting up and his erection pressing against her center. "Pull your pants down." His hands gripped the waistband and pulled.

Fuck. She should have pinned his hands over his head instead of pressing on his shoulders.

Grinding against him to distract him, she kept gulping down his blood while he pulled her pants down her hips, but he was too lost in the act to master the coordination needed to lift her, so he couldn't pull them all the way down to her thighs and expose her.

Jade moaned deep in her throat and ground against him some more, and as his hands left her hips and his arms plopped weakly on the floor, she wanted to smile but kept on sucking.

"That's enough," he mumbled. "You're taking too much."

As she kept going, he lifted his hands in a last-ditch effort to get her off him, but he was too weak and about to lose consciousness. She didn't need to apply much pressure on his chest to keep him pinned to the floor and stay exactly where he was.

When he stopped struggling, she could hear his heartbeat, and when it slowed down to a crawl, she pulled her fangs out and licked the puncture wounds closed.

If Jade could vomit what she'd taken, she would have done it, but the Kra-ell digestive system didn't allow that. It was too damn efficient.

She could rinse out her mouth, though.

After a quick visit to Valstar's bathroom, she pulled the shirt back on and looked at her watch.

It was only fifteen minutes past midnight.

Tom's people would start scrambling the compound's communications at one forty-five, and only then would Pavel incapacitate the guard downstairs and bring her a set of titanium chains to bind Valstar with.

Regrettably, there was no chance that Valstar would stay down for an hour and a half. His body would regenerate the blood faster than that.

She would have to drain him at least two more times.

"Dear Mother of All Life, please, give me strength to do what I must."

She also needed to light the fire in the trash can to signal Tom that everything was going as planned. Hopefully, Pavel had already incapacitated Boris and got it ready for her.

Marcel

Marcel tried to get comfortable in the so-called command post, which was a beat-up old soviet-era armored personnel carrier that William had filled with so much equipment that there was barely any room for them to sit.

They were parked inside the last tunnel, hidden from the compound's watch towers until it was time to attack.

Bhathian sat up front with the Guardian driving the vehicle, and in the back William, Morris, and Charlie sat in front of their electronic equipment.

He and Sylvia were all the way in the back, crowded in the little space that remained behind William's enormous console, but unlike Roni's mate, who had a job to do, Marcel wasn't sure why Bhathian had stationed him in the command post of the tunnel team.

He had no special task assigned to him.

Bhathian just didn't want him to be in the first wave of Guardians storming the compound because he hadn't had enough practice with the exoskeleton suit. It was bullshit because he had as much practice as Kalugal's men, and they were going in the first wave.

Bottom line, he was there to observe, to keep Sofia updated, and when the active Guardians and Kalugal's men took control of the compound, he was to help with collecting the Kra-ell's tranquilized bodies and taking them somewhere to be locked up.

He was also in charge of the tranquilized tunnel guards, who were bound and gagged in the last truck of the convoy. They would also need to be moved to a secure location once the compound was taken.

By one-thirty in the morning, both teams were at their designated positions, waiting for William to take down the compound's communications.

Onegus's calm voice sounded in Marcel's earpiece. "The countdown starts in fifteen minutes. Last equipment check."

"On it, boss." Marcel heard Yamanu and Bhathian's nearly simultaneous replies.

Bhathian headed the tunnel team, as they called it, and Yamanu headed the river team, which would attack from the hunting grounds' side.

"William?" Onegus asked.

"I'm ready," William said. "I'm checking my equipment."

"Pilots?"

"I'm ready," Charlie said. "I just hope this old bird and the soviet bunker-busting munitions will do the job."

The plan was for the two Russian military drones that Turner's contact procured to launch a simultaneous missile attack, blowing off the gates at both ends of the compound along with sections of the fortified wall flanking them. Both openings needed to be wide enough for roughly forty men in exoskeletons to make it through all at once and get in position in under fifteen seconds.

"The drones will do fine," Morris said. "My concern is not that they won't suffice for the job, but rather that they will prove too powerful and create a crater and a debris field that will make it harder for the teams to get in position within the tight window of time they've got. But that's what we have, so let's hope they will do the job."

"I did what I could with them." William leaned back in his seat. "At least the guiding system is top-notch."

Onegus sounded again. "Is everything ready?"

Morris replied. "Everything is a go on my and Charlie's end. The birds are circling in the ten-mile radius. You give the signal, and the birds will be on target. Missiles are armed, and we will launch both at precisely 2:00 as planned. To all the hotshots listening, you need to stay back and enjoy the fireworks from a safe distance."

Yamanu cackled in Marcel's ears. "I just hope that you remember how to shoot. Did you practice with Parker on his new game console as I told you to? I bet he kicked your ass. The kid can fly these things better than you and Charlie. Hell, I can do a better job than you."

"I can beat both Parker and you blindfolded," Charlie said.

Marcel could hear the muted laughter coming from both teams. Yamanu's teasing was the perfect antidote for the pre-battle jitters everyone was feeling.

They were about to face an enemy none of them had ever fought before, an enemy that was stronger, faster, well trained, and under compulsion to defend the compound at all costs.

He was jerked out of his reverie when Onegus's voice came through again. "It's 1:45, and the signal from Jade is on. Time to flip the switch on the communication disruptor."

"Done," William said. "Communications are down. We are good to go."

"Done as well," Charlie said. "The drones' ETA over the compound is one minute."

As the driver rolled the vehicle down the fourth and last tunnel, Marcel watched the countdown on William's screen.

"We are in range and ready to launch the missiles," Morris announced.

Marcel couldn't help but be impressed by how calm everyone was despite the unknown they were about to face. They had a solid plan, and everyone knew what they were doing, but to quote the Prussian Field Marshal Helmuth von Moltke, no plan of operations extends with any certainty beyond the first encounter with enemy forces.

But then, von Moltke had never met the likes of Turner.

Morris's dry voice broke the stretching silence. "Launching missiles in 3, 2, 1, launch."

Marcel stood up so he could see the impacts on William's split screen, but he should have followed the pilots and William's example and put on goggles. As the missiles hit their targets within a fraction of a second apart, he was momentarily blinded. As his vision cleared, two gaping holes appeared where only seconds before stood massive gates supported by reinforced concrete walls.

Toven

Yamanu whistled in Toven's earpiece. "Man, that missile did the job and then some."

The ground still shook, and they felt the blast quite intensely despite their protective gear, but there was no time to wait for the dust to settle to confirm the damage. They had fifteen seconds to close the distance to where the gate was, enter the compound, and get in position.

The purebloods were amazingly fast, so even if most of them were fast asleep, it wouldn't take them long to grab their weapons and charge forward to defend their turf.

"On my mark," Yamanu said. "Go!"

As the team sprinted full speed ahead, the ground thundered under their heavy exoskeleton suits. To those who were proficient in using them they provided speed in addition to strength and protection, but Toven struggled to keep up.

"We are in position," Bhathian's voice sounded in his earpiece.

"So are we," Yamanu said.

They had to overcome several disadvantages. The purebloods and the hybrids were significantly stronger and faster, and they outnumbered the Guardians and Kalugal's men two to one.

Including the females, there were roughly a hundred and sixty purebloods and hybrids. Based on Jade's assessment, some of the females would stay to protect the children, but most would join the first response warriors and fight just as fiercely as the males to protect the compound.

On top of that, the Kra-ell were intimately familiar with every nook and cranny of the compound, while the Guardians were only familiar with the general layout.

To compensate, the clan had the technology, modern weaponry, a brilliant strategist, and the element of surprise.

Turner's plan was as simple as it was brilliant.

Enter the compound from both ends to force the defenders to split up, and spread out in a wide semicircle formation, so that when the Kra-ell rushed out to meet them, they would have to spread apart as well and, in so doing, would make it easier for the teams to target individually.

If possible, it was better to avoid shooting darts into a cluster and potentially hitting one person twice.

The darts were calibrated to incapacitate a feral animal, which might be too much for the Kra-ell slim frames, but since their bodies had self-repairing capabilities, one dose wouldn't kill them.

Two doses, however, could prove lethal.

During the planning of the attack, a concern had been raised about a tactic that depended on the Kra-ell's disorganized rush to meet their attackers. A smart commander would hold the warriors back to better assess who and what they were facing, so betting on all of them charging ahead was risky, but ultimately, the consensus had been that this was precisely what the Kra-ell defenders would do.

The reasoning was that the Kra-ell were habituated to defer to Igor in everything, and since he was absent and so were his second- and third-in-command, they wouldn't know what to do and would react instinctively rather than strategically. In addition, Igor's compulsion would drive them to defend the compound at all costs without regard for their own well-being, and that would spur them into mindless action as well.

As the team spread out in a semicircle, Yamanu stretched out an arm and motioned for Toven to get behind him, but Toven ignored the command and stood beside the Head Guardian.

It didn't take long for the defenders to show up.

No more than ten seconds passed before a group of fierce-looking warriors galloped toward them at breakneck speed. Surprisingly, not all were armed with swords as they had expected. He could clearly see Kalashnikovs in the hands of several warriors. From a distance, he couldn't tell whether they were male or female, not because of the protective goggles he wore that made everything seem even darker, but because there wasn't much difference. They were all tall, slim, and had long dark hair. As they got closer and their faces became clearer, he identified at least two females among them.

"Grenade launchers at the ready," Yamanu commanded.

Bhathian's command echoed in Toven's ears.

"Fire," Yamanu barked.

Twenty grenade launchers discharged at once.

William's modified stun grenades exploded in a blinding light and deafening boom that would have damaged human eyes and ears permanently, but on the Kra-ell the effect would last only a few seconds.

The distance, along with the exoskeleton suits, the goggles, and the specialty earpieces that were fitted with active noise-cancelling circuitry, protected the teams, but even with all that, Toven felt the impact of those grenades as if he had been punched in the gut and hit over the head.

As one, the advancing Kra-ell stopped as if hit by a wall. Disoriented and off balance, they became perfect stationary targets.

"Fire at will," Yamanu commanded.

Jade

As soon as the twin explosions erupted, Pavel burst into Valstar's quarters with a bunch of chains looped over one arm and two swords strapped over his hips, one on each side.

"You did it." He grinned at Jade before baring his fangs at Valstar. "The bastard sentenced me to a whipping because I didn't respond with a *yes, sir,* fast enough." He kicked the male in the gut. "He considered it disrespectful."

The bastard was still too weak from blood loss to react.

Was it an act? Or did Pavel really hate Valstar that vehemently?

Hopefully, it was the latter. Jade had no choice but to leave the boy in charge of guarding Igor's second, and she wasn't too happy about trusting Tom's compulsion to make Pavel obey her commands to the letter.

Taking the chains from him, she bound Valstar, locked the chains, and put the key in her pocket. "Watch him." She looked around the room for something to use as a gag. "Don't move. Don't even go to the bathroom. If Valstar somehow gets free, he will detonate the explosives and kill all of us." She pulled Valstar's underwear from his discarded pants and stuffed them into his mouth. "I need something to tape it with."

She walked into his office and started opening drawers. Finding a roll of masking tape, she returned to the bedroom, tore off a large piece, and wrapped it around Valstar's head twice.

"Don't remove the gag even if he starts choking on it. I don't know how strong of a compeller he is."

"Don't worry." Pavel handed her one of the swords and a dagger with its sheath that he'd hidden inside his shirt. "What happened here?" He pointed at the glass.

"I don't have time to stand here and chat." She strapped the sword onto her hip, and the knife went inside her waistband. "I have some killing to do."

"Don't kill my father," Pavel surprised her by saying. "He's not a bad guy."

She wasn't sure about that. He was one of Igor's inner circle cronies, but he hadn't been one of the murderers of her tribe, so she had no beef with him.

"I won't. He did nothing to my people. But once the other females are free of Igor's compulsion, it's out of my hands. He might have killed their families."

Pavel nodded, dragged a chair closer to where Valstar was on the floor but had the presence of mind to keep out of reach of the unconscious male, and sat down.

She cast one last glance at the murderer lying on the floor and walked out.

Not killing him had been one of the hardest things she'd ever had to do.

No one deserved to die by her hand more than Valstar, but they needed him alive to catch Igor, and that was more important than her impatience to exact vengeance. Catching Igor was crucial.

Still, it might be a mistake to let Valstar live even for a few more hours.

As the human saying went, a bird in the hand was worth two in the bush, and one kill was better than none.

But it wasn't just about revenge.

If Igor got a whiff of anything being amiss in the compound and ran, her people would never be safe. He would find a way to rebuild his force. By locating the other pods and compelling the survivors to serve him or, if he didn't know where the others were or he knew and they were all dead, by renewing his breeding program and producing as many hybrids as he could until he had a force large enough to come after his former subjects.

Marcel

The scenes unfolding on the screens in front of Marcel were mesmerizing.

The Kra-ell charged as predicted, splitting their force to deal with the invaders on both sides.

The Guardians and Kalugal's men must have seemed like aliens from a nightmarish sci-fi movie with their imposing exoskeleton suits and weaponry.

It was a testament to the Kra-ell's courage and ferocity that they hadn't even paused before charging the invaders. Or maybe it was Igor's compulsion at work.

Morris and Charlie guided a couple of small surveillance drones equipped with infrared cameras over the main building of the compound, looking for potential snipers or for other warriors lying in wait for any who might make it through the main body of defenders.

He spotted two splinter groups that were stealthily approaching their teams' flanks. They melted into the night and moved like animals on a hunt, but they were no match for the infrared cameras of the night-vision drones.

"Over there." Marcel pointed at them on Morris's screen.

"I see them," the pilot said. "We need the big bird back."

"Mine is on the way," Charlie said.

Marcel wondered how the two managed to fly two drones each. Their computer screens split between the view from the small surveillance drone and the large military one. It required amazing coordination.

"Do we fire at them or just around them?" Morris asked. "Those drones are not equipped with tranquilizer bullets."

"Aim at the ground around them to distract them," Onegus said over the com. "The Guardians are aware of their approach, and they need them distracted. Make sure to aim behind the Kra-ell, so you don't hit any of ours."

"Roger that," Morris said as he brought his drone right above the Kra-ell's heads.

"I got the group approaching Yamanu's team," Charlie murmured.

"Fire at will," Onegus commanded.

A staccato of rapid fire from the anti-aircraft gun on board each of the drones lasted for all of twenty seconds, but that was all the distraction the Guardians needed.

Once the dust settled, four shadowy figures twitched on the ground in one location and six in the other.

The tranquilizer worked quickly, paralyzing them almost immediately, but it took up to several minutes for the drug to knock them out completely.

The Guardians didn't wait, though. Pulling titanium cuffs from the pockets of their suits, they bound the Kra-ell's wrists and ankles and connected the two with a chain in the back. They weren't taking any chances. For now, it didn't matter whether they were purebloods or hybrids. They were all bound in the same way. Later, when it was time for Toven to work on their minds, they would be separated into two groups.

Transfixed by the action on the video feed, Marcel might have missed the drama unfolding on the other side of the courtyard if not for Morris's whistle.

"Look at her fight." He pointed to where two Kra-ell were engaged in a fierce sword battle.

A male and a female were going at each other with vicious stabs, and watching their deadly dance was mesmerizing.

"Is that Jade?" William asked.

"It's either Jade or Kagra," Marcel murmured. "They are both free of Igor's compulsion and eager to get the revenge they've been craving for over two decades."

William let out a breath. "I wonder if the older kids will join the fight. Jade's daughter is only sixteen. I hope she's not out there while her mother is on a killing spree."

Jade

Down in the courtyard, Jade saw several warriors lurking in the shadows, the lack of collars identifying them from afar as Igor's lackeys.

Most of the others must have rushed toward the attacking forces, and she wondered what was on the minds of the purebloods hiding in the shadows. Did they plan to take the invaders from their flanks?

As if that would do anything to the suits those warriors were wearing.

It was an exercise in futility.

That surprised her. She hadn't thought they would have the presence of mind to devise a strategy without Igor and Valstar directing them.

But that was the invaders' worry. Or rather, the liberators.

She shouldn't think of them as invaders, or she might say that to her people who needed to believe they were being freed.

But that was a worry for later.

Right now, she had murderers to kill and revenge to exact.

Pretending to join their efforts, she slunk behind Artuom and slit his throat. He did not deserve an honorable death, and she had no qualms about robbing him of the privilege of a duel.

Besides, his buddies were near, and she couldn't take on all of them at once.

The scent of his blood was overpowering, but that was only because she was right behind him. The compound was saturated with residue from the explosions, and the dust was still heavy in the air.

Nevertheless, the Kra-ell senses were designed to follow the smell of blood, and as Distor turned around and sniffed, Jade pressed herself against the building's wall, cursing silently that she hadn't had time to drag Artuom's body further into the shadows. He was sprawled on the ground, his legs illuminated by the moonlight, and his gaping neck bleeding profusely.

Lucky for her, right then a large drone passed overhead, distracting Distor momentarily, but as she was about to leap at him, Kagra sprung out of the shadows and slit his throat without making a sound. She lowered him gently to the ground and smiled at Jade.

She saluted her second and headed toward the pure-bloods' living quarters. The place seemed deserted, but she knew they were hiding, and she wanted to check on Drova. She was only sixteen, so she should be hiding with the other kids, but she might have done something stupid and gone out to fight.

"What's going on out there?" Vombad stepped out from behind a column.

There was a sword in his hand, and a gun was tucked into his belt. Was he there to defend the children? Or was he just hiding and leaving the work of defending the compound to others?

He was near the top of her kill list, but she wouldn't do that here where the children could see it. They were Kra-ell, but they were still soft-hearted, and there was no need to show them the cruelties of life just yet.

"Isn't it obvious? We are under attack. Why are you here instead of out there?"

"I could ask you the same question."

She looked down her nose at him. "I'm checking up on the children."

"They are safe in the basement, and several females are guarding them."

They weren't safe, and he knew it. If Igor could activate the explosives, they would all be dead.

"Then my question still stands. Why are you here?" She walked out the door, hoping he would follow.

When he did, she decided that there was still a smidgen of honor left in his body, which earned him an honorable death in a duel.

When they were at the edge of the courtyard, Jade turned around. "I'm no longer restricted by Igor's compulsion, and I've waited for over two decades for the day I'll get to avenge my sons and my males." She unsheathed her sword. "Make your peace with the Mother, though I don't think it will save you from spending eternity in the valley of the shamed."

Looking amused, he pulled out his sword. "When I kill the traitor who betrayed us to our enemies, I'll be guaranteed a place in the fields of the brave."

He veered to the right and swung his sword with incredible force toward her neck. Anticipating the move, she swiveled away while swiping the sword at his calf, but he jumped out of the way, and the cut she inflicted was only superficial.

Baring his fangs, he growled and pressed on, with a dagger appearing in his left hand. When she parried his sword's swing, he brought his knife in an uppercut motion in an attempt to gut her.

Jade somersaulted backward, landing on her feet long before he closed the distance between them, and threw her dagger at him. He shifted, and it was embedded in his shoulder instead of hitting him in his heart.

His fangs bared, and his eyes fully red, he yanked the dagger out of his shoulder and threw it at her.

His aim was messy, probably because of the wound to his shoulder, and it barely grazed her arm, cutting through her shirt and scraping her skin.

With the dagger lost in the dirt she was left with the sword only, but that was enough to finish him.

Vombad was bleeding from his calf and shoulder, while she had only suffered a scratch.

Advancing in a flurry of blade motion in order to draw his attention to the sword, she got in range and kicked his injured calf with the force of her momentum.

As his leg buckled, he instinctively reached with one hand to break his fall and lifted his sword to protect his head.

She moved sideways, and rather than going for the obvious, she sliced down at the hand holding the sword.

He lost his hold, falling on his ass.

It should have been easy for her to finish him right then, but he wasn't as easily defeated as she'd hoped.

Moving faster than a viper, he twisted and caught his sword with the other hand, immediately shooting forward and thrusting it where she'd been just a split second ago, but she was right behind him.

Again, it would have been easy to thrust her sword into his back, but then she wouldn't see his eyes as she delivered the death blow, and that wouldn't be satisfying enough.

She'd waited a very long time for this moment and wasn't willing to compromise.

Instead, she delivered a roundhouse kick to the back of his head.

Vombad was built like a brick wall, but the loss of blood and the mighty kick to the head were clearly taking a toll, and he fell to his knees.

He tried to push back up, but his legs refused to accept the load. He leveled his eyes at her. A look of pure hate and evil.

She knew that he was still dangerous, even on his knees, and it would have been foolish of her to underestimate him.

But he'd already lost, and he knew it.

Jade smiled. Bless the Mother for the strength she'd gifted her with.

Vombad parried her swings, and for a few brief moments, Jade toyed with him, letting him believe that he was holding her back. But when the glimmer of hope appeared in his eyes, she delivered a hard blow to his sword hand, forcing him to let go.

Standing tall in front of the murderer of her people, she waited for him to do the honorable thing and offer her his throat, but in his heart Vombad was a coward, and he instinctively lifted his hands to defend his head and his neck.

"You were always a worthless coward, Vombad." She swatted away his defending hand with her sword and delivered the killing blow.

Kian

Kian had watched the mission unfold through the video feed from the drones, but once the drones were no longer needed and the battle continued on the ground, he had to rely on listening to the com.

Next to him, Onegus was talking to Yamanu, getting an update.

"When all was said and done, there was really no fighting to speak of," Yamanu said. "The tranquilizer darts did what they were supposed to, but some of the Kra-ell could fight off the effects for longer than we'd expected, so we had to knock them over the head. After that we bound them with the titanium cuffs and brought them down to the basement of the office building. The guys were squeamish about doing that to the females, but we had no choice. They fight as viciously as the males. I'm proud to report that we managed not to kill anyone, not even those we had to fight after we dispatched the first wave of defenders. The only casualties the Kra-ell suffered were the work of Jade and Kagra. They dispatched six of Igor's inner circle males."

"What about Valstar?" Onegus asked.

"She made good on her promise and didn't kill him. She left the guard who Toven released from Igor's compulsion to watch him while she went on her killing spree."

"How is Toven doing?" Kian asked.

"Toven was never in real danger, and for the most part, he behaved. He refused to stand behind me when the Kra-ell attacked, but with the suit on, the few bullets they managed to discharge before we blinded them with grenades just bounced off him."

"I'm glad you convinced him to wear it."

Yamanu chuckled. "I told him that he would have to stay in the amphibian and wait for us to secure the compound, and then I added a few gruesome descriptions of what the Kra-ell could do to him, and that sealed the deal. Toven agreed to wear the suit, Bhathian lost the bet, and now he owes me a case of Snake Venom."

"Did he start freeing the people from Igor's compulsion?"

"Not yet. We are waiting for Mia and Sofia to arrive. We didn't approach the humans yet, either. We figured it would be better if she did it."

"Good thinking."

Yamanu chuckled. "I love these damn suits. They are hot, cumbersome, and they get stinky after wearing them for over an hour, but none of ours has suffered even a scratch."

Kian smiled, a knot in his stomach easing. "I consider those suits the best money we've spent."

"Jade's second got injured pretty badly, though. One of her designated victims almost finished her."

"I heard," Kian said. "How is she doing?"

"She'll live. Merlin patched her up. Several purebloods and hybrids are in the infirmary as well."

"How did they get hurt?"

"We ran out of darts after shooting the first wave of defenders. We had to either shoot or quash the rest. The bastards kept fighting until they were knocked out."

"They didn't have a choice," Kian said. "It was the compulsion."

On his other side, Turner shook his head. "It's not just the compulsion. It's their tradition. They fight to the death."

"Wasn't that outlawed?" Onegus asked.

Turner shrugged. "What we know, we've learned from Emmett, Vrog, and Aliya, who repeated what they were told. I would love to hear what Jade promised to tell Toven. When that conversation starts, I want to be part of it, and I don't care what time it is."

"Same here," Kian said. "It's not that I don't trust Toven to tell us everything, but like Turner, I prefer to hear it as it is told by Jade."

"I'll let Toven know that you asked that. Are our four compellers ready to assist him?"

"They are all on standby," Onegus said.

Kian turned to the chief. "Can you put everyone on the com? I want to thank them for a job well done."

Onegus nodded. "Go ahead."

"Great job, everyone," Kian said. "You all did your part admirably. I want to thank Kalugal's men for volunteering their help, and special thanks to Toven and Mia, who've agreed to undertake the monumental task of freeing the minds of everyone in Jade's compound. We still have a long night ahead of us, and Igor is still out there. Hopefully, he will be apprehended when he returns to the compound and brought to justice by those he enslaved and whose families he slaughtered."

Toven

By the time the van with Mia and Sofia arrived at the compound, the Guardians had removed the bodies of those killed. There hadn't been many; five purebloods had died at Jade and Kagra's hands, and the sixth had been dispatched by Kalugal's lieutenant when he'd saved Kagra from the male.

There were several injuries, though, with Kagra's being the most severe.

She and Jade had fought with swords, probably because those were the only weapons they'd had access to, and the last pureblood Kagra had taken on dealt her a blow that would have been fatal to a human. He was about to finish the job when Kalugal's lieutenant leaped and smashed his exoskeleton's reinforced fist into the male's head, saving her life and killing the pureblood.

Toven hadn't seen the event and had only been told about it after the guy had brought the injured female to the compound's clinic.

With everyone wearing identical suits, it was impossible to distinguish who was who. Only Bhathian and Yamanu wore a colorful band around their arm that identified them as Head Guardians.

When the van came to a stop next to him, Sofia opened the side passenger door, waved at him, and then bolted toward the human section of the compound or maybe to search for Marcel.

Mia leaned forward and smiled. "Hello, my love. I'm glad to see that you are really unharmed."

"Did you doubt it when I told you I was fine?"

"I did," she admitted. "You sounded off."

"I called you as soon as the compound was secured, and there was still a lot to do. I was in a bit of a rush." He pulled her wheelchair from the back and unfolded it.

Lifting her into his arms, he hugged her to his chest for several long moments before lowering her to the chair.

She smiled up at him. "You hugged me as if you missed me terribly."

"Of course, I missed you." He crouched next to her chair. "I'm just glad that it's over. I've never been fond of battles."

"Who is?"

"You'd be surprised." He turned to look at the Guardians, who were still patrolling the grounds in their exoskeletons.

Jade had assured them that all the purebloods and hybrids were accounted for, but they didn't want to take any chances.

Toven had removed his suit as soon as he had deemed it safe.

Mia put her hand on his shoulder. "Let's get to the compulsion part. The faster we have everyone compelled, the sooner William can stop scrambling the compound's communications. Where is Igor's second? He's the first on the list, right?"

"He's on the second floor of the office building. The Guardians have him contained."

She turned her chair toward the building. "Wasn't that guard you compelled at the tunnel entrance in charge of that?"

"He was until the Guardians took over. We don't know where Pavel stands yet. He helped Jade because I compelled him to obey her. I don't know if he would have done it of his own free will."

They met Jade in the lobby of the office building. "How do you want to do it?" she asked. "Do you want them brought to you individually or in groups?"

All the Kra-ell were locked in the office building's basement, so if they set up shop in one of the offices on the first floor, it wouldn't take long to bring them up.

"You can bring three at a time. But first, let's take care of Valstar."

She grimaced. "You have no idea what I had to endure to keep him alive. His vile blood is souring my digestive system."

"It was unavoidable."

"I know." She let out a breath. "After Valstar, I'll bring up my daughter. She's terrified and won't calm down no matter what I say to her. When you free her from Igor's compulsion, can you do something to ease her?"

"I'm not a therapist, but I'll do my best."

"Thank you." She shifted her eyes to Mia. "They are all terrified. Even those who pretend to be brave. I know we are pressed for time, but if you can say a few encouraging words to help them calm down, it would make my job easier. Igor has them all under his compulsion, even the children, except for the very young ones."

"What are you planning to do?" Mia asked.

"Assemble the females of my former tribe and get them to help me sort this place out."

"How is Kagra doing?" Toven asked.

"Your doctor assures me that she will live."

Sofia

"Sofia! Wait up!" She heard Marcel calling behind her and slowed down.

He caught up to her, snagged her from behind, and twirled her in a circle. "Everyone you care for is safe."

"I know." She wiggled out of his arms. "You told me." She'd been so relieved when he'd called her that she'd felt faint. "But they must be terrified. Did anyone talk to them?"

"I did, but they wouldn't open the doors. I yelled and told them that we were liberating them, but no one answered."

"Were you still wearing your exoskeleton suit?"

"I took it off, but since no one saw me anyway, that wasn't very helpful."

When they reached the group of buildings that housed the humans, she first noticed that all the shutters were closed, and no light was coming out.

Her gut squeezed with anxiety. "I hope they are just holed up and that nothing happened to them. What if the purebloods had orders to kill the humans if there was an invasion?"

Marcel shook his head. "Just go, knock on your father's door, and tell him it's you."

"Yeah. You're right." She tried to open the front door of the building. "It's locked."

"Let me try." He did, but the door was barricaded on the other side. "I'll ask a Guardian still wearing the exoskeleton to open the way for us."

"Hold on." She took a couple of steps back, cupped her hands on the sides of her mouth, and yelled, "Helmi! It's me, Sofia. These people are with me. Open up so I can explain!"

"That's her room." She pointed. "She should have heard me."

"Maybe she can't see you." Marcel pulled out his phone, activated the flashlight, and shone it at her face.

The shutter on the second floor moved a fraction of an inch and then banged open.

"It is you!" Helmi pushed her head out. "Who's the guy?"

"That's my fiancé, Marcel. He and his people came to free us from the Kra-ell."

"How?"

"It's a long story, and I don't want to keep shouting. Where is my father?"

"With my mom and Isla. Do you know if Tomos is okay?"

Sofia turned to Marcel. "Tomos is her hybrid boyfriend. Did any of the hybrids get hurt?"

"None of the hybrids died," Marcel said loudly so Helmi could hear him. "Some are injured and are being taken care of in the infirmary, but only Kagra is seriously hurt. The other injuries are not life-threatening, and I don't know if your boyfriend is one of the injured."

"Can I go to the infirmary?"

"Sure."

She leaned out the window and looked around. "Where are the aliens?"

Marcel lifted his hand. "Here. I'm one of them. What you saw were protective exoskeleton suits that made us stronger than the Kra-ell."

"Oh." Helmi smiled sheepishly. "So you're human. Is it safe outside?"

Sofia was glad that Helmi followed her statement with a question, so she didn't need to answer it. This wasn't the time to explain about immortals and gods and how they were related to the Kra-ell. They needed to get all the humans ready for Toven, so he could release them from Igor's compulsion.

Marcel nodded. "We have the compound secure, and all the Kra-ell are either in the infirmary or the basement of the office building."

Helmi's eyes widened. "Including the kids?"

"We figured they would feel safer with their mothers."

"Let me talk to the others." Helmi disappeared.

Nearly fifteen minutes passed before Sofia heard movement on the other side of the door and then dragging sounds as things were moved to clear the way.

When the door finally opened, and her father stepped out, she flew at him with her arms outstretched.

"Sofia." He crushed her to him. "I was so worried."

"I was worried too."

When he let go of her, she turned to look at Marcel. "Marcel, this is my father, Jarmo. Dad, this is Marcel, my fiancé."

Her father gave Marcel a brief once-over before offering him his hand. "So those are your people, the ones dressed like aliens."

"Yes. We came to free you from Igor's tyranny."

Jarmo tilted his head. "And replace it with what?"

"We are not sure yet," Marcel said. "It was all done in a rush."

"Can we go inside?" Sofia asked.

Her father took a step back and motioned for them to enter.

Marcel

The only thing Sofia had inherited from Jarmo was her blue eyes. He was balding, but what remained of his hair that hadn't turned gray was blond.

He led them to a communal living room with several worn-out couches, armchairs, and two round tables, one holding a chess set and the other a deck of cards.

As they sat down, wide-eyed people started to drift in.

"Do you speak Russian?" Jarmo asked Marcel.

"I understand some if it's spoken slowly, but I can't speak it."

Jarmo nodded. "You probably don't speak Finnish either, right?"

Marcel shook his head.

"Then we will speak English, but also slowly. Many of us don't know it." He smiled at Sofia. "You can translate. Yes?"

"Of course." She motioned for a plump, rosy-cheeked woman to come closer. "This is my aunt Hannele, Helmi's mother. And that's Isla, my other aunt."

The three siblings looked a lot alike. They were also close in age, late fifties or early sixties.

"Hello." Isla dipped her head and offered him her hand.

"Nice to meet you. I'm Marcel, Sofia's fiancé."

Smiling shyly, she turned to Sofia. "*Chto takoye fiancé?*"

"*Zhenihk.*" Sofia took his hand as she translated.

"*Kongra.*" Isla smiled brightly. "*Ohn krasavchik.*"

"She says that you are handsome."

He knew enough Russian to understand that. "Thank you."

Helmi entered the living room with a coat draped over her arm. "I'm going to look for Tomos." She gave Marcel a small wave. "I'll come back later."

He gave her the thumbs up.

Other people came in and took seats wherever they found them, but Jarmo didn't introduce any more of them.

"I know you are all under Igor's compulsion," Marcel said. "And you can't say anything bad about him or leave this place if you want to. This ends today. We brought a powerful compeller who will free you from Igor's compulsion. He has already freed Sofia, Jade, Kagra, and Pavel, and he's freeing more people as we speak. By morning, everyone in this compound will be able to speak freely and decide on the future they want to pursue."

"Where is Igor?" Jarmo asked.

"He's not here. But when he returns, we will be waiting for him, and he will be brought to justice. You might not be aware of it, but he committed heinous crimes against his people. He killed the males of Jade's tribe, enslaved the females, and he compelled them to keep silent about what happened to them. He did the same thing to other Kra-ell tribes."

Jarmo didn't look surprised. "I was born in this compound and saw those females when they were brought in. I knew something terrible had happened to them."

Marcel waited for Sofia to translate, and several of the older ones nodded when she was done.

Evidently, Jarmo wasn't the only one who had noticed.

"Who will lead in Igor's place?" Jarmo asked.

"As I said, it will need to be decided in a vote. Will Jade be an acceptable leader?"

Jarmo shrugged. "I don't know if she'll be better. She's good to the children but has no respect for adults."

When Sofia translated, Isla huffed a breath and said something too fast for him to follow.

"My aunt says that the Kra-ell are all the same and that one is not better than the others, but the people here don't have anyone on the outside, and they wouldn't know what to do and how to provide for themselves."

Her other aunt added to her sister's assessment, and he caught a few words here and there, but not enough to understand what she was saying.

Sofia turned to him. "Hannele says they can be happy here if we take the Kra-ell away. They can grow crops and tend to the animals. That's what they were doing anyway, and it's enough to put food on the table for the humans living here. They will need to find a way to pay for the other things they need like clothing and other necessities." She leaned closer and smiled. "I don't think my aunt realizes how much more goes into running a place like this."

"We will help you figure it out," Marcel said. "I'm not the boss of this operation, and I'm not making the decisions. I'm here to help you get organized so you are ready when our compeller comes to free you. As I said, we need everyone to be freed of Igor's compulsion by morning."

"What do we need to do?" Jarmo asked.

"Make sure that everyone is awake and ready in about two hours."

Jade

It was morning when Tom and Mia finished with the last of the humans, and William, their tech guy, had removed all the collars. Valstar had provided the key, so the process should have been easy, but Jade had still experienced a few anxious moments when the damn thing hadn't opened as smoothly as it was supposed to. She'd volunteered to go first, and after William had figured out how to maneuver the tricky locking mechanism, he'd had an easier time with the others.

Turned out that the collars contained location trackers, explosives, and a trigger mechanism that could be activated remotely, but as she'd suspected, they had no listening capabilities.

Jade was exhausted, but she'd promised Tom a story, and she never went back on her word, so she'd dragged herself to the human quarters and sat across from him.

Tom's mate lay on the couch with her head resting on his thigh, and a blanket spread over her child-sized body. She was so petite that she would still be small even after her legs grew back.

Jade was about to thank Tom for all the work he had done, but then the Head Guardian with the pale blue eyes and long hair walked in and plopped tiredly on one of the couches.

"We blocked the gates with the vehicles," the Guardian said. "And we put Kra-ell guards at the entrances to the tunnels. We have snipers hiding in the trees and a team inside each tunnel. We are ready for Igor."

He was one of the two Head Guardians who had introduced themselves to her as Bhathian and Yamanu, but she'd forgotten who was who. The other one was a mountain of a man, with muscles the size of a professional bodybuilder, and he was just as cordial as this one, but not as easy with his smiles.

"What about the cameras?" Jade asked.

"All the camera feeds are broadcasting prerecorded stuff on a three-hour loop. All Igor will see are empty tunnels and empty corridors. The same goes for his and Valstar's offices. We also checked the entire compound for hidden cameras and listening devices."

"Did you find any?"

The Guardian nodded. "Quite a few. They are taken care of as well. We need to thank Igor for being paranoid and not allowing anyone to have cell phones in the compound. We verified that all the phones were locked in the safe in Valstar's office, and we searched everyone and all the rooms to ensure no one was hiding a communication device. We've left nothing to chance." He flashed Tom a teasing smile. "The only wild cards are the guards you compelled. How good is your compulsion? Are they going to follow the script we gave them?"

Tom leaned back and sighed. "I was still in good form when I compelled the purebloods and the hybrids we needed for the tunnels, so you have nothing to worry about them singing the tune I taught them. I wasn't as good with the others, but since all I had to do was remove Igor's compulsion, and our other compellers did the rest, it's all good. Regrettably, Igor didn't have a contingency in place in the event of disruption in the compound's communications. Getting someone to call him from one of the surrounding villages would have bought us more time, and we might have learned when he was planning to return."

When it seemed like the two were done talking, Jade dipped her head at Tom. "Thank you for what you did for us. You and Mia and your warriors worked hard to save my people, and you made a great effort not to harm anyone. You've exceeded all of my expectations, and you have my eternal gratitude."

"You're welcome," Tom said. "How is Kagra doing?"

"She's asleep. Your doctor assured me that she's healing at a good pace for a Kra-ell." Jade chuckled. "He was so excited about getting a peek at her digestive system. He said that he understands now why our waists are so slim. Our stomachs are tiny, and our intestines are much shorter and narrower than that of immortals and humans because we live on a liquid diet. I told him that he could have just asked me, and I would have explained, and he said that it was not the same as getting to see the insides of Kagra's gut."

"Doctors are all weird," the Guardian said. "And Merlin is weirder than most."

Tom smiled. "I like Merlin. He's unconventional."

Jade didn't have any experience with human doctors, so she had nothing to add to his comment. "I'm ready to deliver my end of the bargain." She glanced at Mia. "Do you want to wake your mate up?"

He smoothed his hand over Mia's short black hair. "I'll tell her everything later. She's exhausted."

"Kian and Turner asked to listen in," Yamanu said. "You can put them on a video call." He turned to Jade. "Is it okay with you?"

"Why wouldn't it be? I promised Tom to tell him the history of his people, and he can do with it whatever he pleases."

The guy shrugged his broad shoulders. "Some people get shy when the camera is on them."

She narrowed her eyes at him. "Your communication is secure, correct? Because this information should never reach the humans."

Tom chuckled. "We are in their quarters."

She waved a dismissive hand. "You can cast a silencing bubble around us, can't you?"

"Yamanu can do that. I'm too tired to even think."

The Guardian nodded. "It would be my pleasure. But first, I'll call Kian."

As he placed the call, Sofia came down the stairs with her immortal boyfriend. "Can we join you? Or is it a secret meeting?"

"What I'm about to tell Tom is information that I didn't even share with my daughter, but when I promised him the story, I failed to make it contingent upon him keeping it a secret. It's up to Tom what he wants to do with it." Jade looked at him. "Do you have a problem with that?"

"The only problem I have is keeping my eyes open. Yamanu will shroud us so no one else can listen in, and I'll make sure that Sofia keeps what she hears to herself."

"Would you like some coffee?" Sofia asked.

"That would be great."

She turned to Jade. "What about you?"

Jade nodded. "Black with nothing added."

"I know." Sofia pushed to her feet. "Purebloods can't tolerate dairy or sugar."

"I'll help you." Her boyfriend followed her to the kitchen.

Jade shook her head. "After I fulfill my promise, I want to hear how Veskar got to know a god, how he got a god to help him, and how Sofia ended up with an immortal boyfriend."

Yamanu chuckled. "We will be here all day and all night."

"When Igor walks into the trap we set up for him, I'll take a break to fulfill the last part of my revenge. Other than that, I'm at your disposal."

Toven

"Before I begin," Jade said. "I want to warn you that the history I know is what I was told." She put her coffee cup down on the table. "I suspect that a lot of it is not true. As you know, history is written by the victors, and most of the time, it was the gods." She snorted. "You probably think that humans called you that because they were awed by your powers, but that's the name you gave yourselves. In the gods' language, the name for your people means 'we are gods.' I guess the ability to manipulate genetics and create new species at a whim made you think that you are entitled to that designation."

Toven shrugged. "In a way, it makes sense. We might not be the creators of all life, but we are the creators of some life."

Jade regarded him with an amused smile. "That can also be said about procreation, which would make every living creature a god."

He didn't necessarily disagree with that observation, but it wasn't entirely true, and he didn't want her to think that she had won the argument. "That's multiplying what was already created. It's not creating something new."

"What do you call hybrids, then? They are something new."

Yamanu lifted his hand. "Let's agree to disagree on the definition of creating life. That argument alone will take all day. Please, continue the story."

Jade nodded. "We shall revisit that some other time. Many millions of Earth years ago, before the gods had interstellar travel capability, they mastered genetic manipulation. Their history claims that they had always been the way they were and that they used their superior genetic material to create the Kra-ell. It was supposedly their first attempt at creating intelligent life by enhancing an animal that was already closely related to them genetically. But after my years on Earth, I began to question that story."

"Why?" Sofia asked. "It makes sense. They did the same thing with humans."

"The gods created humans for the same reason they supposedly created the Kra-ell. They needed workers to do all the things that the gods considered beneath them. They didn't want to get their hands dirty."

"What do you believe is the real story?" Toven lifted his coffee cup, but there wasn't much left.

"I'll make more." Sofia rose to her feet.

Jade took a small sip from her coffee and put the cup back down. "I think that the gods were originally like the Kra-ell, or very similar, and that they manipulated their genes to become better." She winced. "Or what they considered superior."

"What makes you think that?" Marcel asked.

"The Kra-ell didn't have written history per se. We had myths and legends, and one of them told a different story, but I thought it was just a myth, our way to aggrandize our kind. The legend was that a long time ago, Jombil, who is like the god Loki of Nordic folklore, offered the same deal to the Kra-ell queen and the gods' king. According to the legend, the king accepted the offer, but our queen rejected it because the price Jombil demanded was too steep. It meant changing our entire way of life and giving up our traditions, and that was an insult to the Mother of All Life who had created us."

"What did Jombil demand?" Toven asked.

"Basically, everything that gave us an advantage over the gods in exchange for every advantage they had over us. We have speed and strength, and we hunt and drink blood. They have eternal life, but what is the point of living forever when they hide like Veskars in underground dwellings and eat like scavengers? I prefer to live out my lifespan serving the Mother, and after I die, spending eternity in the fields of the brave."

Toven wouldn't have traded places with her, but she was right about the myth hinting at a different story than the one recorded by the gods.

"Do the gods and the Kra-ell come from the same planet?" Marcel asked.

Jade nodded. "That was another falsity that the gods propagated. They claimed that the original animal they used to create the Kra-ell came from a neighboring planet. The gods didn't have interstellar travel capabilities back then, but they had already mastered interplanetary travel."

Toven lifted a brow. "Was there an animal like that on the neighboring planet?"

"There was," she admitted. "But that doesn't mean that the gods used it to create us. Both our kinds could have that animal as a distant relative. Anyway, they used the explanation to treat us as a subclass of beings the same way they later did with humans and many other species. They claimed that they created the Kra-ell to be their slaves. The Kra-ell did everything for the gods. They planted and harvested, worked in their factories, cleaned their homes, and did everything else that the gods deemed beneath them."

Toven frowned. "How did the Kra-ell become slaves in the first place? If the gods claim that they created them for that purpose is true, then it's self-explanatory. But if we give credence to your legend, you started out on equal footing with the gods. You had your own queen."

Jade smiled. "The legend says that Jombil was offended by the queen's refusal of his offer, and he punished the Kra-ell. A terrible disease infected all the animals that used to be their source of blood. Most of the animals died, and those that didn't were too sickly to take blood from. The gods offered their help, but it came with a price. They had the knowhow and the means to manufacture synthetic blood that could sustain us, but we had to pay for our food with labor, and that's how the Kra-ell slavery started."

Kian

Kian suspected that the gods had something to do with the disease that targeted the animals. They were experts in genetic manipulation, so creating a virus that would selectively affect just the larger hot-blooded animals that the Kra-ell fed on shouldn't have been much of a challenge, and that was how they had secured a slave workforce.

Nasty.

The gods who had been sent to Earth had obviously lacked that ability. Otherwise, they wouldn't have sent a flood to cull the spread of humans. They would have sent a virus.

The angle at which Yamanu's phone was recording the conversation provided him a good view of Jade and Toven, the coffee table, and Yamanu's huge feet. The others were not on the screen.

His phone had the camera off and was muted, so he and Turner could talk while listening to Jade's story.

"Did the animals ever recover?" Sofia asked as she bent over to refill Toven's cup with fresh coffee.

"Eventually, they did." Jade lifted the cup for Sofia to pour into. "But it took a very long time for the animal population to sufficiently replenish its numbers to feed the Kra-ell population, especially since that population had nearly doubled in size since the gods took over their lives. There were no more tribal wars, and the gods didn't permit duels to the death except on special holidays, so there was nothing to cull the male population. The gods were happy to accommodate the additional workforce, and the growing disparity between males and females didn't bother them.

"On the contrary, they used it to get better control over the males. It's also possible that the gods did something to alter our genetics, so we produced many more males than females and blamed it on nature. At that stage in our history, we were under their complete control."

"Whose history is that?" Toven asked. "I assume that the gods would try to put a more positive spin on these events and portray themselves as the benevolent saviors of the Kra-ell."

Jade cast him a smile. "You are absolutely right. My story might have led you to believe that it all happened during one lifetime, but it spans hundreds of thousands of years. You won't find this version in their recorded history, but at some point the Kra-ell started recording their own history, and the gods who were opposed to slavery recorded their opinions as well. Not that I got to read any of them, but I was told that they still exist but are difficult to access."

"Like the Vatican documents?" Sofia asked.

"Not exactly," Jade said. "Even though the gods were ruled by a king, they pretended to be a democratic society, and things got voted on by an elected council. But they had a way of dealing with those who disagreed with the majority. Those rebel recordings were deemed dangerous propaganda threatening the peaceful coexistence between the gods and the Kra-ell, and they were eliminated from all official publications."

"The Kra-ell were physically stronger," Yamanu said. "They were a warrior race that probably chafed at being captive. Didn't they try to rebel?"

Kian had a feeling that he knew the answer to that, and it had to do with the Odus.

"In the beginning, the Kra-ell depended on the gods' synthetic blood to survive, so they didn't rebel. Those who did were dealt with harshly, but their biggest hold on the Kra-ell males was the females. Only the adult males were employed by the gods, while the females and the children were kept in seclusion, supposedly for their own good." Jade's lips twisted in a grimace. "The official explanation was that the underground cities of the gods were not suitable for the young Kra-ell, who needed the outdoors to thrive. The unofficial reason was that the gods didn't want the two races to mix. The Kra-ell didn't want that either, but the gods' council feared that some of the gods might try to seduce Kra-ell females, and it was better not to allow them free access."

"What about the other way around?" Toven asked. "Didn't they fear that the goddesses would seduce the Kra-ell males?"

Jade shrugged. "For some reason, they weren't concerned with that."

Kian suspected that the mate addiction worked differently at the beginning, affecting only the female gods, but not the males.

"Anyway," Jade continued. "By keeping the females and children out of the underground cities and in special above-ground reservations, the gods had full control over the males. If they misbehaved, they didn't get access to their females, and if they did something really bad, the gods would take it out on their families."

"What did they do to the families?" Sofia asked in a near whisper.

Kian wanted to know that too.

"They limited their supply of synthetic blood." Jade's eyes flickered red. "They starved them."

Jade

Tom looked doubtful. "Was that also in the historical records?"

"It was implied, but I don't have proof." She glared at him. "I don't have any proof for any of the things I'm telling you, so you are free to choose what you want to believe."

She was too tired and too hyped up at the same time to play games. If he wanted to believe that his people weren't capable of such cruelty, it was his prerogative.

"I believe you," he surprised her. "They were capable of much worse."

"The flood," Yamanu murmured. "Everyone thinks that it was a natural phenomenon and that the gods just used it to their advantage to cull the human population, but even if it was nature's doing, they could have warned people to seek higher ground."

"I wouldn't put it past the gods to have caused it," Jade said. "They had the technology, but they must have taken it with them when they left, or those who remained on Earth didn't have the tools or knowhow to maintain it." She turned to Toven. "Which one was it?"

"A combination of both, I suspect. Please, continue your story."

It was an evasive answer, but he hadn't promised to tell her anything. He'd promised to free her people, and he had done his part. Now it was her turn to do hers.

"The males were allowed to visit their tribes when the females were in their fertile cycle, which all the Kra-ell females of breeding age entered simultaneously. But since there were many more males than females, there was fierce competition. Games were organized for the males to fight each other and to participate in other contests of strength and endurance. Only the winners got invited to breed with the females."

"I hope it was the females' choice and it wasn't forced upon them," Mia murmured sleepily.

"The gods didn't go that far," Jade said. "The females chose who they wanted to invite to their beds. In fact, contests like that used to be deadly before the gods enslaved the Kra-ell, but the gods outlawed fighting to the death. Then again, it could have been part of their effort to rewrite history to make themselves look good. But since the fertility festival continued to be celebrated for thousands of years after the Kra-ell were freed, and fights to the death were no longer prohibited, it's possible that the gods' records were truthful on that."

"Finally, we get to the interesting part," Yamanu murmured. "I want to hear how they were freed."

Tom chuckled. "I have so many questions before that. Why did the gods live underground? When did they start interstellar travel? Where is their planet?"

"I can answer some of that," Jade said. "Our sun is what you call a red giant, and our planet is hot, humid, windy, and dark, so the gods are more comfortable in their underground cities. I can't tell you where it is because I was never shown a map of the galaxy with our planet and Earth marked and directions on how to get from point X to point Z. All I know is that it's hundreds of light years away."

"How do you know that it's hundreds of light years and not thousands?" Tom asked.

"I know how long we were supposed to be in stasis, and it was in the hundreds of light years, not thousands, but then our years are not the same as yours. They are significantly longer."

"What do you mean by supposed?" Tom asked.

"It took thousands of years instead of hundreds. I think we were tricked, but it could have been a malfunction."

"Tricked by whom?" Tom asked.

She smiled. "The gods, of course. Who else? It was their ship. But I'm getting ahead of the story." She turned to

Yamanu. "You wanted to know how the Kra-ell were freed."

"Most definitely."

"The Kra-ell hated living underground. They loved being outdoors, and they lived for the hunt. Those who worked the fields for the gods were not as miserable as those who worked in their factories and homes. The festivals were the only times those who worked underground got to be outdoors.

"Their liberation happened in three stages. A movement started among the gods to better the Kra-ell's conditions and end their slavery. By then, the animal population had rebounded, not enough to fully sustain all the Kra-ell, but enough for them to enjoy the occasional hunt. The young gods helped the Kra-ell negotiate a new deal. They would still work for the gods during the day, but at night they would be allowed to go topside and hunt if they wanted to. They were given building materials to erect lodging for themselves, the females and children could come live with them, and they could elect a new queen. It was an improvement, but their living conditions left much to be desired, especially compared to how the gods lived."

"They could have built the things they needed," Tom said. "After all, they worked in the gods' factories and produced all of their goods."

"The Kra-ell received only basic education and didn't know how to create the things they built for the gods. They only knew how to put them together."

Yamanu nodded. "It makes sense. The workers who put together cellphones don't know how to design them."

Tom looked like he wanted to say something but then decided not to.

Jade continued. "The young gods who initiated the change realized that it wasn't enough, and they demanded that the Kra-ell be given complete autonomy. The older gods claimed that the symbiotic relationship was beneficial to both people, and to sever it would destroy both societies. The gods needed the Kra-ell labor, and the Kra-ell needed the goods that the gods manufactured because the planet's wildlife could not sustain their population. They still needed the synthetic blood that the gods produced. One of the young gods leading the movement was a gifted inventor, and he proposed to replace the Kra-ell workforce with smart robots that were just as strong and could perform all the menial tasks the gods needed the Kra-ell for."

Toven

"The Odus were invented," Toven said. "I can see how that could solve the gods' problem, but what about the Kra-ell? They still needed to buy synthetic blood and other goods from the gods, but if they couldn't work for those things, how were they going to get them?"

Jade leaned back and crossed her arms over her chest. "Things like that don't happen overnight. Someone still had to build those smart robots. On top of that, they weren't easy or inexpensive to make, and the gods couldn't replace the Kra-ell workforce without creating a huge drain on their resources, which were needed primarily to develop their interstellar fleet. The idea sounded good in theory but wasn't economically or practically viable. The gods still needed the Kra-ell workforce."

"So nothing really changed," Sofia said.

"The change was gradual." Jade stretched her booted legs in front of her. "The newly elected Kra-ell queen negotiated with the gods' king for the Kra-ell to be paid actual wages, not just in goods. They were no longer forced to work for the gods. They could choose where they wanted to work, negotiate their wages, and use their earnings to buy whatever they pleased from the gods. Over time, the Kra-ell built better dwellings for themselves, and their living conditions improved significantly."

"What did the gods do with the Odus?" Yamanu asked.

"They were modified to be house servants only. The factory robots didn't need to look like people, and they cost much less to make."

"So that's the end of the story?" Marcel asked. "The Kra-ell were given equal rights?"

Jade laughed. "Not even close. The Kra-ell were free, they had their tribal grounds, and the gods didn't interfere in their affairs, but they were regarded as second-class, or rather as savages, and from their point of view, the gods were not wrong. For many generations following their emancipation, the Kra-ell were ruled by a dynasty of queens who were happy to let the tribal wars resume. It was our tradition, our nature, and the Kra-ell celebrated the freedom to kill each other. Most wars were over hunting grounds, others were about revenge, and some were fought just for the sake of fighting. The male population began to shrink again."

"Did the gods step in to stop it?" Mia asked. "That must have affected their workforce."

"By then, the gods had automated almost everything, and they no longer needed as many workers. They were happy for the Kra-ell to kill each other. They supplied the tribes with primitive weapons like swords, knives, and javelins, which would be useless if the Kra-ell ever turned against them."

"That was my next question," Toven said. "The Kra-ell were warriors, the gods had resources they needed, why didn't they attack?"

"The gods had superior technology and weapons." She waved a hand around. "It's the same old story, and Igor learned nothing from history. You came in with your spacesuits and subdued a force twice as large as yours with hardly any effort." She closed her eyes. "I made the same mistake. Perhaps if I'd had better weapons and more advanced surveillance at my compound, Igor wouldn't have had such an easy time killing my people."

"How did they do it?" Yamanu asked.

She waved a dismissive hand. "That's not part of the story I promised Tom."

What Jade had promised was the history of the gods, not the Kra-ell, but that was the history she knew, and the two were intertwined.

"Still, despite the tribal wars and deadly duels, the Kra-ell greatly outnumbered the gods, whose birth rate was a tiny fraction of the Kra-ell. But when a progressive queen outlawed the tribal wars and duels, our population exploded, and things got really bad. There weren't enough jobs, and the Kra-ell lived in abject poverty. Thankfully, enough time had passed for the animal population to grow and flourish, so they didn't starve, but things were bad. The gods started to fear them, while the young gods started to demand that something be done about the Kra-ell plight."

"I don't understand," Toven said. "After so many generations of being free, they should have built their own economy independent from the gods. Why didn't they?"

For the first time since he'd met Jade, her proud expression turned embarrassed. "We didn't have the right set of tools. We lacked education."

Jade

"The gods valued education and technology. We valued nature and staying true to our roots. We lived like primitive humans did a long time ago, while underground, an advanced civilization thrived. The gods who had supported the Kra-ell all along realized that our queen's progressive ideas would fall apart if we stayed rooted in our traditions, and the tribal wars would return. The only solution they could see was to make us more like them, not genetically because that was anathema to us, but by providing us with an education above the basics, so we could start building our own economy."

Tom nodded. "I bet there was a big resistance to the idea. Access to education is critical for removing class barriers, and the ruling class seldom grants it without a fight. Human history is rife with examples."

"You're right. The progressive gods demanded equal rights for the Kra-ell and access to the same education the gods had, but the king and the gods' council refused. They reasoned that if the Kra-ell wanted a better life for themselves and their children, they needed to develop their technology from scratch like the gods had done."

"That wasn't smart," Yamanu murmured. "They were sitting on top of a powder keg. They should have made at least a token concession."

"They didn't," Jade said. "The movement grew, and as rumors of impending uprising started, the king ordered all the Odus delivered to the capital, and they were reprogrammed to defend the gods. I won't bore you with the war details, but the gist was that the Kra-ell were stronger, faster, and outnumbered the gods twenty to one. Even with the Odus and the advanced weaponry, the gods barely stood their ground, and the casualties on both sides were staggering. The king of the gods agreed to meet the queen of the Kra-ell and negotiate a peace treaty."

Tom shook his head. "I find it hard to believe that the gods let the situation escalate like that without trying to defuse it or launch a preemptive strike."

Jade glanced at Yamanu's phone, which was propped on the coffee table. Yamanu and Tom were still wearing their earpieces, so it was possible that the comment had originated from whoever was listening on the other side, but she was surprised that Tom, a god, deferred to anyone.

"As I said before, this is the history I know. Things might have happened differently, and perhaps the gods had made some halfhearted offer that the Kra-ell refused. The agreement they reached was that the Kra-ell would receive an education that would allow them to advance faster, but they would not be privy to the gods' genetic knowhow and their most advanced technology. In exchange, the king demanded that the Kra-ell submit to genetic manipulation to control their population growth. The queen refused to budge on that, fearing that the gods would manipulate more than the reproduction rate. The king responded that the only other option was for the Kra-ell to colonize other planets."

"I assume that the queen agreed," Tom said.

"She did. As part of the treaty, the Odus were decommissioned, and the technology to make them was banned. The gods replaced them with simpler robotic servants that were not nearly as strong and were easy to destroy."

"We suspected that was what happened to them," Yamanu said.

"You knew about the Odus?"

Yamanu nodded. "But I don't understand why the gods would agree to decommission the Odus. What if the Kra-ell rebelled again?"

"I suspect the king wanted to get rid of the technology and used the treaty as an excuse. The Odus could potentially be used against him by his own people."

Tom lifted his hand. "So that was why the Kra-ell were sent to Earth? To colonize it?"

Jade smiled. "Not yet. There is still more to the story, and you'll find the next part most relevant to you. It explains why you are here."

He arched a brow. "That's indeed interesting."

"After the treaty was signed, the purging started. The gods were angry and divided, the older gods blaming the young ones who had sided with the Kra-ell for stirring up the rebellion and causing all the bloodshed. But the gods did not believe in capital punishment, and the king needed to keep up his benevolent façade, so to get rid of the troublemakers, he exiled every god who had taken part in the rebellion, including three of his children. He called it a research expedition, but everyone knew he was punishing them."

"Why Earth?" Tom asked.

"Why not Earth? By then, the gods had found many planets that supported life, and they created intelligent life by enhancing local creatures on several of them, including Earth."

"Why were you sent to the same place?" Yamanu asked.

"That's a story for another time." Jade looked out the window. "It's morning, I'm tired, and I want to check on Kagra." She turned to Tom. "Did I uphold my end of the bargain to your satisfaction?"

He chuckled. "You've just given us a taste. There is so much more that I want to know, but it can wait. We are all tired, and we need to get some rest."

"I'm hungry," Yamanu said. "Where can I get some food?"

Sofia rose to her feet. "I can make you something in the kitchen."

Jarmo entered the living room. "Can I come in?"

Jade glanced at Tom. "Can he hear me?"

The god nodded. "Yamanu dropped the bubble."

"You can come in. I'm done."

"Thank you for sharing your history with us," Tom said.

"You're welcome. But if you can, don't share it with my people. I want my daughter to hear the story from me first."

He nodded. "You have my word."

"I appreciate that." She cast him a tight smile and rose to her feet. "If anyone needs me, I'll be in the infirmary."

Kian

As Kian disconnected the call, he looked at Turner and Onegus, who had joined them during Jade's story. "That was quite a tale. The gods were not painted in complimentary colors."

"Don't forget who told the story," Turner said. "That's how the Kra-ell recorded the events."

Onegus shook his head. "It was so similar to what the gods did with humans that it rang true. But since those sent to Earth were the progressives, they treated humanity much better than their elders treated the Kra-ell."

"I have many questions for Jade," Kian said. "But right now, we need to decide what to do with the compound's money."

Toven had compelled Valstar to reveal all the bank account numbers and where their stock portfolio was located, but Valstar only had access to the operating account, representing a small fraction of the holdings.

Turner leaned back in his chair and crossed his arms over his chest. "Roni can probably break into those accounts and transfer the money, but that would alert Igor. If we leave the funds and assets where they are, and Igor gets a whiff of what happened to his stronghold, transferring everything to different accounts would be the first thing he'll do, and the compound will have no source of income. Given the size of that portfolio, they can support themselves just from the dividends and the interest earned."

"It's a difficult decision," Kian said. "The community needs the money to survive, so taking the money out might be more important than catching Igor. But that will guarantee that Igor will bolt. However, if we don't empty the accounts, we will still know where the funds are, and Roni can track them, so if Igor bolts anyway, we will be able to follow the money."

"If he bolts, " Turner said, "we will have to relocate everyone in the compound. The problem will be moving them all out to a secure location without him being able to track them. We will have to put them all through an MRI and take out their trackers, and what's worse, we will have to keep those loyal to him imprisoned until we catch him. On their own, there isn't much they can do, and Toven's compulsion will keep them in line. But if Igor returns and gets a hold of them, he will break through Toven's compulsion as easily as Toven broke through his."

Thankfully, Toven had had the foresight to compel that information out of each person he freed from Igor's compulsion, so they knew who they needed to watch.

"Let's see." Onegus pulled up the list on his laptop. "Out of Igor's original group, Jade and Kagra killed six, and they are adamant about executing his second and third once they are no longer needed. Three are traveling with Igor. That leaves five who we know are still loyal to him. The four females in his original group want to see him dead. Of the forty-one purebloods born on Earth, twenty-three are loyal to him, and the rest hate him and his band of cronies. Eight of the twelve female purebloods born on Earth are loyal, including Igor and Jade's daughter. The hybrids are unhappy about being treated as second-class, and none of them is a fan of Igor, but they don't expect another pureblood to treat them any better."

Kian let out a breath. "That's a lot of people to keep locked up until we catch him. I'd rather risk losing the money than risk letting Igor get away. When we eliminate him, we can leave Jade in charge of the compound, sign a treaty of cooperation with her, leave a couple of people to monitor her, and be done with this mess."

Turner pursed his lips. "But if we don't move the money, and Igor still figures out that the compound was compromised, we won't have the funds to relocate them. It's either a win-win or a lose-lose. I don't like these odds."

"Neither do I. Let's hope the Fates shine upon us and lead Igor into our trap."

Sofia

Yamanu wiped his mouth with a napkin and pushed away the plate with the chicken carcass. "Thanks for the meal, Sofia. The chicken was delicious." He turned to her father. "Do you grow them here? I heard a rooster crow."

The Guardian had demolished an entire hen with a mountain of potatoes on the side. The quantity could have fed four humans, but he didn't look full. Sofia would have offered him more, but that was all the cooked food she'd found in the refrigerator.

"We do." Her father smiled. "Wait until breakfast is made. I'm told that our eggs taste better than anything you can get in a supermarket."

"They do," Sofia confirmed. "Our eggs are delicious, especially when fried with homemade butter."

Yamanu sighed. "I wish I could stay and enjoy breakfast with you, but I need to check on my men." A guilty look crossed his handsome face. "All they have to eat are field rations." He rose to his feet and bowed his head to her father. "Thank you for feeding me."

Her father inclined his head. "Thank you for freeing us."

"You are welcome."

When Yamanu walked out of the kitchen, Sofia pushed to her feet. "Does anyone want more coffee?"

She had a feeling that her father was forcing himself to stay up so he could have a private talk with Marcel. It was sweet of him to do the fatherly thing.

He lifted his cup. "Please. I can't keep my eyes open, but how can I go to sleep when there is so much going on?"

"You can't stay awake for much longer." She lifted the carafe and poured more coffee into his cup. "You should get some sleep. I'll wake you if something happens that needs your attention."

"Aren't you tired?"

She smiled. "For me, this is daytime. I'm still on Oregon time."

"I see." He cast a sidelong glance at Marcel. "Maybe now you can tell me how you met Marcel, and how and why you two got engaged so quickly."

There were so many things that Sofia couldn't tell him. Her potential immortality was the most essential part because without it she couldn't explain the special bond between truelove mates, and without that it was difficult to explain why she and Marcel were technically engaged but didn't plan on getting married anytime soon.

Not that she was sure that she and Marcel were indeed bonded. It was supposed to happen between immortals and Dormants, but not Kra-ell Dormants.

She refilled Marcel's cup and her own before sitting back down. "I'm not pregnant, if that's what you were worried about."

He laughed nervously. "I wasn't worried. I was hopeful. I imagined a new life for you away from this place with a nice husband and a child. My grandchild."

"Fates willing, it will happen." Marcel took her hand and lifted it to his lips for a kiss.

The display of affection was a little embarrassing in front of her father, and she pulled her hand away. "The mission I couldn't tell you anything about was to spy on Marcel and his people." She cast an apologetic smile at Marcel. "Long story short, we fell in love, but then I was found out, we had a rough patch, but love triumphed."

"That's a very short story." Her father cut a reproachful look to Marcel. "What is Sofia not telling me?"

"A lot. She's under compulsion not to reveal certain things. I can fill in the blanks for you, but I will have to erase them from your memory."

Her father lifted his hand. "One moment. How will you erase things from my memory, and why?"

"What happened here tonight needs to remain a secret. Tom has the ability to compel, and I have the ability to reach into your mind, erase recent memories, and replace them with false ones."

"What about my old memories?"

"Those are tougher to erase, so Tom's compulsion to keep what you know about the Kra-ell from anyone who's not in this compound at the moment will have to suffice."

"Then what good will erasing the recent memories do? I will still know about the aliens living among us, and the others will remember too."

Marcel nodded. "That's true, but the Kra-ell don't know some of the things I'm about to tell you, and those things need to remain a secret from them. The only reason I'm sharing the information with you is that they have to do with Sofia and her future."

The resigned expression on her father's face made him look older than his fifty-seven years. "Do what you must."

Sofia put her hand on Marcel's arm. "It doesn't make sense to tell my father about what might be in my future and then thrall him to forget it. Can't Toven compel him to keep this a secret as well?"

"Who's Toven?" her father asked.

"Oops." Sofia slapped a hand over her mouth. "I shouldn't have said that."

Marcel

Marcel sighed. "I'll take care of it."

Reaching into Jarmo's mind, he plucked the name Toven from his memory and replaced it with Tom.

Sofia's father shook his head. "What just happened?"

"A small mishap." Marcel turned to Sofia. "You are right. I wanted to avoid asking Tom to do that after all the work he had done, but I will. I'm also going to cast a silencing bubble around us, so we are not overheard."

"What is a silencing bubble?" Jarmo asked.

"One more trick of mine." Marcel cast the bubble. "Can you feel it?"

Jarmo's eyes widened with wonder. "Even the Kra-ell cannot do that."

"No, they can't." Marcel took a sip of his coffee to wet his mouth for the extended version he was about to deliver.

When he was done, Jarmo gaped at Sofia. "You will become like them?"

"It's not a sure thing, Isi."

Marcel frowned. "Isi?"

"It means daddy in Finnish."

"Oh, I see."

Jarmo was still speechless.

"What's the matter?" Sofia asked him.

He shook his head. "I'm glad that you will have a long life, but I am not glad that you will become like her."

"You mean my mother?"

He nodded.

"Even if I grow fangs, I will still be the same person I am now. The transition will change my body, not what's in here." She put her hand over her heart.

"Here you are!" Sofia's cousin burst into the kitchen, her eyes red-rimmed, either from crying or lack of sleep.

Dropping the silencing bubble, Marcel pulled out a chair for her.

"What happened?" Sofia asked. "Why are you crying?"

Helmi rubbed her eyes. "They put handcuffs on Tomos and are keeping him locked in the hybrids' quarters together with all the hybrids. I tried to tell them that Tomos was a good guy and that there was no need to keep him in cuffs, but they wouldn't listen. The big guy with the huge muscles told me that it's temporary, but he didn't tell me for how long." She glared at Marcel. "I thought that you came to free us? Did you mean only the humans?"

He wasn't sure how to answer that. "We came to free Jade and her people, and that includes you and probably Tomos. I hope he isn't loyal to Igor."

Helmi threw her hands in the air. "He isn't. He didn't have a choice and had to obey Igor and his men. All of us had to. That doesn't make him or us Igor's supporters."

"I know. The question is how he feels now. I wasn't there when Tom and the others compelled the hybrids to tell them the truth about their loyalties, but I would be surprised if Tomos or any of the others liked Igor."

"Of course, they don't. They were treated even worse than us." She shifted her eyes to Sofia. "Did you talk to your mother?"

Sofia shook her head. "Is she handcuffed and locked in her quarters as well?"

"They all are." Helmi rose to her feet and walked over to where the cups were stored. "I heard that the purebloods are locked in the basement. That's even worse." She poured herself a cup and sat back down.

"It's safer that way," Sofia murmured. "I wonder how my mother feels about her father."

Helmi's eyes widened. "Is he dead?"

Sofia grimaced. "Not yet, but he will be soon. Jade will kill him to avenge her sons and all the males of her tribe whom Igor and his cronies murdered. Igor enslaved her and the other females, and as if that wasn't enough, he stole all of their money."

"Oh." Helmi shook her head. "Those are many horrible things. I'm so happy that I'm human." She finished the rest of her coffee and got to her feet. "I'm going to sleep, and I hope not to have nightmares after what you told me."

Sofia

After Helmi left, Sofia leaned over and kissed her father's cheek. "Get some sleep, Isi."

"Not yet." Her father leveled his eyes at Marcel. "What will happen to my daughter? What if she doesn't turn? What will happen to all of us?"

"Sofia will always be safe with me. Even if the induction doesn't work, she will live with me as my mate, and I'll cherish the years she can give me." Marcel took her hand and gave it a gentle squeeze. "But I strongly believe that she will transition, and we will have at least a thousand blissful years together."

As her father looked at her, tears misted his eyes. "I'm happy you found love, but I don't want to lose you. I want to be part of your life. I want to see my grandchildren born, and I want to be there to help you raise them. Don't you want to have me, your aunts, and your cousins in your life?"

She looked at Marcel. "Do you think your boss will allow them to live in his village? They don't have anywhere else they can go."

Marcel let out a breath. "I don't know. Maybe Kian will allow me to stay with you here. If Jade takes over command of the place, he will not leave her to do whatever she wants. They will sign a cooperation treaty, and Kian will need someone to be the clan's liaison to the Kra-ell. Perhaps I can get nominated to the post." He smiled. "After all, who else is better suited for the job than the guy who is mated to one of Jade's subjects?"

Sofia's heart soared with renewed hope. "That would be perfect. But won't you miss your people?"

"We can visit from time to time." He leaned closer and planted a kiss on her lips. "I love you, and if this is where you'll be the happiest, then this is where I'll be to share that happiness with you."

Her throat tight with emotion, Sofia leaned her forehead on his. "I love you so much. I can't believe you are willing to do this for me." She leaned back. "Living with the Kra-ell is not easy, and I don't know how things will change with Jade in charge. Listening to her story, I saw her in a different light, and I believe that she can be a good leader for the purebloods, but she needs to change her attitude toward the humans and the hybrids. Given the history of her people, she shouldn't treat anyone as second-class."

"You are absolutely right." Marcel shifted his gaze to her father. "We will elect a council, and each group will have the same number of representatives. Jade will have to get the council's approval for every major decision. That's how our clan is governed, and it works very well."

Her father nodded. "I like your suggestion." He rose to his feet and offered Marcel his hand. "Welcome to the family, Marcel. Can I call you son?"

Marcel shook his hand. "You can, but I will not call you Dad for obvious reasons. So maybe we should stick to our given names."

Understanding dawning, her father paled. "How old are you?"

"Much older than you."

"By how much?"

Sofia chuckled. "You don't want to know, and it doesn't matter. Even though Marcel has lived for a very long time, I am his first real love, and he is mine, and that's all that matters."

Her father nodded. "You are a smart lady, Sofia. And you make me proud." He leaned and kissed her cheek. "Now I can get some sleep. I'll see you both in a few hours."

"Hold on." Marcel pushed to his feet. "Tom needs to compel you to keep everything we told you a secret."

"Of course."

"It will only take a moment." Marcel led her father to the common room.

It took a little longer than that, and when Marcel returned to the kitchen alone, he sat back down and pulled her into his lap. "I like your father."

"And he likes you." She wrapped her arms around his neck. "Thank you for offering to live here with me, but we don't even know if any of us can stay here. We didn't catch Igor yet."

"I know. But your father needed to hear that. I will not take you away from him. No matter what happens, I will find a way for you to have everything you ever wanted, including having your father, aunts, and cousins near you."

"I love you." Her voice wobbled as happy tears spilled from the corners of her eyes. "I really don't want to ask and spoil this wonderful moment, but what about your guilt and your need for atonement? Are you ready to let it go?"

"My heart is lighter than it has ever been, but I still need to confess my crime and redeem myself either by punishment or service. Hopefully, our judge will show me leniency and choose service for my redemption."

Sofia grinned. "Isn't being the liaison to the Kra-ell a great service to the clan? I doubt anyone else would want the job."

"I hope Edna agrees with you."

"Let me talk with her, and I'll convince her." She cupped the back of his neck. "You are no longer alone, Marcel. We are a team, and we will face the future together, with love and devotion, for better and for worse and for everything in between."

THE ADVENTURE CONTINUES
JADE & PHINAS'S STORY IS NEXT
The Children of the Gods Book 68
DARK ALLIANCE KINDRED SOULS

TURN THE PAGE TO READ THE EXCERPT—>

JOIN THE VIP CLUB
To find out what's included in your free membership,
flip to the last page.

Dark Alliance Kindred Souls

A daring operation half a world away devolves into a full-scale crisis that escalates rapidly, requiring the clan's full might and technological wizardry to manage and survive.
Hardened by duty and tragedy, Jade is driven by a burning desire for revenge. When Phinas saves her

second-in-command, Jade's gratitude quickly becomes something more.

Jade

Jade strode into the infirmary and surveyed the cots that had been arranged in two neat rows in the center of the room. Several had been vacated, but many were still occupied.

Immortal Guardians watched over the injured, and for some reason, one of them was sitting on a chair next to her second-in-command's cot and was holding her hand. With his back turned to her, she couldn't see his face, but given the breadth of his shoulders, he wasn't a Kra-ell. The males of her species were much stronger than the immortals, but they were built slimmer.

Besides, no Kra-ell male would have shown Kagra such disrespect.

Mothers held their children's hands when they were small and frightened, but Kagra was a grown female and a warrior, and according to the liberators' doctor, she wasn't dying.

Liberators.

That still remained to be seen.

So far, the god who called himself Tom had done what he'd promised and more, freeing her people without a single unintended casualty, but Jade didn't trust gods, and that included the scions of the progressives who'd fought alongside the Kra-ell in the big rebellion back on the home planet.

Even when their intentions were noble, the gods' patronizing attitude toward the Kra-ell was offensive, and their ingrained belief in their own superiority was infuriating.

Jade had no choice but to accept Tom's help, and she still needed him to catch Igor so she could finally avenge her sons and the other males of her tribe. But once that was done, she wouldn't let the god or his immortal companions rule over her and her people.

Given that Tom was a powerful compeller on a par with Igor, that might not be easy to do, but she'd be damned if she lived another day enslaved to a male or a female, for that matter.

If Jade ever served anyone again, it would be by choice, and she would only serve a worthy Kra-ell ruler like the queen and her children, who Jade had sworn to protect.

Well, she'd only sworn to protect the queen, and she was no longer in the queen's service, but once a vow was made it never expired, and it didn't matter that she wasn't supposed to even know that the royal twins had been onboard the ship heading to Earth.

She'd failed to protect them just as she'd failed to protect her people, but there was no guilt associated with that failure because there had been nothing she could have done to prevent their ship's destruction, and without the mother ship, there was no way for her to locate the other escape pods.

In all likelihood, the twins and most of the other settlers hadn't survived.

Walking over to Kagra's cot, Jade grabbed a stool on the way and placed it next to the immortal's chair. "Does my second-in-command require a dedicated guard?"

It would have been better to conduct this conversation while she was looming over him, but the effect would have been lost if she had wobbled on her feet.

How long had she been awake?

It felt like she hadn't slept for days.

Given the copious quantity of Valstar's blood Jade had gorged on, she should have felt energized, but his blood must have been contaminated by the drug she'd put in his drink, and she could feel its effects. It was only by the Mother's grace that she'd functioned as well as she had and killed four of her sons' murderers. Kagra had dispatched two more, but she'd nearly lost her own life in the process.

Nevertheless, Jade wasn't going to get any sleep until Igor showed up. It was already eleven o'clock in the morning, and she was starting to get worried.

The immortal tilted his head and smiled. "I'm not here to guard your second. I'm checking on the female whose life

I saved." He let go of Kagra's hand and offered his hand to Jade. "I'm Phinas."

So he was the one she'd heard about. The Guardian who'd leaped from fifty feet away and smashed his exoskeleton-reinforced fist into Gorven's head, killing him on impact.

From what Jade had been told, it was no small feat to perform such acrobatics with the tremendously heavy suit on.

The immortal was an impressive warrior.

"I'm Jade." Shaking what he'd offered, she dipped her head in respect. "Thank you for saving Kagra. I owe you a life-debt."

He held on to her hand. "You don't owe me anything because I didn't do it for you. But just out of curiosity, what does a life-debt mean?"

She liked his reply. But even though he hadn't saved Kagra for her, she still owed him a life-debt, and once it was offered, it had to be paid. "It means that I will defend you with my life if needed, and anything you ask of me is yours."

He arched a brow with a sly smile lifting one corner of his full lips. "Anything?"

Males.

No matter what species they were, they had only one thing on their minds. Although with how exhausted and dirty Jade was, the evidence of what she'd done crusting over her leathers, Phinas must be either teasing or just not very discriminating about the females he flirted with.

Then again, warriors pumped up from the battle were more lustful than usual.

To answer his question, though, anything meant anything.

Jade held his gaze. "That's what I said."

"What if I ask for your firstborn?"

She winced. "Too late for that. Both my first and second born sons are dead, slaughtered by Igor and his cronies."

The smile died on his lips, and he inclined his head. "My apologies. I didn't know."

"I thought that the Guardians had been briefed about the history of my tribe. Tom knew about my sons even before he got here, and so did Marcel, Sofia's boyfriend."

"I'm not a Guardian," Phinas said.

Was he a medic? That would explain why he was checking up on Kagra. Military medical staff received the same training as warriors, but if he were a medic, the doctor would have introduced him to her. Maybe he was in charge of munitions, or a tech?

"I was told that the one who'd saved Kagra's life wore an exoskeleton suit. Did the techs and medics get to wear them too?"

He smiled. "I'm not a tech or a medic. I'm first and foremost a warrior, but I'm not a Guardian because I'm not part of the Guardian force. I'm part of a group of volunteers." He glanced at one of the Guardians standing watch over the injured. "What do you call me and my men?"

"Kalugal's men," the Guardian said.

"Who is Kalugal?" Jade asked.

When Phinas glanced at the Guardian again, the guy shook his head.

"I'm sorry." Phinas smiled apologetically. "I'm not at liberty to discuss the clan's inner politics with you. You will have to ask Yamanu or Bhathian. They are in charge of this operation."

"I thought Tom was in charge."

Phinas shrugged. "I can't comment on that either. All I can tell you is that Tom is not a Guardian."

"That makes sense." He was a god, but the other Kra-ell in the infirmary didn't know that. She couldn't say it out loud. "He wouldn't be part of the military arm of the clan. That would be left to the descendants."

"That's correct." Phinas flashed her a charming smile. "It's a pleasure to talk to a female who is a warrior herself and knows how those things work."

"I assume that your females are not fighters."

He shook his head. "That's another thing I cannot comment on. All I can say is that I haven't had the pleasure of chatting with a female fighter before." He turned his gaze to Kagra. "Watching her fight was awe-inspiring. I have been trained to fight with swords and daggers, and I recognize skill when I see it. She's incredible."

Pride filled Jade's chest. "Kagra is exceptional. That's why I chose her as my second-in-command. When she wakes up, she will be upset about letting herself get gutted."

Jade turned around to look for the doctor the Guardians had brought along. She found him on the other side of the large room, checking on one of the injured hybrids.

When he felt her gaze and lifted his head, she asked, "Why is Kagra sleeping so much? You said that she's healing well."

He smiled sheepishly. "I gave her sedatives so she'd sleep."

"I thought you were only giving her painkillers."

He put his hand in his coat pocket. "I gave her both. Sleeping will help her heal faster."

Phinas

Phinas took the opportunity of Jade talking with Merlin to adjust himself and cross his legs.

From the moment he'd laid eyes on her, he'd been sporting a hard-on that he'd been desperately trying to hide. Despite being exhausted, dirty, and covered in dry blood splotches, the female was so damn hot that she made him as randy as a buck in heat.

It wasn't his style.

Phinas was coolheaded and reserved, and he'd never let females get under his skin.

Perhaps the spike in his libido had been caused by the testosterone still coursing through his blood after the battle, or maybe it was the fault of those damn tight leather pants and sheer mesh shirt of hers, or maybe the turn-on was the sword sheathed in a fancy scabbard and hung low on her hips, her swagger as she'd walked into the infirmary, the palpable power radiating from her, or all of the above.

Regardless of the trigger, though, the result was the same. He'd had trouble stringing two coherent thoughts together, as evidenced by his unfortunate blunder.

He'd heard that the males of Jade's tribe had been slaughtered by her captors, and he should have realized that she could have had a son or sons among them. But that was what happened when his mind was occupied by thoughts of stripping her naked.

He would leave the sword belt and boots on, though.

Jade was tall and slim, and her face was beautiful despite her huge eyes and hard expression. She had no breasts to speak of, but her ass was round and firm, just the way he liked it. However, the disturbing truth was that he was more turned on by her inner power than by her enticing feminine assets, and the fact that she was a ruthless killer only added to her dangerous allure.

That was strange as hell for him and entirely out of character.

Despite having been raised in Navuh's camp among males who believed that women were created to please and serve them and breed, Phinas wasn't a misogynist.

He'd never been one, but he was old, and in days past, women and men had very different roles in society.

Female warriors did not exist in his world, but he'd always believed that being mothers and caretakers was no less important, probably more so, but like other males of the time, he believed that motherhood was a female's ultimate calling and that women weren't suited for jobs that men performed.

Warriors took lives. Women created life and nurtured it.

After he'd been recruited by Kalugal and escaped Navuh's camp, Phinas had traveled to the US, where at the time women had been regarded with a little more respect, but not by much.

It had taken many more years for Western society to realize what had taken him mere weeks.

As soon as Phinas had been able to interact with women who were free to express themselves, he'd realized that they were as smart and as capable as men, just not as physically strong and aggressive, and that was fine. Not every male was born to be a fighter, either.

That being said, he was a dominant male by nature, and he'd never thought he would be attracted to someone like Jade. A female who could hand him his ass.

"Are you going to sit here all day?" Jade asked him. "Aren't you needed somewhere else?"

He arched a brow. "Does it bother you that I'm watching over Kagra?"

What he'd really wanted to ask was whether she was jealous of the attention he was giving her injured second.

"Kagra has the doctor to watch over her." Jade hung her head and let out a breath. "I'm so damn tired, but that's not an excuse. You're not one of my subjects, and what you do with your time is none of my business."

"You're not one of my subjects either, but my advice to you is to get some sleep."

"I can't. There is still so much to do, and Kagra is out, so I have no one to assist me. But even if she was fine, I still wouldn't go to sleep. I'm waiting for Igor's capture so I can finally kill him."

As a vicious expression twisted her lips, her fangs made an appearance, and her eyes blazed with red light, but even that wasn't enough to diminish his attraction to her.

On the contrary, he wanted her even more.

"You won't be much good to anyone when you fall flat on your face. You need to sleep for at least a couple of hours to recharge." He waved his hand at the empty cot next to Kagra's. "You can lie down right over here, and I'll wake you up the moment Igor is captured."

"I also need to talk to my daughter." She looked at the cot longingly. "But maybe I should rest for a few minutes before I do that." She pushed to her feet and walked to the other cot.

"How old is she?"

"Drova is sixteen." Jade unbuckled her sword belt. "She's a fine female with a lot of potential, but we don't get along, and I'm about to kill her father, which isn't going to help make things better between us." She put the sword under the cot and lay down with her boots on.

He had a feeling that Jade wouldn't have shared that information if she wasn't so tired, which made her less guarded.

It probably wasn't a secret that Igor was the father of her daughter, but it wasn't the kind of thing a woman told a stranger she'd just met.

The murderer of her sons had forced her to breed with him.

Jade must be forged from titanium alloy.

"Is she close to her father?" Phinas asked.

Jade snorted. "No one is close to Igor. He's a sociopath. But he's still her father." She closed her eyes. "Maybe I should kill him first and talk to her later?"

She turned on her side, giving him a great view of her gorgeous ass. "I'm just going to rest for a few minutes."

"You should rest for longer than that. I'll watch over you," he said with such conviction that she turned around and looked at him.

"Thank you. But that won't be necessary." Jade waved her hand at the Guardians. "I'm sure they can protect me if needed."

He doubted she would rely on them to defend her. Her sword was right there under her cot, reachable in a split second.

"I'm not going anywhere." He crossed his arms over his chest.

"Suit yourself." She turned around again.

Phinas wanted to learn more about Jade, to find out what kind of hellfire had forged such a tough female, but it would have to wait until after she'd exacted revenge for the slaughter of the males of her tribe and the subjugation of its females.

Kian

The last person Kian had expected to walk into the war room at one o'clock in the morning was his mother.

He pushed to his feet, walked over to her, and leaned to kiss her cheek. "Did you have trouble sleeping, Mother?"

A goddess only needed a few hours of sleep, but his mother was an early riser, and she enjoyed walking outside when the sun was just cresting the horizon. Her eyes were too sensitive for the harsh Southern California sun, even in the winter, and she liked being able to forgo the goggle-like sunglasses that she needed to wear other times when getting out of the house.

"I brought you coffee and pastries from the vending machines." She motioned for her butler to come in.

"Good evening, Master Kian." The Odu put the tray with the coffees and the wrapped pastries on the conference table, bowed, and headed out the door.

Kian pulled out a chair for her. "You still haven't told me why you are up and about so late."

She shrugged one delicate shoulder. "I could not sleep, and I did not want to call you in case you were in the midst of directing the battle, and I didn't want to call the house and wake Syssi up either. So I came to see if you were still here and whether the evil Igor was captured." She smiled. "If I had known that you were all alone in here, I would have come to keep you company earlier."

She could've texted him, but she just hadn't wanted to give him a chance to tell her not to come.

After he'd told her about Jade's promise to Toven, Annani probably couldn't contain her curiosity. She wanted to hear what Jade had told Toven about the gods, the Kra-ell, and their home planet.

Kian took one of the paper cups and removed the lid. "Turner and Onegus went home to shower and change and catch a couple of hours of sleep, but they are coming back."

"You should have done the same."

"Until Igor is caught, someone needs to be in the war room at all times. Roni is in the lab, monitoring Igor's bank accounts, and I'm getting updates from the compound."

"How is Toven doing?" she asked.

"He and Mia worked all night to free everyone from Igor's compulsion, and last I heard, they were asleep on the couch in the common room in the human section. William removed everyone's collars, and he's resting as well. The Guardians are taking turns watching the purebloods and the hybrids, and Merlin is taking care of the injured. Did I cover everyone?"

"You didn't mention Marcel and Sofia."

Kian smiled. His mother was well-informed, and she had everyone cataloged in her brain. He could throw at her the name of any clan member, and she would know everything about them, down to their favorite foods and where they had visited on their last vacation.

Remembering that many details about so many people was a truly remarkable ability, but what was even more remarkable was how much she cared about each member of her clan.

"They are also in the human quarters, helping calm people down."

"How is Jade?"

"The last I heard, she took a nap on one of the cots in the infirmary. Her second-in-command was badly injured. Merlin patched her up, and she's going to be fine."

He'd already told her that there were no casualties on their side and that on the Kra-ell side, only Igor's inner circle cronies had been killed by Jade and Kagra, and several purebloods and hybrids were injured.

Annani smoothed the folds of her gown, readjusting it over her knees. "You know what I really want to know. You were too busy before, but this seems like a quiet time, and you can spare a few minutes to tell me what Jade shared with Toven about the gods."

Kian winced. "You're not going to like what I tell you."

"I want to hear it anyway."

"The gods weren't nice people, and those who they sent to Earth were rebels, banished here for their part in a rebellion."

Annani nodded solemnly. "I had a feeling it was something like that. Otherwise, they would not have been abandoned on Earth with no ability to return home or even communicate with their families."

"There is one part that you're going to love, though. You are most likely the granddaughter of the gods' king. Some of the rebels were his own children, and he sent them to Earth along with the others. Given that Ahn, Ekin, and Athor were all leaders of the gods' local community, each in their respective field of authority, they were no doubt royalty."

Annani smiled. "I had a feeling about that as well. My father wore the mantle of leadership with such inborn grace and dignity, but he never called himself king. Nevertheless, my mother insisted that I behave like a princess." She smoothed her skirt again even though it didn't need it. "What was the rebellion about?"

"The Kra-ell. Turns out that the Kra-ell were the gods' first attempt at creating a hybrid creature to serve them. But the old gods were not as progressive as your father and his siblings. They treated the Kra-ell like slaves. The young gods did not approve of the way the Kra-ell were being treated or rather mistreated. First, they demanded better conditions for the Kra-ell, and when that was achieved, they demanded equal rights and access to education, but the king and his council refused." Kian paused to unwrap a pastry. "Jade said that hundreds of generations passed between the stages of the Kra-ell emancipation, so it wasn't like those demands were made one right after the other."

"What happened during the rebellion?" Annani asked.

"The Kra-ell were stronger physically, which was probably by design because they were meant to be laborers, and back then, the gods didn't include susceptibility to mind manipulation in their genetic enhancements, so they couldn't defend themselves by seizing the Kra-ell minds. The gods had superior weapons, and their underground cities were fortified, but the Kra-ell had the numbers. The king mobilized the Odus, who were originally designed to be house servants, and they were converted to be defenders of the gods against the Kra-ell. But even with the Odus, the gods couldn't win, and the casualties on both sides were staggering. The king of the gods and the queen of the Kra-ell negotiated a peace treaty, and part of it was the decommissioning of the Odus." He leaned back and took a sip from his coffee. "In my opinion, the only reason for the king of the gods to agree to decommission the Odus was fear of them being used against him in another rebellion. Otherwise, it makes no sense for the gods to give up their best defensive weapon."

Annani tilted her head. "It might not be their best weapon anymore. Once the rebellion was over, they probably developed something better than the Odus and made sure that it could not fall into the wrong hands, or what they considered rebel hands."

"I agree."

They were probably both right. Kian wasn't much of a politician, but he knew how they operated, especially those who had been in power for too long and had no intentions of losing their seat to another. After the king decommissioned the Odus, most likely with a lot of fanfare and publicity for the consumption of his public, he must have started developing an alternative in secret. There was no way he'd left himself exposed to the possibility of another rebellion.

The next time someone dared to oppose him, he would have had a brutal and efficient response at the ready, one that was entirely under his control.

In fact, with the genetic manipulation mastery of the gods, he'd probably ordered another species to be altered for that purpose—creatures who were as strong as the Kra-ell but susceptible to mind manipulation and easy to destroy.

Was Kian letting his imagination run away from him?

Maybe.

But as it'd been proven time and again, reality was stranger than fiction.

"Was that the full version or a summary of what Jade had told Toven?" Annani asked. "So many questions remain unanswered."

"It was a summary, but Jade's full version was far from complete either. There are many things she probably doesn't know, and her spin is obviously tilted in the Kra-ell's favor. After Igor is apprehended and Jade takes charge of her community, we will ask her to tell us more."

Toven

"I'm worried." Toven ran his fingers through his hair. "Igor should have called by now."

It was almost two o'clock in the afternoon, and it was becoming clear that Igor was onto them. There was still a chance that he was on his way, maybe flying back from Moscow or some other distant location, but the fact that he hadn't tried to call Valstar or anyone else was telling.

That was why Toven had called the meeting. He, William, and the head guardians had assembled in the human quarters' common room, with Kian, Onegus, and Turner participating in the meeting via the tablet propped on the coffee table.

The humans stayed away, giving them the privacy they needed, and Yamanu had encased them in a bubble of silence to make sure no one could listen in on them.

Bhathian nodded. "What really bothers me is that when we turned the compound's communications back on, there weren't any missed calls from him in the logs."

As all eyes turned to William, he rubbed a finger over the bridge of his nose as if he was pushing his glasses up, except he wasn't wearing any. "I don't know what to tell you. I double checked all the transmissions, and everything is working fine. At six o'clock in the morning, we switched on the recorded footage and set it to transmit normal Monday morning activity. He shouldn't have noticed anything amiss unless he spent hours watching and noticed that it was going on a loop."

"Did he try to detonate the explosives?" Kian asked.

William shook his head. "He didn't. Neither did he attempt to detonate the collars. I checked."

"What now?" Toven asked. "Until Igor is caught, we have to keep the purebloods and the hybrids on lockdown. How much longer do we wait?"

"We can't wait," Turner said. "It's true that Igor has only one pureblood and two hybrids with him, but he could use his compulsion power to bring the Russian Army to storm the compound or even their air force to bomb the place, although I doubt he would go that far. I assume that he wants his people back alive."

"I'm not so sure," Kian said. "If he had the entire place rigged, he has no qualms about bombing the compound and killing everyone."

Turner shook his head. "He can't do that. I think the rigging was meant as a last-stand kind of thing, and he didn't intend to implement it unless all hope was lost. According to what Jade told us, it seems that Igor doesn't know where to find more of the surviving Kra-ell, and without his people, he has nothing. He needs the females to keep breeding more Kra-ell, and he even needs some of the males to provide the necessary genetic variety. He would do anything to get his people back, or at least some of them."

Yamanu stretched his long legs in front of him. "I still don't get how he figured out what was going on here. Even if he noticed something was off with what the hidden cameras were transmitting, he couldn't have guessed that a stronger compeller took over his people, because he couldn't possibly have known about Toven. Igor would have assumed that he could just walk back in and compel everyone to his will."

DARK ALLIANCE KINDRED SOULS

JOIN THE VIP CLUB
To find out what's included in your free membership, flip to the last page.

The Children of the Gods Series

Reading Order

THE CHILDREN OF THE GODS ORIGINS

1: Goddess's Choice

When gods and immortals still ruled the ancient world, one young goddess risked everything for love.

2: Goddess's Hope

Hungry for power and infatuated with the beautiful Areana, Navuh plots his father's demise. After all, by getting rid of the insane god he would be doing the world a favor. Except, when gods and immortals conspire against each other, humanity pays the price.

But things are not what they seem, and prophecies should not to be trusted...

THE CHILDREN OF THE GODS

Dark Stranger

1: Dark Stranger The Dream

2: Dark Stranger Revealed

3: Dark Stranger Immortal

Dark Enemy

4: Dark Enemy Taken

5: Dark Enemy Captive

6: Dark Enemy Redeemed

Kri & Michael's Story

6.5: My Dark Amazon

Dark Warrior

7: Dark Warrior Mine

8: Dark Warrior's Promise

9: Dark Warrior's Destiny

10: Dark Warrior's Legacy

Dark Guardian

11: Dark Guardian Found

12: Dark Guardian Craved

13: Dark Guardian's Mate

Dark Angel

14: Dark Angel's Obsession

15: Dark Angel's Seduction

16: Dark Angel's Surrender

Dark Operative

17: Dark Operative: A Shadow of Death

18: Dark Operative: A Glimmer of Hope

19: Dark Operative: The Dawn of Love

Dark Survivor

20: Dark Survivor Awakened

21: Dark Survivor Echoes of Love

22: Dark Survivor Reunited

DARK WIDOW

23: DARK WIDOW'S SECRET

24: DARK WIDOW'S CURSE

25: DARK WIDOW'S BLESSING

DARK DREAM

26: DARK DREAM'S TEMPTATION

27: DARK DREAM'S UNRAVELING

28: DARK DREAM'S TRAP

DARK PRINCE

29: DARK PRINCE'S ENIGMA

30: DARK PRINCE'S DILEMMA

31: DARK PRINCE'S AGENDA

DARK QUEEN

32: DARK QUEEN'S QUEST

33: DARK QUEEN'S KNIGHT

34: DARK QUEEN'S ARMY

DARK SPY

35: DARK SPY CONSCRIPTED

36: DARK SPY'S MISSION

37: DARK SPY'S RESOLUTION

DARK OVERLORD

38: DARK OVERLORD NEW HORIZON

39: DARK OVERLORD'S WIFE

40: Dark Overlord's Clan

Dark Choices
41: Dark Choices The Quandary
42: Dark Choices Paradigm Shift
43: Dark Choices The Accord

Dark Secrets
44: Dark Secrets Resurgence
45: Dark Secrets Unveiled
46: Dark Secrets Absolved

Dark Haven
47: Dark Haven Illusion
48: Dark Haven Unmasked
49: Dark Haven Found

Dark Power
50: Dark Power Untamed
51: Dark Power Unleashed
52: Dark Power Convergence

Dark Memories
53: Dark Memories Submerged
54: Dark Memories Emerge
55: Dark Memories Restored

Dark Hunter

56: Dark Hunter's Query

57: Dark Hunter's Prey

58: <u>Dark Hunter's Boon</u>

Dark God

59: Dark God's Avatar

60: Dark God's Reviviscence

61: Dark God Destinies Converge

Dark Whispers

62: Dark Whispers From The Past

63: Dark Whispers From Afar

64: Dark Whispers From Beyond

Dark Gambit

65: Dark Gambit The Pawn

66: Dark Gambit The Play

67: Dark Gambit Reliance

Dark Alliance

68: Dark Alliance Kindred Souls

69: Dark Alliance Turbulent Waters

When a dangerous foe turns the tables on the clan, complicating the Kra-ell rescue operation in unforeseeable ways, Kian and his crew bet all on a brilliant misdirection.

On board the Aurora, Phinas and Jade brace for battle while enjoying a few stolen moments of passion.

Drawn to the woman he sees behind the aloof leader, Phinas

realizes that what has started as a calculated political move has evolved into a deepening sense of companionship.

Jade finds reprieve in Phinas's arms, but duty and tradition make it difficult for her to accept that what she feels for him is more than just gratitude and desire.

After all, the Kra-ell don't believe in love.

70: Dark Alliance Perfect Storm

After two decades in captivity, Jade is finally free, her quest for revenge within grasp, but danger still looms large. A storm is brewing on the horizon, gathering momentum and threatening to obliterate Jade's tenuous hold on hope for a better future.

Dark Healing

71: Dark Healing Blind Justice

The sanctuary is Vanessa's life project. The monumental task of rehabilitating the traumatized victims of trafficking doesn't leave much time for personal life, let alone dating or finding her one and only.

When Kian asks her to help the Kra-ell, she's torn between her duty to the sanctuary and a group of emotionally wounded aliens who no other psychologist can treat.

She's the only immortal with the necessary training to get it done.

The Kra-ell culture and the purebloods' nearly androgynous alien looks shouldn't appeal to her, and yet, she finds one of them disturbingly attractive.

Is it the dangerous vibe he emits?

Does it speak to her on a subconscious level?

Or is it her need to put the broken pieces of him back together?

And why is he interested in her?

She cannot offer him a fight for dominance like a Kra-ell female would, but some strange and unfamiliar part of her wishes she could.

72: Dark Healing Blind Trust

Riddled with guilt over the crimes he was forced to commit, Mo-red is ready to stand trial and accept the death sentence he believes he deserves, but when the clan's alluring psychologist offers a new perspective on his past and hope for a better future, he resolves to fight for his life.

73: Dark healing Blind Curve

Kian is still reeling from the shocking revelations about the twins when a new threat manifests, eclipsing everything he's had to deal with up until now. In light of the new developments, Igor, the other Kra-ell prisoners, and the pending trial are no longer at the forefront of his mind, but the opposite is true for Vanessa. As her relationship with Mo-red solidifies, she is determined to save the male she loves, even if it means breaking him free and living on the run.

Dark Encounters

74: Dark Encounters of the Close Kind

Convinced that her family is hiding a terrible secret from her, Gabi decides to pay them a surprise visit.

Something is very fishy about the stories her brothers have been telling her lately. Her niece, a nineteen-year-old prodigy with a Ph.D. in bioinformatics, has gotten engaged to a much older guy she met while working on some top-secret project, and if Gabi's older, overprotective brother's approval of the engagement wasn't suspicious enough, he also uprooted his family and moved to be closer to the couple.

What Gabi discovers when she gets to L.A. is wilder than anything she could have imagined. Her entire family possesses godly genes, her brothers and her niece have already turned immortal, and she could transition as soon as she finds an immortal male to induce her. Finding a suitable candidate in a village full of handsome immortals shouldn't be a problem, but Gabi's thoughts keep wandering to the gorgeous guy she met on her flight over.

Could Uriel be a lost descendant of the gods?

He certainly looks like them, but that doesn't mean that he's a good guy or that he's even immortal. He could be a descendant of a different god—a member of an enemy faction of immortals who seek to eradicate her family's adoptive clan, or what is more likely, he's just an extraordinarily good-looking human.

75: Dark Encounters of the Unexpected Kind

Who is Uriel?

Is he a lost descendant of the gods or just a gorgeous and charming human who has rocked Gabi's world?

76: Dark Encounters of the Fated Kind

As Aru and his team embark on a perilous mission, their past and present converge in a meeting that holds the key to their fate.

Dark Voyage

77: Dark Voyage Matters of the Heart

As Annani and Syssi set out to unravel the mysteries of Syssi's visions about the gods' home world, the long-awaited wedding cruise sets sail with Aru, Gabi, and Aru's teammates on board.

While the gods find themselves surrounded by immortal clan ladies eager for their affections, they soon discover that destiny has a different plan for them.

The Children of the Gods Series Sets

Books 1-3: Dark Stranger trilogy—Includes a bonus short story: **The Fates take a Vacation**

Books 4-6: Dark Enemy Trilogy—Includes a bonus short story—**The Fates' Post-Wedding Celebration**

Books 7-10: Dark Warrior Tetralogy

Books 11-13: Dark Guardian Trilogy

Books 14-16: Dark Angel Trilogy

Books 17-19: Dark Operative Trilogy

Books 20-22: Dark Survivor Trilogy

Books 23-25: Dark Widow Trilogy

Books 26-28: Dark Dream Trilogy

Books 29-31: Dark Prince Trilogy

Books 32-34: Dark Queen Trilogy

Books 35-37: Dark Spy Trilogy

Books 38-40: Dark Overlord Trilogy

Books 41-43: Dark Choices Trilogy

Books 44-46: Dark Secrets Trilogy

Books 47-49: Dark Haven Trilogy
Books 50-52: Dark Power Trilogy
Books 53-55: Dark Memories Trilogy
Books 56-58: Dark Hunter Trilogy
Books 59-61: Dark God Trilogy
Books 62-64: Dark Whispers Trilogy
Books 65-67: Dark Gambit Trilogy
Books 68-70: Dark Alliance Trilogy
Books 71-73: Dark healing Trilogy

MEGA SETS

INCLUDE CHARACTER LISTS

The Children of the Gods: Books 1-6
The Children of the Gods: Books 6.5-10

TRY THE SERIES ON

AUDIBLE

2 FREE audiobooks with your new Audible subscription!

PERFECT MATCH SERIES

Vampire's Consort

When Gabriel's company is ready to start beta testing, he invites his old crush to inspect its medical safety protocol.

Curious about the revolutionary technology of the *Perfect Match Virtual Fantasy-Fulfillment studios*, Brenna agrees.

Neither expects to end up partnering for its first fully immersive test run.

King's Chosen

When Lisa's nutty friends get her a gift certificate to *Perfect Match Virtual Fantasy Studios*, she has no intentions of using it. But since the only way to get a refund is if no partner can be found for her, she makes sure to request a fantasy so girly and over the top that no sane guy will pick it up.

Except, someone does.

> **Warning:** This fantasy contains a hot, domineering crown prince, sweet insta-love, steamy love scenes painted with light shades of gray, a wedding, and a HEA in both the virtual and real worlds.
>
> Intended for mature audience.

Captain's Conquest

Working as a Starbucks barista, Alicia fends off flirting all day long, but none of the guys are as charming and sexy as Gregg. His frequent visits are the highlight of her day, but since he's never asked her out, she assumes he's taken. Besides, between a day job and a budding music career, she has no time to start a new relationship.

That is until Gregg makes her an offer she can't refuse—a gift certificate to the virtual fantasy fulfillment service everyone is talking about. As a huge Star Trek fan, Alicia has a perfect match in mind—the captain of the Starship Enterprise.

The Thief Who Loved Me

When Marian splurges on a Perfect Match Virtual adventure as a world infamous jewel thief, she expects high-wire fun with a hot partner who she will never have to see again in real life.

A virtual encounter seems like the perfect answer to Marcus's string of dating disasters. No strings attached, no drama, and definitely no love. As a die-hard James Bond fan, he chooses as his avatar a dashing MI6 operative, and to complement his adventure, a dangerously seductive partner.

Neither expects to find their forever Perfect Match.

My Merman Prince

The beautiful architect working late on the twelfth floor of my building thinks that I'm just the maintenance guy. She's also under the impression that I'm not interested.

Nothing could be further from the truth.

I want her like I've never wanted a woman before, but I don't play where I work.

I don't need the complications.

When she tells me about living out her mermaid fantasy with a stranger in a Perfect Match virtual adventure, I decide to do everything possible to ensure that the stranger is me.

THE DRAGON KING

To save his beloved kingdom from a devastating war, the Crown Prince of Trieste makes a deal with a witch that costs him half of his humanity and dooms him to an eternity of loneliness.

Now king, he's a fearsome cobalt-winged dragon by day and a short-tempered monarch by night. Not many are brave enough to serve in the palace of the brooding and volatile ruler, but Charlotte ignores the rumors and accepts a scribe position in court.

As the young scribe reawakens Bruce's frozen heart, all that stands in the way of their happiness is the witch's bargain. Outsmarting the evil hag will take cunning and courage, and Charlotte is just the right woman for the job.

My Werewolf Romeo

The father of my star student is a big-shot screenwriter and the patron of the drama department who thinks he can dictate what production I should put on. The principal makes it very clear that I need to cooperate with the opinionated asshat or walk away from my dream job at the exclusive private high school.

It doesn't help matters that the guy is single, hot, charming, creative, and seems to like me despite my thinly-veiled hostility.

When he invites me to a custom-tailored Perfect Match virtual adventure to prove that his screenplay is perfect for my production, I accept, intending to have fun while proving that messing with the classics is a foolish idea.

I don't expect to be wowed by his werewolf adaptation of Red Riding Hood mesh-up with Romeo and Juliet, and I certainly don't expect to fall in love with the virtual fantasy's leading man.

The Channeler's Companion

A treat for fans of *The Wheel of Time*.

When Erika hires Rand to assist in her pediatric clinic, she does so despite his good looks and irresistible charm, not because of them.

He's empathic, adores children, and has the patience of a saint.

He's also all she can think about, but he's off limits.

What's a doctor to do to scratch that irresistible itch without risking workplace complications?

A shared adventure in the Perfect Match Virtual Studios seems like the solution, but instead of letting the algorithm choose a partner for her, Erika can try to influence it to select the one she wants. Awarding Rand a gift certificate to the service will get him into their database, but unless Erika can tip the odds in her favor, getting paired with him is a long shot.

Hopefully, a virtual adventure based on her and Rand's favorite series will do the trick.

Note

Dear reader,

I hope my stories have added a little joy to your day. If you have a moment to add some to mine, you can help spread the word about the Children Of The Gods series by telling your friends and penning a review. Your recommendations are the most powerful way to inspire new readers to explore the series.

Thank you,

Isabell

FOR EXCLUSIVE PEEKS AT UPCOMING RELEASES & A FREE COMPANION BOOK

Join my *VIP Club* and gain access to the VIP portal at itlucas.com
To Join, go to:
http://eepurl.com/blMTpD

INCLUDED IN YOUR FREE MEMBERSHIP:

YOUR VIP PORTAL

- Read preview chapters of upcoming releases.
- Listen to Goddess's Choice narration by Charles Lawrence
- Exclusive content offered only to my VIPs.

FREE I.T. LUCAS COMPANION INCLUDES:

- Goddess's Choice Part 1
- Perfect Match: Vampire's Consort (A standalone Novella)
- Interview Q & A
- Character Charts

If you're already a subscriber, and you are not getting my emails, your provider is sending them to your junk folder, and you are missing out on **IMPORTANT UPDATES, SIDE CHARACTERS' PORTRAITS, ADDITIONAL CONTENT, AND OTHER GOODIES.** To fix that, add isabell@itlucas.com to your email contacts or your email VIP list.

**Check out the specials at
https://www.itlucas.com/specials**

Made in the USA
Monee, IL
10 March 2025